AD ARNOLD

Detective Clover and the Mystery of the Manor

To every bullied child, to every lonely child; to everyone who dreamed more than they studied.

Contents

Prologue

Poppy

The blood stained like ink on aged paper; thunder roared and plates shattered. When moonlight shone through the clouds and trees for the first time that night, enlightening the large bedroom, there was not a single word in my vocabulary that could describe how I was feeling. I tried to see through the crowd, but the group smothered any sight of him. I closed my eyes momentarily, and as I did I heard a soft voice cry out over the echo of the storm.

"Dad?" The girl's voice said, muffled by the storm.

It was almost funny in a way, the way his body laid there. So vividly real, and yet not at all. My vision wavered as I stared out the window, mouth ajar, but inside my chest, there was nothing but a cold, sleek, hollowness.

I wondered if this secret would ever leave my brain, my lips. The king was dead. Finally, Augustus was dead. I tried with great effort not to laugh and give myself away. Now, I am king; *I am king.*

People left the room, not because they were uncomfortable, but because they knew they did not deserve to stay any longer. Away went the doctor, in her beaked mask. The girl's governess went second. Then the chef, the footmen, the ancient royal painter, and finally– his daughter.

Mysteries lurked throughout the breathing walls of this palace, of this world. If it weren't for my situation I would've appreciated it more; I have always had a sense of morbid aestheticism.

Nonetheless, I was fascinated by the colours of my brother's face, how his nose and lips flushed brighter in death than they did in life. His skin was almost pearlescent. I pulled at his brow, and his eyelid lifted to reveal the grey of his eyes. His pupils were dilated, and drool dribbled along his chin, but not enough for them to notice, not enough for anyone to care. *Malum*. It was strenuous not to whisper the word, and while I knew I mustn't, it was the sole thing in my mind.

With only one spoon– one colourless spoonful of concentrate– I was able to slip in a sickness too vague to have a name put to it, but I knew. Created from fane, malum had been my first choice ever since his coronation.

I began to plan my first act of business as King, which I supposed would be to lock up the gardens, for it was far too easy to acquire enough malum to kill a man. It truly was one of my kingdom's greatest accomplishments.

For all the colours they made in this kingdom, I have yet to see one so magnificent, as the one Augustus created. So radiant in the moonlight, I took it in as I dreamed of my future. He had no wife, no one but a young daughter, nothing that would be a threat to me.

He should've known I would betray him, maybe he did all along. It was an obvious cliche, people expected the jealous brother, but *I am not jealous*. I am not taking something out of greed, or malice. I am the only one truly made for that crown, the only one built for the glory it withholds, the only one who truly understands. It was he who took it, it was he who stole it from my ready and trained hands. It was he who let me be blamed for it. And I would no longer sit and wait as he took what was mine and pretended that he deserved it. I was raised for it, I was built for it. It was no longer a betrayal in my eyes, it was no longer revenge.

It was destiny.

Not just destiny, it was something more than that. It was the circulation of lives that did not know what they revolved around; it was a story. A story of great hope and loss. I longed for the vines of my destiny to hold the world, for all to look at me and know that I was the one in the centre of it all, the one which connected them, the one they revolved around. I am what everyone waited steadily for like a barn cat waiting to pounce on a mouse. They wait with their hands sweaty, and their mouths salivating, until they drool onto their chin, all grotesque and primal.

I am the opponent in this game of chess that they didn't know they were playing. I am the one pulling the strings. A simple decision on my end could create paradoxes and universes splitting and stretching beyond even my own comprehension. My destiny, my loyalty, my blood. I will revel in each disgusting article in the post, and laugh until I get sick at the children with their rampant rebellious minds. I have waited, stalked, and sat in the scalding water of this kingdom's indecency, and I will not stand for it any longer, my destiny has called for me to make this change. To be the one in the history books. To spit in the face of all stupid enough to challenge my destiny.

In my haze, I seemed to have forgotten that my hand still rested on his face, my nails creating the slightest crescent moons near his scalp. It was no matter, no one would want to look at him a second time, not even the doctors.

Wiping the drool off of his face with my handkerchief, I looked at my brother one last time, my little brother.

"Goodbye, Your Majesty."

How the mighty fall; how the worthless flail.

Chapter I: The House and its Occupants

Snowdrop

B right; that was all Clover could see. Warm, bright light. It held everything in its palm, past, present, future. Its fingers stretched on endlessly, dancing above a great flame. A strange green light grew behind their eyes. It was beautiful. It consumed their mind, like a candle burning to the wick. Slowly, agonisingly, the wick was consumed, with no chance of escape.

The green light drew closer, and with each moment Clover could feel their body burn. The light lit their nerves ablaze, eating up every non-feeling that Clover had ever experienced. Their body drew closer to the outskirts of the light, where fear raced faster than blood. They didn't know what was outside the light, but only that it would prove to be terrible. That was all they could feel. They wondered if it even mattered.

It didn't.

Clover forgot it all when they awoke.

The first sensation Clover felt was the overwhelming feeling of *noise*. Everything was buzzing, sudden, jarring. It was the marching of machinery. Their face itched, so they scratched it. That was their first movement in the new world.

Opening their eyes, Clover's first sight was an elegant room. The walls around them were embossed with grey flowers which bloomed as if it were a warm spring day, but the window next to them said otherwise. Through the floor-length glass roared a violent blizzard which engulfed the room. White flakes moulded onto the frame, seeking vengeance on the building for daring to stand.

They were strangely at peace with it all.

Once again, the loud stomping rang out into Clover's room, and while they had not heard it the first time, they made the immediate connection that it was the very same noise which led to their sudden consciousness.

Clover was quickly aware of the coldness of the room, which created chills so extreme it felt as if pins and needles were stabbing their skin with great repetition. The cold was dry and brushed against Clover's eyes as if it were envious of their moisture. It had no regard for the quilt around them. After forcing their eyes closed, Clover began to breathe in a way so unnatural, they struggled to recall where they had learned it. In for three seconds, out for four.

The door creaked open, and another blast of cold air hit Clover's face.

Stay asleep, a voice in their head warned, and Clover listened as they attempted to cease the rapid beating of their heart.

Harsh, heavy footsteps hit the room's wooden floor and approached the canopy bed until Clover could no longer feel the frigid breeze against their face, signifying that something was in front of them. Clover could feel their hands sweat viciously despite the cold, and dug their nails into their palms to keep a steady, unconscious-like breathing pattern. The trick must've worked, as Clover heard the footsteps patter away. They allowed a shaky breath of relief to escape their lips and propped themself up on their bed before almost shrieking at the sight that befell them.

Standing in the doorway was a tall person with unnaturally yellow hair and dark eyes, one of which was covered by a monocle that looked right out of an ironic parody made to insult the upper class. She readjusted the monocle as she scanned Clover's face.

"I knew you weren't asleep," a strange voice said, one that was at complete odds with the body it came out of, "she's never been wrong, doubt she'd start any time soon."

The person collapsed into the plush armchair next to the bed, letting out a sigh. Clover could not get past the vibrancy of her hair. It was the colour of the light around them, like golden thread.

"She?" Clover replied, not out of an actual wanting to know, but because they felt the need to respond. The word sounded harsh, which made sense, as it was their first one.

Blondie didn't reply, but Clover saw a glare forming on her face. Her cheeks were flushed red, cold and poreless– like a doll– and the features above her cheeks were painted haphazardly, with uneven eyebrows and blotchy freckles. Her eyes were dark, like the shadows of the very room they sat in. There was no warmth in her eyes, human or not. *She wants to kill me,* they thought. *She wants to kill me in this beautiful room.*

"This was my room, you know." Blondie spat; Clover wondered if she could read minds, "They made me sleep in the library *forthwith.*"

"Forthwith?" Clover interrupted.

3

"I am tired of your questions." Blondie fidgeted with her monocle with one hand and gestured to the bedside table with the other. She looked young, too young for a monocle (how Clover knew this, they had no idea.) "Food," Blondie clarified.

Bright fruits and a glass of a strange purple drink were placed carefully on a silver tray; loose petals decorated it like snow. They traced the metal details with their hands as they set it onto their lap. It soothed their sweating palms.

Clover wanted to ask for her name, but when they turned to her Blondie was already gone.

Blondie would enter the room three times after that, two times to bring food, but the third to bring another person.

Clover had finished poking at their third full tray (the thought of eating the strange food made them ill) when it happened. They were still confused and resting, mind reeling with restlessness, and there was a silence all around, so the sudden knocking struck a pang of fear into Clover's heart; it rushed through every vein and released out of Clover's palms as sweat. They looked at the tray of mysterious pink jelly, swirling its cubed fruit like a poisonous, sugary sludge.

Clover had not left their bed all day, paranoid of what would happen if they did, but the knocking continued. The person expected to be let in.

Clover crept out of bed, their legs creaking as they did, and watched as their diaphoretic hand hovered over the doorknob, awaiting their instruction. Swallowing their fear, they opened the door, revealing the perpetrator of the persistent rapping.

A girl of short stature stood before Clover with bandaged eyes. Her short hair was cut choppily, and her bangs were so short that they stuck out like antennae.

With an eerie voice, the girl spoke.

"Will you let me in?"

This was how Clover found themself with another stranger sitting in the chair next to their white canopy bed. Clover had the urge to lead her to the chair until the thought emerged that perhaps she would've found it rude. Alas, she made it to the chair without Clover's help.

Fidgeting with the hem of their shirt, they read small embroidered initials on the wrists: *R.W.*

"You are silent," the girl said.

Clover shook their head in an attempt to shake out their fear, not that she would've seen it.

"Hello." It felt strange to speak.

"The fabric was from some of my old dresses, my brother altered them for you since your other clothes are drying, I'm sorry."

The girl seemed to enjoy wearing bright, frilly things, which was proven by the fact that Clover's sleeves had three layers of lace on the cuffs, matching the girl's superfluous pink gown.

"Thank you," was all Clover could come up with. They didn't understand why she was apologising.

"Do not thank me." She paused for a moment before adding in a whisper, "We are being watched."

Clover looked up to see Blondie standing in the doorway. The contradiction of the two girls perplexed them, Blondie large and imposing, and the dark-haired girl seeming so small. Somehow, they both intimidated Clover. They wiped their hands on their nightgown.

"Is that all?" Blondie asked, her voice solid and unmoving.

"Yes... I am tired," the girl replied, her sentence halved by a yawn.

When she stood from her chair she faced Clover one last time.

"It was nice speaking with you, Clover, I do hope you'll stay."

Before Clover could mention that they barely spoke, she left with a sweep of her gown. It was long after the door shut that Clover realised they had never told her their name, somehow it did not shock them.

The next day there was yet another knock on the door, however, it was unable to stir Clover from the depths of slumber that embraced them. It was far into the morning when Clover woke up, and when they did, they found a note on their left bedside table and a bundle of fabric at their feet.

"Be downstairs at eight," the note told them, and Clover had reason to believe that being late would not end well for them. Clover thought of how peculiar it all was as they opened the bundle. It was filled with fabric (clothes, they soon realised), a silver pocket watch, and a note with handwriting that did not match the other. It read,

"I don't have the time to come and check on your health today, but according to Dorothy, you've been doing all right. Here are your clothes and the possessions we found. You must have many questions. Please be patient with me. (P.S. Don't mind Dorothy, she doesn't mean it.)"

The sentences were choppy and hurriedly written– ink was smudged across the page– but the new stranger was correct. Clover was confused.

They knew they weren't as scared as they were supposed to be, but perhaps that was intentional. Perhaps they were being lulled into a false sense of security.

The note also mentioned someone named Dorothy, who was either Blondie or the girl with black hair. Clover assumed it to be the former. The dark-haired girl didn't seem to match such a name.

Buttoning up the grey waistcoat over their new shirt made Clover uneasy, for they knew it wasn't new, nor was it new to them. They tied a yellow bow tie around their neck with muscle memory. They slid the pocket watch into their waistcoat and focused on steadying their breathing. One thing at a time.

The windows beside them were still frosted, and through it was a colourless nothingness. There may have been land beneath all of the white, or perhaps the house resided upon a cloud, lost and untouched. The light reflected off of it like a great candle in the sky.

With those thoughts racing through Clover's mind, they walked out the door of their room and realised that they did not know where to go. The hallways were endless and narrow, and on the walls were tall, wooden bookshelves filled with tomes, art, and... *dolls*?

Upon closer inspection, Clover deduced that they were most definitely dolls, but they were not the fabric ones given to children. They were alike nothing Clover had seen before. A rainbow of eyes looked back into Clover's own, each detail painted beautifully, each joint meticulously carved, yet each one was unique, the details were not perfect in an identical sense, but they were perfect for what they were: man-made, human.

"They're nice, are they not?" A voice uttered, snapping Clover out of their daze. This voice was different from the girl– or Dorothy– it was somehow softer, sadder.

"Yes," Clover replied, their voice still hoarse from lack of use. However, after looking around the hallway, they couldn't find the source of the voice. A creeping feeling appeared along their spine.

"Thank you, they took me a long time," the voice said again, echoing, still hidden. Clover looked at the candle-lit ceiling above, at the dingy maroon carpet below, and all in between, and still, there was no sign of who was speaking. In a panic, Clover stumbled past a bookshelf in the narrow hallway, revealing an opened door that was covered by the shelf. It stood hidden from the rest of the hall.

Inside the door stood a figure not much taller than Clover, but their silhouette was all that was visible in the shadows. The only other thing they could make out was long wisps of white hair peeking from the darkness; it was like wind was emanating from the room. Clover felt an eerie chill trickle down their spine.

"Hello?" Clover gasped.

"Oh! I'm sorry, did I startle you?" The person squeaked. A gloved skeleton of a hand extended from the shadows, lightly grazing Clover's shoulder before whipping back to the darkness. "I suppose I'm used to being seen no matter where I am."

"Whatever do you mean?" Clover heard their voice choke out. Despite the voice changing to speak in a friendlier tone, it was still hard to make out the face that belonged to it. They saw a large mass of hair consume what little sight they had of the person's face, and a sharp nose could be seen if they squinted.

Loud footsteps stomped up the stairs across the hall, echoing loudly through the corridor. Dorothy must've been looking for Clover. The person squeaked again and turned to close the door, but not before whispering, "You'll see me again soon, then we can speak."

He held out a hand, which Clover took. The man's hand felt brittle in Clover's, but his handshake was firm. Was this the gentleman of the house?

"I must leave now," he turned away momentarily before adding, "You may call me Teddy."

"Clover."

"I know," he said, returning to the shadows.

Clover's feet hit the hardwood staircase in a solemn pattern, left foot down, right foot down, until the guest and occupant descended to the bottom floor in complete silence. Dorothy seemed to be the sort of person who preferred not making conversation, or maybe she wasn't and was purposefully trying to make Clover uneasy. Whichever one it was did not matter, for either way they were silent.

Dorothy's tall boots made loud, cascading noises beyond the dining room staircase. Clover had assumed before that she was more vertically inclined, but walking next to her only cemented that fact. They barely stood at her shoulder.

As the two entered the dining room, Clover's past anxiety returned. Something was wrong. Every room had the sour smell of mould, but it was the strongest there. They tried with great difficulty not to scrunch their nose in front of their hosts. Or were they captors? They still weren't quite sure. There was no doubt in Clover's mind that the house was as old as the very dirt it was built upon. It seemed as if the walls were one harsh breath away from total collapse. That was, of course, assuming that the house was not in the clouds.

If they thought the hallways were cluttered, it was nothing compared to the dining room. Dust clung to all as if glued in place, and vines grew from the ceiling so thickly that they covered most of the windows, resulting in the candleless ceiling being consumed by never-ending darkness.

Bookshelves once again stood at every wall, and yet there were still never enough. Stacks of books swallowed each morsel of empty space in the large room, with many various antiquities using them as convenient display pedestals. There were rolls of old paper and fabric of all colours hanging from the shelves. The room was so overwhelming that Clover barely realised that there were already people sitting at the dining table, old and rotted.

Sat there was the girl from the day before, head tilted downward. Her hair was different than it had been the last time Clover saw her. Gone were the choppy bangs, and in its place was a curly mop of dark, styled hair. Half of the hair had been curled and cascaded down her back, while the other half was brought into a bunch on the top of her head and tied with a ribbon. Clover was unable to look away; the style was too impressive to call anything but positive attention to it.

Beside her sat a tall stuffed animal, but Clover was unable to deduce the species. It looked like a cat– or maybe a fox– but with *hands*. They couldn't figure it out.

Their footsteps echoed in the large room as they made their way to the table and took their seat. The questions regarding new species of animals were not important, so Clover tried to steady their gaze on their hands.

The stuffed animal stood from the chair, as every normal stuffed creature of unknown origins would. Clover sat frozen, confused on whether or not this was supposed to be happening. They also wondered if the girl sitting at the table was a doll as well, due to how still she sat. It wouldn't have been the weirdest thing by far.

Clover kept surprising themself with how calm they felt. Their hands were shaking in the cold, but apart from that, nothing about them could indicate that they were feeling anything but confusion.

They disliked the silence given by the house, and they disliked the mystery even more. *What a strange group of people*, they thought endlessly.

"Your stuffed animal moves?" They asked, which was less of a question and more of a statement of the obvious.

The girl looked up, indicating that she was, in fact, alive. Clover found this fortunate. Her eyes were grey, and two large scars ran down her eyelids. *Like a clown*, a hidden, vindictive part of their brain supplied.

"He isn't mine, he's his own stuffed animal."

Clover was beginning to grow tired of everyone's riddles.

"Well all right, then your friend– who is a stuffed animal– moves?"

"Yes."

Clover shuffled anxiously in their chair, they *really* didn't like silence.

"My brother made him for me," she said in a voice that seemed to disturb all chatter, no matter where in the house it was heard.

"That's lovely."

Dorothy sat next to Clover and glared. They wanted to say something, but the words were trapped in their throat.

"Might I ask why...?" Clover began to say before a crash bellowed from upstairs.

11

"Sweet Vera!" Dorothy shouted, pushing the chair away and falling when one of her large sleeves caught on one of the wooden arms. Clover could barely see her run up the stairs through the stacks of books and clutter. The thumping of her shoes was magnified by her anger and the echo of the dining room, and it would've been a comical sight if not for the setting it was placed in, and the situations that led Clover to see it.

Soon the animal returned with a large silver tray with many plates of food. Clover looked at their surroundings once more and saw a large painting of something they couldn't understand behind the young girl. Clover tried to ignore it, but the painting kept drawing their gaze.

"Could you pass me that, please?" Clover asked her, pointing to a plate across the table. It was filled with a variety of cooked meats: bacon, ham, and sausage. Like the rest of the plates, the smell that wafted from it was entrancing, but dangerous. Clover's stomach growled with a deep, conscious yearning, but they were adamant on their refusal to eat. Poison was not a memory they could recall, but an all-too-familiar sensation they could feel on their tongue.

The girl didn't move for a moment before reaching to the other side of the table. Clover looked behind her at the newly revealed portrait while she was occupied. It looked abstract at first glance, almost nonsensical, but on second glance, looking closer, they began to see a small, red, winding pattern that reminded Clover of a web. Once they saw the web they noticed the colour shift between the lines of the web, revealing the overall image.

Two red eyes pierced through Clover, and all at once, they felt their senses return to them. The fear, the emotions, and the largely delayed reaction to the overwhelming situation that Clover finally found themself worried about. They were not in their house. They did not know where their house was, or if they even had one. They needed to know what was going on.

The girl set the plate in front of Clover, but it was obvious that they had not noticed. After a choked whisper which was supposed to be *"Sorry!"* Clover attempted to leave the table with whatever dignity they had left.

"What are you doing?" Dorothy demanded, but when she noticed their face she stepped aside, allowing them to leave in silence.

That was the last thing Clover remembered before they felt a sharp stabbing pain in their head and fell to the floor, down like a stack of books. The voice in their head spoke once more.

You asked a blind girl to pass a plate to you, have you ever heard of something so foolish?

The other parts of their body murmured in agreement.

Chapter II: The Manor Grounds

Hawthorn

Once again, Clover found themself in the canopy bed without knowing how they arrived. They were tired of sleeping, but they were also tired of the house's mysterious nature. With a burst of determination, they decided that they would be tricked no longer. They understood, with the strangeness of their mind, that they must first learn the way of the manor.

On each side of Clover's canopy were wooden bedside tables. The bed they sat on was wide and comfortable, and the wardrobe opposite it was opened slightly, revealing many coats and dresses. The room was bathed in its entirety by warm, yellow light from lamps perched on their bedsides, shrouded with lace woven to depict a forest scene. Light flickered out of small bird-shaped gaps in the thread, white rabbits hopped across the snow-like lace, and fabricated flowers thrived despite the cold. The beautiful creations distracted Clover from the growing ache forming in the back of their head, and for a moment Clover did not worry about where they were; it was the room of young dreams.

When they stood– huffing as they did– they were hit with

something they were not used to, warmth. Looking out the window, Clover noted the missing snowfall. It did not make any sense, earlier that day there was a blizzard, and now the outside world was green and unblemished by snow. Clover went to the window and sat in front of it, overcome with how beautiful the view was.

There was a city far north of Clover's window. Brick buildings peeked from behind the city's walls, past the winding path leading east, towards the ocean. Clover longed for the ocean breeze. The smell of salt which they could not imagine, but felt familiar to their nose. Far away in Dreamland, they almost missed the sight of a shining, bright green light near the beach.

Standing up once more, Clover looked to see a balcony door which had not existed when they first awoke. There was a mirror beside it, and for the first time, they were allowed sight of the body holding their brain.

They were a physical thing once again. Tall and muscular– or were they short and frail? It was still difficult to say, their sense of self not aligning with what they saw. Perhaps they were tall, perhaps they were not. Perhaps they were strong, perhaps they were not. They felt their face and saw their fingers do so in the mirror. It was as if their brain muddied their sight, for they knew that what they were looking at was their flesh, but they could not process it. They squished their nose, felt the lids of their eyes, pressed against their lips, but to no avail.

With a sense of failure, Clover looked instead at their clothed body. They wore a nightgown similar to the one the girl was wearing before. Did that make them a girl, as well? *No*, a voice in their head said. *You are something quite different.*

"What am I?" Clover asked the mirror.

"You?" The mirror said. "Why, you are a detective!"

"Yes… that does make sense, I suppose." What a detective was, they had no idea.

Clover was hit with a strong burst of wind as they opened the door, and the smell of the ocean was almost overpowering. It was as if they were drowning in the sea.

The light was emanating from a lantern held by someone creeping closer and closer to the manor. They were wearing a wool coat and a mask resembling a bird with purple splotches. Their first thought was to be afraid, but pushed it down until the only emotion they felt was indifference. How easy it was to do so.

"It's quite cold out here!" Clover called out to the person, unsure of what to do otherwise. This seemed to shock the person, as they dropped the light they were carrying momentarily.

"It's all right; I'm used to it!"

The person was now close to the balcony and reached for their mask before unhooking it from around their head, revealing long white hair. It was Teddy.

Clover's eyes widened. They felt strangely pleased with this revelation, at least now they wouldn't have to worry about warding off evil visitors from someone else's house.

"I told you we'd see each other again!" he said with a laugh, holding the light up to his face.

"Teddy? Is that you?"

"As it is, and as it always will be!" Teddy exclaimed proudly while relighting the candle in his lantern, for it had gone out in the fall.

"What are you doing?" Clover asked, taken aback by Teddy's burst of energy. His laugh was small and squeaky, almost muffled by the sound of nearby rustling leaves.

"Making the house safer, " Teddy said as he attempted to close the latch of the light. He might've been handsome, had he not been so translucent.

"With a lantern?"

"With a lantern," Teddy paused for a moment before saying, "Would you like to join me?"

Clover stared at him for a moment before nodding. It was clear Teddy *didn't* expect them to fall as they climbed vines down the balcony, and he most definitely *didn't* laugh when they inevitably did so.

"It isn't as easy as you would think," Clover exclaimed as Teddy helped them to their feet with a smug look on his face. Again, his handshake was gentle.

"Of course." He laughed again, and with that, Clover took back any thoughts of his handsomeness. He was a silly man, a very *pale* silly man, which were two things Clover found concerning.

And so the two went, with Teddy lighting pillars surrounding the house with his lantern, and Clover struggling to keep up. Not only was this due to darkness, but also because they were trying to find the right questions to ask. Instantly Clover felt more comfortable with Teddy than the rest of the house's people, as he seemed much less intimidating. Perhaps this was Clover tapping into humanity's ability to find comfort and romance in even the strangest of circumstances. Or perhaps– more reasonably– it was their curiosity in his nerves which kept them from running in the opposite direction. *He could be of use. Use his weakness to your advantage!*

Clover blushed at the thought.

The green light from the lantern filled the area between the two as Clover struggled to try to find the pockets on their nightgown. Teddy's mask stayed at the bottom of his chin, creating ominous shadows on his face which reminded Clover of the young girl in the manor; their faces rested in the same solemn look, despite looking nothing alike. His eyes were doe-like, wide, and looked straight ahead as if determined to find something specific. The light matched those eyes with the same familiar shade, and Clover was unable to answer the question of where they had seen it before. There was a magic to it.

"You were the one who wrote that note, yes?" Clover asked, faking nonchalance. Yes, that seemed like a good start to the thousands of questions they needed to ask. Teddy looked up from the current pillar he was lighting and glanced at Clover before nodding. The purple flowers embroidered on the mask moved in the light. Clover continued with their questions. "Where am I?"

Teddy looked at Clover, and when they met eyes Clover was overwhelmed with just how much pity they saw.

"Let's go inside first," he said with a quick smile.

Teddy led Clover into a study after helping them back onto the balcony. Books of every colour lined the walls surrounding a dark wooden desk in the centre. A large brick fireplace cast a lonely shadow over the room, and the fire's low tendrils grasped for any further sustenance. He pulled his mask off and hung it on a hook on the door, and beside it, he set a wooden cane. Clover had not realised that Teddy had used it during their walk.

He gestured for Clover to sit at the desk as he hauled logs from a woven basket on the floor, throwing them into the almost-smothered fire. He rubbed his hands together before blowing into them in a motion that resembled an attempt for warmth, but when he placed his hands above the hollow flame it began to burn a faint green. The green quickly muddled out and turned yellow. Teddy, unaware of Clover's shock, hoisted himself off of the ground and began to rummage for something on the shelves near the desk. The green was nostalgic, like the sight of an old friend.

Clover noticed a small drawing which lay centred on the desk, recently abandoned. It was a sketch for a likeness. There was an outline for dark hair sketched atop the paper, but the face and all other defining features were lost, known only to the mind of its artist. They were so caught up in staring at the outlined person that they almost didn't notice the sounds of rummaging had stopped. *Almost.*

"Did you draw this?" They asked once the study was quiet.

With an unblinking stare, Teddy nodded with hesitancy. The warmth of the fire had not spread to his cold gaze, and he stared with the same air a rabbit would as it looked out of its borough into the eyes of something dangerous. It was as if he was afraid of Clover's attention– or opinion– of the drawing. Or, perhaps more likely, he feared Clover. If so, the feeling was mutual.

The curiosity of his look did not leave Clover's mind, and they could feel those eyes follow their hands as they stared at the drawing. The feeling of being observed was unlike most feelings, but they were not afraid. Eyes they could handle, Dorothy's shouting they could not.

They knew it was best to act oblivious in case Teddy was a threat. He was still a stranger, after all, even if he didn't look to be a strong one. They knew not to put their guard down.

"Is something wrong, Teddy?"

He stared at Clover, his eyes widened in an incomprehensible expression. Clover looked away, back at the likeness. Teddy tapped on the desk absent-mindedly until a green light began to emerge from his hand. After tapping twice, one of the chairs that had been leaning against the wall at the other end of the room was pulled next to him in an instant. Teddy sat in it, not noticing Clover's expression. He cracked his knuckles before reaching into his coat pocket.

After laying a piece of crumpled-up parchment onto the desk, he held his head in his hands for a few seconds before closing them in front of his mouth. The movement reminded Clover of the bird mask that was currently hung up on the door. Teddy's eyes remained closed.

"Well?"

"Well?" Clover copied.

"Are you going to look at it?" Teddy said, and his voice grew colder with every syllable. Clover flinched, picking up the paper in haste. Unfolding it revealed something wonderful: Clover's name.

Clover Page-Bettencourt was their name. It was printed at the top of the page, which was the only thing that wasn't partially burned, ripped, or ruined by water. From the limited information that was saved, Clover learned that the document, in all of its crumpled glory, was some sort of licence of identification for a detective.

"You really don't remember anything? About your past?" Teddy asked.

"No," Clover felt choked looking at the document, "I do not."

For a long time, Teddy did not speak. He simply stared at the floor. If Clover hadn't been so preoccupied, they would've taken more time to be confused about how he knew their memory was lost in the first place. Perhaps he was a doctor.

"Are you sure?" He said. Clover thought it seemed redundant.

"Some things, but they come and go, and are mostly of no use to me." *What is a girl?*

His eyes stared holes into the floor before glancing at the desk.

"Well," he began, "You are in a kingdom called Terra Florens, your name is Clover Page-Bettencourt, and you are experiencing memory loss. Most likely concussed."

"What day is it?"

"I think about May the twenty-third, 1894."

Clover didn't know why they asked for the date, it meant nothing to them.

"Maybe try explaining what happened, perhaps it'll jog my memory," Clover thought it was strange that they were the one having to remind him. Teddy was silent for some time before speaking.

"Yes, of course. I apologise. It was a cold night, which isn't rare. I was paroling just as I was tonight when I heard a crash near the beach. Of course, I went to check to see if it was something malicious, and I hid behind the tree when I realised there were people." Teddy began, gesturing with his hands with every word, if Clover wasn't so intrigued they might've laughed.

"People?" Clover asked. Teddy nodded before continuing.

21

"I can't remember their exact words at the time, but you can ask Rose about it later, you've met Rose, right? The one with short black hair, I cut it for her, actually, it usually isn't that bad. I've been having a tough time focusing lately."

"Teddy?"

"I'm sorry, I'm rambling aren't I?" Teddy began to apologise hysterically.

"The people, Teddy."

"Right, yes, of course. They were talking about how they were looking for something but they couldn't find it– thieves I think– so I waited for them to leave once I learned that they weren't a threat to us, it's unwise to go around picking fights with thieves, especially when there were so many, I could've maybe asked Dorothy to help, but she's been so busy as of late. So I waited until I was sure they were gone to look around at what they were looting. That's where I found a carriage and– well– *you*."

"*I* was in the carriage?" It was difficult to follow what Teddy was saying.

"Pretty beaten up too, by the looks of it, but I think I did a pretty good job at healing you back to health– I mean, by the looks of you– you know, you're walking and everything."

It took Clover a long time to process what Teddy said,

"How did my injuries heal so fast if they only happened a few days ago?"

Teddy looked up at them with that same inexplicable expression.

"Two reasons probably, one a little easier to explain than the other."

"What do you mean?"

"First of all, my name isn't actually Teddy, that's just what

Rose calls me, and–"

"Is she your daughter?" Clover interrupted without thinking, and Teddy looked at them with a mix of amusement and confusion before replying.

"Sister. Do I look that old?" *Yes*, Clover wanted to say but thought against it.

"No, I'm sorry, please continue."

Teddy paused. Clover could hear a soft hum rumble from somewhere in the house, and it rang in their ears like a long drawn-out note on the violin.

"Could you first promise me something?" He said, his voice suddenly solemn.

23

Chapter III: A Childhood

Baby's Breath

Lethe, forever breathing, was not a stranger to misery. Terra Florens in particular was a land rarely spared. In their history, monsters born from caverns too deep for the goddess Vera to see terrorised the human population. Civil wars raged on for decades, over subjects ranging from religious freedoms to violence against another's farm animal. After hundreds of years of violence, Terra Florens finally found peace under the reign of King Augustus. The kingdom took one collective breath of anguish when he passed, and mourned just as a family would mourn.

The second son of Augustus– Augustus II– brought the sun back to Terra Florens. Kind was the only word that could've described him. His smile shone over the population. The kingdom found that the flowers grew brighter, and the birds sang sweeter under his reign.

When his brother, Valentijn, came to power, the land turned sour. It was an unspoken sourness, one no one dared to utter aloud. There wasn't any legal reason why he shouldn't have been just as fit to rule, but he lacked the warmness Augustus II brought.

Dangers were never-ending during the time of King Valentijn's reign. Whether it was animals, natural disasters, or even other people, countless things could harm the common citizen. Among all of those, however, was one predator of mankind that succeeded them all: their own paranoia.

There had been a nationwide phenomenon of cursed people sent to strike fear in the human population. Most people took it as something made to stir up fear, but others took it as a sign of the apocalypse. Magical people, once a rare sight in Terra Florens, were now feared and despised.

On the June solstice of that year, two years after Valentijn came to power, a baby boy was born.

Aster Williams lived in the apartment on top of his family's toyshop with his mother, father, and dog, Antigone, in the large city of Solle, located in western Terra Florens. They were a happy family– unusually eccentric, sure, but if anyone were to ask any of their neighbours, they would've referred to the Williams as the happiest family in all of the city, perhaps even the kingdom. That was not to say that they had an easy life, but it was not so rampant with tragedy to make them different.

That was until Aster started to grow up, and the changes began.

It started small, with his houseplant (who he named Diana) starting to flourish after being dead for many months. It was easy for his parents to deceive themselves into thinking that it was a coincidence, but his experiences were not unique. The streets filled with newspapers stamped with titles such as *"The Dangers of Magical Children!"* and, *"How to make sure your child hasn't been replaced with an evil fairy child!"* It became harder and harder for the Williams to pretend that Aster was normal.

Changelings, as some called them, had become such a threat that word spread of royally funded schools meant to teach the children how to suppress their power. Mr and Mrs Williams were afraid to admit they didn't want to send Aster to such a place, for they knew he wouldn't be able to handle it. He was weaker than the other children, easily bullied and easily pushed around. He was also stranger than the others, unable to follow the schoolteacher's lessons as fast as his peers. Without the safety of his home, he would have no place to go.

So when the day came to bring Aster to the town centre, they kept him upstairs. If their neighbours noticed Aster not going out as much, they didn't say anything, and soon the memory of the family became as faint as old paint on a toy train.

"These children are different from all other magic we have encountered," declared the king. "They are dangerous, they will destroy us all."

The crowd cheered, despite not understanding his words.

"Pa," Aster asked one day as his father showed him how to build a figure of a horse, "Why can't I go to school anymore?"

His father sighed and patted Aster on the back. The dark-eyed gaze of his father disarmed the stubborn questions that bubbled up from Aster's rebellious mind.

"You were too smart for it," replied he, which seemed to work well enough, as Aster went back to painting his little toy horse and trying to stop a certain mischievous dog from chewing on the wooden limbs. He was unable to hear how his father's voice caught on the words, nor how his father held back a sob when he left the room.

Aster loved nothing more than his parents' toy store, with the only thing tied with it being his parents themselves, strong, generous, and people who stood up for others who couldn't. They were like the heroes he read about at school, back when he had to go.

Aster's favourite part of helping his parents were the dolls. He loved sewing clothes for them, and to see them wear his creations was almost as satisfying as if he had worn it himself. Obviously, he couldn't wear what he made, as they were far too small, but it did not stop him from pretending.

He had a sheltered, but otherwise happy childhood with only the smallest amount of magic that he legally shouldn't have, but that was all right. His parents reminded him that his magic wasn't dangerous like the stories in the newspapers, and he felt safe.

When Aster turned twelve, his mother gave him a stuffed bear that he had named after Antigone, who had run away months prior, putting the whole family in a bit of a slump. If he held the bear close enough, it almost felt as if she were still there.

A strange sickness was spreading about Solle, reaching its claws into the darkest corners of the city. A dark shadow of soot and ash lodged into the lungs of the misfortuned. When it found the Williams' household, it had no name. At first, the doctors claimed it to be a dust-induced cold, but soon enough, the once bright house over the toyshop became filled with the echoed coughs of the undead. Aster especially was affected. *Miasma* was all the name it deserved. Bleeding lungs revealed themselves upon greying handkerchiefs placed over his mouth. While he was at first most attacked, the more he recovered the more his parents fell to it.

27

Aster, not yet adolescent, crawled from his bed every few hours to give rusting cups of water to his mother and father, ignoring the sway and shake of his small hands. His stuffed bear lay forgotten on the floor. His vision blurred, but still he persevered. His home fell into disrepair, the ground covered in bloody rags and blankets.

The doctors did not come to treat, but instead to bury, even Aster understood that. Despite it, as he woke up one bleary, aching day, he found himself unable to detach himself from his dying parents. His dead parents.

They were lost sometime in the night.

"Serves them right," whispered a masked doctor. "Having a child as strange as *that*. Most definitely magic. Do you see his hair?"

"If he was magic, he wouldn't still be here," replied the other.

"Born of magic then. A grandparent."

They both stared down at him.

"You cannot blame him for what he came from."

"Shall we send him to an orphanage or one of the Juno schools?"

They pointed their beaks at him.

"Leave him on the street."

He could not remember how long it had been since the sickness first started, nor could he remember what happened after the loss of his parents. But Aster remembered the sickly stench of ash, and his childhood home set alight. A precaution of infection, or– perhaps– the punishment for their treason.

He was found on the street by an old family friend, Rosaline, with stuffed Antigone in hand. She was young, about ten years older than he. His hair had grown long and light and his skin became pale in his time spent inside. She gasped when she saw him and exclaimed that he had the hair of an old maid.

Fear glistened in her eyes like fresh paint, but Aster did not cry.

He didn't cry when she hugged him so hard he could barely breathe. He didn't cry when she asked him to help her fill two suitcases with clothes so that the two of them could travel to a small country town, where Rosaline's parents were. He didn't even cry when she cut his hair and hid it beneath a hat crocheted by his mother. This was not to say he wasn't sad, or scared– he was terrified– but he couldn't cry.

Aster had known at this time that he was different, but he didn't think he was dangerous in any way. He wasn't like the stories of the kids who set fire to their governess or the ones who made crops spoil because they were bored, he could help people. If they would only give him a chance.

But the king did not agree with him, and despite the last king being magic himself, King Valentijn despised it.

In the country, Rosaline's mother said there was no room for him in the house, but that he could live in the barn. They had to sell their animals long ago, so it was empty.

Aster tried to cry. Instead, he sat tearless in a barn hidden in the countryside without his parents, and it was all his fault. If only he was normal, if only he did the things every other child did. Sweet, kind, normal children. Aster hated himself, and he knew the world did as well.

Rosaline was kind, and she had always been generous with Aster and his family, but he knew he was a burden to her. She was still young. She had gone to the city in search of her fortune. Now, she was stuck taking care of a child, and what a disappointing child he was.

After many weeks, Aster had got used to his new pattern of life. The routine of it all had helped numb the pain, and sometimes he even caught himself forgetting why he was there. He had a makeshift room in the empty barn, with a bed of stale hay and a table made out of a crate. It was quite cosy, and Antigone seemed to like her spot on the bed. He would start the day by eating with Rosaline. Then, he would sneak out the loft window with Antigone to sit on the roof looking out at the forest. When he was done he would sneak back in to sew, and read until nighttime.

He had learned how to sew from his father at the toy store. Rosaline knew this, and gifted Aster a little sewing set as a little *sorry-your-parents-are-dead* gift. It was a nice little sewing set, three needles, ten pins, four different coloured threads (white, yellow, red, and blue,) and a bundle of fabric scraps from Rosaline's stash.

Only two were big enough to be made into something Aster-sized, which was still much more than he expected, and he worried that Rosaline had spent too much on him. Despite her reassurance that it was not the case, he was far too scared of ruining the scraps to do anything with them. For a month they sat in the cleanest corner of the barn.

He enjoyed making clothes for Antigone. She was a bit larger than the dolls he was used to sewing for– he realised– but erased the thought, lest Antigone could read minds. The last thing he wanted was for her to be self-conscious.

On most days, he would read the books Rosaline gave him. They were ancient textbooks, which collected dust faster than Aster could clean. Rosaline said she had big plans for him.

She gave him her old assignments on maths and literature in hopes that he would continue his studies even out of school. He knew his father lied about him being too smart for school, but he couldn't help but be disappointed. On his broken slate, he would stitch together different sentences from books, and sketch large, looping cursive.

Aster's mind wandered to many places whilst in the barn. It was as if his stories developed faster than his brain. With every new word he learned, enchanted portals opened within the mind of his encaged physical form. He could be wherever he wanted, as long as he had a story.

Aster could not bear to look at numbers for more than ten minutes at a time, and during the time dedicated to his studies in mathematics, he conveniently began to forget his slate outside.

He would put on his hat and sneak off to the main house to speak with Rosaline as a detour; she had many different stories. On that particular day, his mind began to wander to the forest, it seemed as if the birds had slowly begun singing a song different from the one he heard when he first arrived, one not as languid, nor as slow. Not to say it wasn't still a melancholic tune, but it was not so much so as before. Despite the point of the trip being to ignore his studies, he was once again distracted by the many stories that sat dormant in his mind.

He allowed himself to look around at the scenery for a moment, if not to clear his mind, but to procrastinate being told off by Rosaline. Moss clung to the trees around the old Dubois farmhouse almost as fervently as dust would in the barn. The smell of rain filled his lungs, healing them from the inside before being shaken out by a loud noise in the

31

distance, one that sounded like a dragon's roar. Technology had changed drastically since Aster had gone into hiding, and Rosaline had told him of a horseless carriage drawn by a motor. Aster did not know what a motor was, or how strong it could pull a carriage, but knew that the noise must've been one.

A thought quickly came to Aster's mind. Why would a motor-drawn carriage be at Rosaline's house? A question which was quickly answered as the deep voice of a man rose with the wind.

"Mrs Dubois? We're here with the king's police on account of…"

Aster didn't hear anything after that, for he felt as if he were stuck in place, they must have been after him. There was no other explanation.

As the officer entered the home, Aster finally felt the strength go back in his legs, and he ran back into the barn, climbing into the loft window. He tried his best to tremble quietly.

After what seemed like an eternity, Aster heard the officers leave, and he choked out a sigh of relief. He decided at that moment that he would no longer allow tragedy to make him weak.

That was until the barn door opened, revealing Rosaline and an officer. Aster would not be able to recall the officer's face, but only that his eyes were filled with hate.

Aster knew only two things at that moment. He knew that his parents were dead, and he knew that he wished he was as well.

Chapter IV: Penitentiary

Aster

The automobile rattled endlessly on the dirt road to Solle's Orphanage for Magical Children, and Aster could feel himself trembling with mortification. It had been over two hours and his hunger had begun to mix with his fear, creating a stew of treacherous panic. The metal creature roared mercilessly, and Aster's only source of comfort came from the thought that if it killed him, he wouldn't have to worry about the horrors that awaited him in the orphanage.

It was past nightfall when a light began to grow in the distance, a lantern. Aster's head perked up from the lull he had finally drifted to and glanced at the king's policeman. He told Aster two hours before that he was to be called Cornelius, although he said so with such strange hesitancy it was as if he were still getting used to it. As the light grew larger, so did the figure holding it: a cloaked stranger wearing thick wool gloves. Amid the cold bite of nature, they were the only person there to welcome Aster into his new prison.

The cloaked person nodded to Cornelius, who continued to drive deeper into the hilltop forest. Staring at the passing trees, Aster wondered if he had ever been to this part of Solle. Perhaps his family went to the nearby lake when Aster was younger, or maybe he saw it through the window of a train when he would go to school.

He missed going to school, and he missed his parents even more.

In the darkness, Aster began to see the world slow down, and through his tears, he thought he saw something very peculiar indeed: a carving on one of the nearby trees. It looked like a smiling face, and strangely it was a comfort.

Green brick erupted from the centre of the ground and came into fruition as a large building at the top of the hill. It was a stereotypically horrific sight. A barren garden lay dead in the crass of Solle's early autumn outside the front door, and the whole property was surrounded by a tall brick fence. The trees around it shook as they drove past, and erupted from the shaken branches came bells. Those bells rang in his head for the rest of the night.

They snuck him into an empty room and took his bag to be searched. He felt that at any moment he would be yelled at, but they spoke to him with no emotion at all, as if his arrival did not matter. They knew his name– assumedly from Rosaline– but not the ones belonging to his parents. They didn't bother to learn them.

His anger was a feeling he never wished to lose, but as the room got brighter and his eyes readjusted to the silent darkness he realised that he had already lost everything. Even at nighttime, there was a difference. Outside his home, he could always hear the faint humming of factories and high-wheel bicycles. In the barn, he could hear the calming buzz of insects and the occasional howl of wolves in the forest. But in the orphanage, no sound perturbed the stone walls. It was all so silent. He couldn't even hear himself breathe.

They had told him that the orphanage was different from the boarding schools for magic children. Not only was he required to complete the program, but he also had to stay until he came of age. He could leave at sixteen if he could find an apprenticeship, but if not he would have to wait until he was eighteen. Six years.

There– with those strange cold walls around him– Aster cried. Left by his parents, abandoned by his country, he could not think of the future, he could not think of the next day. He was alone. Lost.

Aster didn't realise he had fallen asleep until it was morning; until it was already too late.

Outside the window was a dead forest, the bells still. Aster watched the sun rise, and with it came sweltering heat. He was raced from room to room by the staff, and even then, he knew that his possessions were never to be given back. He was shown the dining room, the many bedrooms, libraries, and classrooms. He could not breathe as he peeked through the classroom windows and saw the eyes of children staring hollowly at the front of the room. Aster wondered if soon he would be the same, if that were to be his fate. If he would have to give up his thoughts and feelings in order to be able to exist.

The library was small, and the books were empty. If they weren't, they were filled with nonsense about simplicity and conformity. Aster knew he shouldn't cry, but there was something about the libraries in particular that made it sink in that he was stuck, all alone. Not even stories could help

35

him.

They took a photo of him when his uniform was given, it was the first photograph he had ever taken, and he was sure he looked dreadful in it. He hadn't slept comfortably for weeks and hadn't eaten as much as he should for longer. The man taking the photo attempted to explain to him the difference between "dry and wet plate negatives" but shushed him when he opened his mouth to reply.

Aster was sure that his hair made him stand out more than he wanted, more than they wanted. He told them his mother had the same shade, and that it was a very light blond. That wasn't the case, but it worked. As he stood for the photograph he thought about the object taking it. How could such a fascinating creation be used for something so horrible? Perhaps that was how the orphanage thought of him.

Aster soon found out that the school he now attended differed from the one his parents spoke of in hushed voices. It was obvious when he thought about it, but somehow he could not think much of anything. The schools for magical children with living parents were run by the church, while the orphanages for magical children were run by the throne.

The children there seemed as dreadful as the staff, and just as dreadful as his hair. They stared at him with an inexplicable strangeness that made his stomach flip with the desire to get as far as possible. He didn't see them as his equals for the first weeks, for they were too different. In his mind, they were an extension of the orphanage. Stone walls, stone floors, stone people.

Days went by quickly for Aster in the orphanage, and yet also painfully, excruciatingly slow. His mind was too cautious to wander, and his legs had grown too used to staying still to the point where if he wasn't seen walking into a room, no one would know he was there at all. His breath was trained to be taken in so slowly that one could never hear it, as if he were a statue.

He was not a normal child before the orphanage, but he– with his white hair and spindly limbs– looked as out of place as could be. Long pale fingers like icicles held things in the wrong hand, his left, and his eyes never blinked when they should. Aster Williams was the opposite of a hearty, good-natured child. He was what the teachers and caretakers considered a particularly tough subject. Quiet and haunted, like the very dolls he drew on his slate when he thought no one was looking.

The orphanage worked in a particular way. Every room had surveillance, and the head scholars always watched the children. This was because the orphanage that Aster was sent to– unfortunately– was one of the eight in the nation created to research and fix orphans with magic. There was one in Solle, Everil, Rosamund, Doveport, Lunaris, Dolston, and two in the royal city. Each orphanage was run by six "head scholars," a term gifted by the government to– in Aster's opinion– the cruellest people in the kingdom. One of the cruellest went by the name of Andreas Hughes, a terrible man with thin hair and an even thinner moral code. He hated the way Aster did anything. The way he cleaned, ate, and cooked, were all incorrect.

Because of this, Aster had been sent down without dinner, past the cupboard, past the thirteen rooms– each holding five children– past the living room, and into the basement, where all of the bad children went. Aster never thought he was a bad child by any means, but he had dropped a bowl and had unknowingly made the situation worse after fixing it "paranormally." He was ashamed of being one of the only children to still use their powers after their first few weeks, Aster heard that those were always the worst.

That night, another person was in the basement, someone he had never seen before. Through tear-filled eyes, he saw a young girl who couldn't have been older than ten. When he got closer, and subsequently dried his tears so he seemed less weak, he saw a horrific sight. Her entire face was bandaged and bloodied, and her body was curled up so small it was as if she could fall between the cracks of the stone floor at any moment.

Aster knew that she was about to die. He was conflicted. He didn't want to get in trouble for using his magic again, the loud screaming and bruises had not yet faded, but he couldn't let this girl die, could he?

All conflict was thrown out the window when her head attempted to tilt upwards before flinching and going limp. Quickly, Aster rubbed his hands together, trying to get as much energy as he could into his fingers and putting them on the top of the young child's head, her hair matted from blood. He closed his eyes and transferred the energy from his body to hers. He knew it was dangerous for him to push himself to that level, but he had nothing to lose. Slowly he could feel her cold body growing warmer, blood slowly going back to her arms and legs. Aster felt fresh stitches on her head and his anger rose, who would do something like this to someone so young? He answered his question, it was most likely the very same people who did that terrible thing to his house and parents.

He attempted to unwrap the bandages around her head but was stopped by her hand holding onto his arm.

"You don't want me to?" Aster asked the small, shaking child. She shook her head so quickly that he almost didn't see it. He looked around the basement, his vision once again going blurry from both adrenaline and exhaustion.

"Do you feel better?"

Aster didn't know if she could see him, but she faced his direction and he watched as the bandages on her face began to grow darker, not with blood, but with tears.

"Are you all right? Is something wrong?" He must've done something wrong, he'd never healed another person before, maybe she still felt pain, despite the wounds looking to be healed. She shook her head and hugged him, still crying.

Aster wondered if that was what it felt like to have a younger sibling. He had wondered about it for a long time, but those specific memories of his life before were the few that weren't pleasant. It only flooded his mind with the reminder of his mother's screams. Sitting down quietly next to the girl he mimicked her, holding his knees to his chest and closing his eyes. However, before drifting off, he heard a distant voice echo throughout the room.

"Thank you."

Aster fell asleep, hungry but proud.

The next weeks were better, although slightly. The cruelty was still the same, and the bruises still stung, but now Aster had a friend. The young girl did not share a room with any other kids, as he had found out that she was not technically a child in the orphanage. One night at dinner he asked the only tolerable person there, a friendly older girl named Iris

Webbleton who had been at the orphanage for around seven years, the question stuck in his head.

"Do you know the girl who's always in the playroom?" He asked her, the playroom was the name for the empty room meant to keep the children under ten when they weren't doing classes or in the outside courtyard. After Aster saved the girl, she began showing up with the other young children. He assumed she was put in the basement on her first day. What could she have done to deserve such treatment?

"Which one? The one with black hair or the one who's always falling?"

"Black hair."

"That's Rose."

Iris explained to Aster that Rose was the daughter of two people who worked at the orphanage. She didn't even have powers. Her parents died when she was a baby in an accident and she had nowhere else to go, Aster was confused.

"She's only just arrived, hasn't she?"

Iris brought a napkin up to her mouth, as if to wipe it, and looked forward away from Aster while saying quietly,

"That's what they'll tell you."

Before Aster could digest what was being said, she began talking about an essay she was writing on the importance of normality and how schedules and societies help more than harm. He felt his stomach sink back to the basement.

One night, after everyone had gone to bed, Aster stuffed a pillow underneath his blanket in trivial hopes of fooling the caretakers. Even if it wasn't convincing, it would at least buy him some time. Leaving the room, he was reminded of how he would sneak out of the barn, he wondered if that was why

Rosaline had sold him out, if she thought he deserved it. He couldn't blame her if that was the case, if it was then he would wholeheartedly agree, but every night as he lay in his bed he cursed her name.

After taking his beloved bear Antigone (which he had snuck into the establishment and kept hidden under his mattress,) he snuck down the hallway and realised he had no idea where he was supposed to go, he never learned where Rose's room was. As he looked at the walls, mildly panicking, there was a creak in the floorboards in front of him. Aster tried his best not to scream as he saw a small shadow at the end of the hallway, he convinced himself that this was the ghost of a child who didn't survive the orphanage, and that they were coming for him to bring him to the realm of the dead, but his doom never came. Aster opened his eyes and saw the young girl, still bandaged but less bloody. Aster was glad. He was proud of himself for being the person he wished he had, even if the thought made him grimace with embarrassment.

He went to speak but was cut off by the child shushing him. Rose walked down the hallway, walking on only specific boards to stay hidden, Aster followed the best he could. His footsteps were soft on the wooden panels, as he had practised. She led him to a painting on one of the large white walls, it was a portrait of the scientist who was put in charge of the project many years ago, next to the portrait of the king. Aster knew he couldn't handle thinking about it for too long, so he didn't. The girl faced the painting, and then Aster, and then the painting once more, and then, in one swift motion, she pushed the painting into the wall, revealing a small corridor hidden behind the canvas.

Aster choked back an exasperated laugh and followed Rose

41

into the corridor, making sure the painting shut behind him with a faint *click*.

The space, which at first was only big enough for Aster to crawl in, slowly began expanding the further they went into the hidden passage. Aster was glad that Rose was able to find it, indicating that she still had some vision behind the bandages. Now the passage had become big enough for Aster and Rose to walk side-by-side, and when he was sure no one could hear him from the outside, Aster said, "Thank you."

"You're welcome!" a cheery voice said back to him, he was shocked that a voice so joyful came out of a body that was so harmed. Aster tried to remind himself that even if terrible things had happened, both to him and her, they were still children. Aster didn't feel like a child, maybe he didn't even count as one because of all of what he did, but he knew that Rose was.

"I like your hair," Aster said to her, trying to mimic her cheerful voice.

Rose spun around to look at him.

"I don't, they had to cut it so the doctor could make me better. I think it's ugly," she stared at him for a few seconds before adding, "At least mine isn't white, though."

Aster was in shock at how offensive a child could become in mere seconds, but he couldn't disagree, his hair was made fun of all of the time by the other students. His peers were almost as bad as the caretakers, but he refused to think of it any further.

The two continued to walk down the corridor, and Aster's worry crept behind him. What if he returned after sunrise? He was sure he would get a terrible punishment, something even worse than when he had dropped the bowl.

It was strange. The farther Aster went from the orphanage, the clearer his mind became. It was as if he had been dreaming for months. They came to a door, and Aster watched Rose open it, revealing something mortifying, something that would haunt him for years to come.

He saw a room with sickly white walls covered in grime, which was everywhere, under every surface. Dirt and rust covered the medical equipment hanging on the walls and sitting on the tables, frequently used. An unwelcoming stench suffocated this room, and there wasn't a single window, no matter how much Aster longed for one. He didn't want to think about what the red stains on the fabric of the medical table were, but he knew.

Rose lingered in the tunnel, slowly pushing him forward. He tried to say something, to tell her no or that he needed to leave but his vocal cords couldn't work, and he couldn't find the words. Words that would be lost for a long time.

He barely heard her whisper, "I'm sorry, *Teddy*. You have to."

Aster wanted, above all else at that moment, for his body to absorb itself so he wouldn't touch any part of the room, but as his shoe hit the hard concrete floor a chill went up his spine, the feeling so real and overwhelming. Shaking, he looked around, hoping to keep his screams silent. The door from the tunnel was another painting, and as it closed his body tensed up completely, the noises of machinery drowning out as if he had fallen into a large body of water, unable to move.

There was a machine in the corner of the room, wires poking out like a stomach full to bursting. He felt his dinner threaten to join the mess, and dug his nails into his palms.

A shrill voice called out from a hallway behind a door, and

footsteps were nearing the laboratory. Aster stared at the door, and his heart dropped, vision blurry. Quickly he ran into a wardrobe and closed the door, the smell unbearable, he didn't dare think of what could be inside it with him.

The door opened, and he heard a heeled shoe hit the concrete floor, along with a flat shoe after it.

"Did you find her?" A deep voice said, sounding stressed and agitated.

"I have staff looking all around the premises, she couldn't have gone far." A different voice replied. Footsteps grew closer to the wardrobe, and Aster choked back a scream and covered his mouth with his hand, feeling warm tears fall from his eyes. The footsteps stopped.

"Oh, no need, I have the equipment out already." the same voice said, Aster almost let out a sob of happiness as he heard the footsteps retreat, far from the closet. A cold chill ran down his spine, taking all oxygen away with it. To say that he was terrified was a gross understatement, his blood cold and his face numb, hands shaking violently. He felt a strange, venomous feeling seep through his bones, it was as if fear was a disease quickly consuming him. Aster wondered what equipment they would be using once they caught Rose. Would it be one of the scalpels, all used and bloodied, or perhaps the large machine in the corner of the room, with its terrifying wires and sharp teeth? Every breath stuck in his throat, and with each one, he felt himself drift farther from consciousness.

Aster couldn't remember when he passed out, as the closet was as dark as behind his eyelids, but when he woke he was in his bed, Antigone in his arms, as if he had never left at all. He would've believed it as well if it weren't for the dirt under his nails and the horrible headache ringing in his ears. When he made it out of bed, his stomach lurched and he could barely hide Antigone before his vision blurred and he hunched over himself, trying hard not to hit the floor loudly and awaken the others.

Throwing up out of a window couldn't have ever been a pleasant experience, but as Aster did, his stomach pressed to the open window's metal sill for support as his body went limp, he was sure it was greater than all other sick feelings he had to date. He saw the sunlight trickle in, eyes warm and dry from unblinking, and slowly Aster shut them and pretended he was somewhere far away. A tree rustled outside the building. Aster didn't remember the last time he left the orphanage, or if he ever had. Perhaps he'd been there his whole life. He thought it was winter, but the outside was blistering and snowless.

"We aren't supposed to have the window open." One of the other kids who shared the room said, Anthony.

"Go back to bed, Anthony." Aster tried to say, but the words were stuck in his throat.

"Are you all right?" Anthony replied to Aster's strange, guttural noise. Aster nodded the best he could, his back to the beds, still facing the window.

"If you say so." Anthony scoffed, still concerned but too tired to care.

Most nights, the difficult ones, he would lay in his creaky bed and close his eyes as hard as he could, imagining he was someone else. As a young child, he had his stories for fun, but as a twelve-year-old, they were his lifeline. He would cover his ears with his hair as a precaution against spiders, and when he couldn't bear the night's chill he would cover his head with the thin blanket, snuggling with himself for warmth. There was a voice in his head that screeched whenever he tried to sleep; it yelled at him without ending. It couldn't stop screaming, "We don't deserve this." Aster wondered if it was Antigone.

As his head leaned out the window in a pathetic attempt to steal some of the air's frigidity, he only knew he preferred the screaming when it went away, and there was nothing but the faint sound of mice in the walls.

The next days were exhausting, and they seemed to get longer each time Aster woke up. He couldn't pay attention in class or answer the teacher, each word coming out unintelligible and scraping against his throat. Most teachers and caretakers were those who had outgrown the orphanage, but they didn't have any empathy for their students. He wondered what he had done to deserve it, to live in such a nightmare. Each thought he had buried for the past months kept crawling up like the dead out of their graves. It hurt to cry, so he didn't.

During his daily lessons, exactly one week after what happened in the laboratory, his teacher tapped him on the shoulder and told him to go to the study, their voice a hushed whisper, as if no one else was supposed to hear. Hear they did, however, and soon the whole class was staring at Aster. When he stood, he felt their eyes follow him to the front of the class and through the door as if he were being led to the slaughterhouse, and in a way, he was.

He walked to the study of the scholars through the hallways of Solle's Orphanage for Magical Children, with his hands shaking and his head heavy on his neck. He stood at the door and wondered if this was his doom. If they had found out that he had disobeyed and found their secret, the fact that they had been experimenting on children, the thought would've made him sick to his stomach if he wasn't already in a constant state of it.

At last, he turned the knob of the study's door, and he heard nothing but his heartbeat as his brain caught up with his eyes.

The scholars sat in a semi-circle in the centre of the room, their faces screwed into expressions Aster couldn't decipher. On the centre of the large desk from which they sat was a small furry lump– Antigone. Aster felt tears well up, the pit in his stomach growing deeper than he thought ever possible. He didn't make eye contact with them, didn't dare look at their faces, his cheeks stinging with both the redness of humiliation and phantom pain of the times he had been punished before.

He tasted blood on his tongue, although he did not know where it came from. Someone with a high-pitched voice spoke, but he could not hear over the buzzing of the walls. Once again someone spoke, louder this time, making Aster flinch, but yet he still couldn't hear them. Finally, a person near the centre of the desk spoke, and this time Aster could hear the words they said.

"Aster," the person said, smoothly, calmly, as if it were a casual discussion between friends and not judgement day. Even if he could reply he wouldn't, because he knew they wanted him to. He painfully glanced at the person in the centre, they had long wavy hair, Aster always loved curled hair, like the kind a doll would have. Some may have considered his hair curly, but he thought it was better described as "pale and wispy," *like a ghost*, he would say, had anyone asked.

Aster took a few steps, keeping his eyes to his feet, and approached the desk. In one quick motion, he grabbed Antigone, only hesitating before clutching her to his chest, apprehensive not at the disrespectful gesture, but instead of the thought that they would find him childish for holding it close to his heart. After holding her to his chest for a long moment, he built up the courage to look back up at the scholars.

They did not look pleased.

The person in the middle looked around at the others as if telepathically communicating what to do with him, but Aster still wasn't entirely sure what was going on. After some time of telepathic communication, they stood, chair screeching in a way that brought back the looming fear that Aster had lost holding Antigone. Would they take her away, the only thing he had of his parents? His only possession? He held her tighter and subconsciously stepped back. They approached Aster and smiled at him the way only a scientist could: professional, slight, and fake.

"Do not fear, Aster, I will not hurt Antigone," the person said, how they knew Antigone's name Aster did not know, but still, he was comforted by the notion. The person opened the leather holster on their leg and took out a gleaming crystalline dagger. They held it in their hands, turning it around and around; Aster stared with both fear and curiosity.

"Do you know what this is, Aster?"

Aster did know what a dagger was, but due to the state of his vocal cords, he instead shook his head in acknowledgement. The person grinned.

"It is said that this dagger was created by the fairy Chrysos in the caves of Aconite. Did you know Terra Florens had caves?"

Once again, Aster shook his head.

The person nodded simply, holding the dagger in their

left hand. They proceeded to make a shallow cut in their right palm. Aster was mortified, but it seemed as if the other scholars, even Andreas Hughes, who Aster thought would've been glaring at him by now, seemed completely indifferent to this, he may have even been *scared*.

They held out their right hand and everyone in the room watched as blood dripped onto the dingy carpet, and with their other hand, they returned the dagger to their holster. *They didn't secure it.*

"Heal it."

Aster stared in disbelief.

"That is your power, isn't it? Prove it to us."

Aster choked out a few syllables slowly.

"Prove?" His throat hurt terribly but he tried to ignore it. The person nodded simply once again. Aster tried to clear his throat but it didn't work. He walked to the outstretched hand and held out one of his own. Aster closed his eyes and tried to summon all of his energy into his palm, but it was like trying to walk after years of sitting. The person stared at him; their face strange. Aster hovered his hand over their palm nonetheless, concentrating all of his power, he felt the energy leave his body, but when he opened his eyes the wound was still there, glistening in his failure.

The person looked at Aster with curiosity, their eyes wide and eyebrows raised. It was then that they began to laugh. Their laughter echoed against the brick walls. They wiped tears from their eyes before shaking their head.

"You can't do it, can you?" They mocked, Aster looked at them, terrified. The person turned to the rest of the scholars, and they too started to laugh, booming bursts of laughter all aimed at Aster, he didn't understand what he did wrong.

Wasn't this what they wanted?

Those questions soon died in Aster's brain and were quickly replaced with something much darker. He stared at the holster, trying not to make eye contact. He was humiliated. He held out his hand again, and once more began to concentrate his energy, snapping his eyes shut at the pain, Antigone still held firm to his heart with his other hand.

He couldn't understand how people could hate him so, how they could see him– he being a child– and see something so disgusting, to look at his actions through a filter of hate until he is nothing but vile, putrid slime upon the orphanage floor. He hated them. He hated them because they hated him. Life had beaten him senseless, and before he was even given a chance to think for himself.

"One day," he thought to himself, "I will be somewhere far from this place, where I am happy, and everyone loves me. Where my hair is clean, and my clothes aren't rags, and the world is alive." He wished it with such power that it became a prayer to the world.

"You are loved, Aster." His dear Antigone said to him. "You are loved, because I love you."

With a newfound determination, he concentrated until his sight gave out and his hands shook. The magic which he suppressed for months left him all at once, and he felt his legs fail him once again.

It felt as if he had been winded, knocked unconscious from an explosion, he was unable to see, unable to hear. When his brain finally caught up he found himself on the ground, but that wasn't all he found.

His magic backfired, and the tips of his fingers were caked in ash. He stared blankly at the person lying on the ground, their long hair splayed out in every direction on the ground and eyes wide and unblinking. Were they *dead*? Did Aster *kill* them? That couldn't be. Aster crawled to them, ignoring the screams of the people around him, Antigone abandoned where he fell. He carefully turned over their hand, the wound was gone. He then fell into a fit of coughing and wheezing. When he opened his eyes he was shocked to find more ash on his hands.

Suddenly he felt arms grabbing him and pulling him off of the ground, he tried to shake them off but couldn't, no matter how hard he struggled. Aster grabbed the dagger from the person's holster and held it up as a threat; he had never been more scared in his life. Looking behind him he saw the scholars' revolted faces, he knew what would happen if he was caught. Aster didn't want to go to jail, he didn't want to go from one prison to another, so Aster did the only other thing he could. Aster fought.

The last thing he remembered– before picking up Antigone, before grabbing the keys off of the desk and opening the front door of the orphanage, and before gathering everyone to the main hall to let them know that they were finally free– was how red the scholars' blood was when he washed it off in a small basin, like wet paint. He didn't throw up. There was nothing in his stomach to lose.

He imagined his escape every night as he tried to fall asleep. In his dreams he was outside, running as fast as he could. He would run until his legs gave out and his heart was unable to keep up with his lungs. Aster could never remember the beginning of the dreams, or how he got out, but he would always remember running.

Finally, he was out, but he was unable to run. He was exhausted in both mind and body, and with each step out the closer he felt to the ground. The caretakers ran as well, and although they were less than accommodating, each of them shook his hand before leaving.

In the corner of his eye, he could see Rose, sitting on the steps. At first, anger was the only feeling he had, but he noticed how everyone ignored her, even as they left. She would be left alone to find the horrific sight Aster created.

No one asked where the scholars went, but no one made eye contact with Aster as he stayed inside, staring at the portrait of the king. He knew what he would choose. He went upstairs for the last time, passing Rose, to find a change of clothes in both of their sizes.

It was cathartic to take the responsibility of someone not much younger, but Aster reassured himself that there was nothing else he could do, he couldn't let them leave her behind.

At the time he didn't know if he could forgive her, but he was thankful for the freedom no matter how it was given. As he grabbed the hand of his new adopted sister, he knew that he would do anything to protect kids like him.

He saw Iris, the girl who had lived there almost her whole life, and smiled as she stood on the doorstep, feeling the wind on her face for the first time in years, bells ringing all around. Her red hair, put in braids that very morning, now looked brighter than ever before, and although she was devoid of hope when she put them in, she would untie those ribbons free.

On a train to a town called Dolston sat two children, a boy

and a girl– siblings, the girl told the conductor. The boy couldn't speak, the girl couldn't see. It was a miracle they had arrived there in the first place. They got through the twenty-hour train ride eating dried oats in their dusty clothes. The conductor could not pinpoint what the uniform belonged to, but only that he was not paid enough to care.

At Dolston, the siblings found a young, silk-stockinged wooden spoon of a man shouting profusely about something or other. He couldn't have been much older than Aster, who that day (unknowingly) turned thirteen. When he saw them he gasped for joy.

"You there!" he shouted, his voice exuberant and booming, making Aster flinch. "Do you have a place to stay?"

The children shook their heads. The man almost jumped for joy.

"I have just been given an old home from my great great uncle," he stated in a dingy eatery as the children gorged themselves on bread and cheese paid for by the man (Aster– of course– checked it for mould beforehand.) "I was simply going to tear it down, but apparently it's a *historical site!* Can you believe that? In a forest of Vera!"

Aster and Rose did not know what that meant, but grumbled in dejected agreement nonetheless.

"So, I need someone to take care of it, it's a bit messy and far from town but I am sure it's better than what you have now," the man continued, clicking his heels underneath the table. He handed Aster a folded-up piece of paper. "The directions. You can't miss it, it's the only thing around for miles."

The trudge out of town could only be described with two words: sweaty and conspicuous. A path from town went south to Palmond Cliff, the name of the empty land, and west to Primrose Peak. A farmer had driven a carriage down this road every week for the past twenty years, and by sneaking onto it, Aster and Rose managed to fall asleep on the hottest day of the year in Dolston.

As Aster and Rose hopped off of the carriage, bags in hand, they found a shocking sight, this was no *manor.* It was a castle! Large wooden doors framed each wall of grey brick; long tresses of ivy curling upward to the sky. The roof was green and glimmering in the sun.

To their surprise, the home was filled with old furniture crusted in the skin of time. Dust caked every surface, and by using the once-white sleeve of his shirt, Aster wiped off one of the chairs. There were beautiful carvings on the backing of the chair and red plush on the seat.

"Do you think we can clean it all?" Rose said, more to the fireplace than to Aster, he nodded nonetheless. This would've been an uncomfortable situation had Rose not had powers, but she knew exactly what he was thinking. She knew what everyone was thinking.

Thanks to the orphanage, Rose was able to know things most humans shouldn't.

"We will manage." Aster thought passively.

There were an incomprehensible amount of rooms by the looks of it. They never thought they could be so lucky.

"I don't think anyone will find us here," Rose stated whilst feeling through one of the seemingly hundreds of bookshelves. "Aster come look! It's a whole collection of C. Richardson! You like him. Or, you *will.*"

The days melted together. They did not clean, they did not

do anything productive. All they allowed themselves to do was sit and explore the house, they lived off of hard bread and cheese in the abandoned kitchen.

Ever since the backfiring of his magic, Aster's condition had worsened drastically, he had taken days laying in pain in the dusty drawing rooms, coughing up clouds in his barren throat as he attempted to read the old medical texts. It was as if a venom had spread throughout his muscles, causing them to become weaker, and no matter how many times he tried he could not heal himself. As his muscles deteriorated so did his vision, but perhaps that was simply puberty. Nevertheless, it was obvious that Aster looked entirely different from when he last saw his parents.

For the first time in four years, Aster Williams felt the overwhelming sensation of serenity, not the weightless kind of a child, but the heavy calmness of finally being away from danger. He was not full, not when he knew that kids were going through the same thing he did. He would never be full, he would never be sated, and he would never feel well rested no matter how long he slept. It was a curse that lingered on every person who experienced the hatred of a country.

Aster didn't speak for almost five years after that, and even when he could once again, he didn't speak as he did before. His mind was filled with nothing but a restless yearning for revenge.

He knew his mind would never clear, and he knew his heart would never be free. Below the beauty of his home country laid a dark secret, and from the hands of fate he was pushed to action. He had aged quicker than he deserved. He would make his disgust apparent to every person in Terra Florens. The orphanages, the government, and lastly King Valentijn; they would all know his name. There was nothing more terrible than a child lost.

Chapter V: A Cottage in the Woods

Queen Anne's Lace

"My name is Aster Williams," Teddy said, and in his words was a drastic sincerity that Clover didn't understand. The veins in his hands were a faint blue, like painted porcelain, and trembled over his stomach like birds anticipating a strike.

Clover recognized the name, but could not place where they had seen it. They vaguely remembered the name Aster Williams on the front page of newspapers, wanted for something or other. Perhaps he was undercover because he was a famous painter or an elusive tamer of small anthropomorphic mice.

Aster stared at his shoes as if his nickname was a mask which had fallen, unable to protect him. Clover was almost embarrassed at his sincerity. It seemed indecent on his face.

"I hope you can look past your fear," he said.

"I beg your pardon?"

His face went slack. It seemed he did not understand the extent of their injury, or simply thought himself more important than he was.

Clover didn't lie to him. They were sure that if anyone in

57

the house wished to harm them, they would've done so long ago. Aster looked grateful as he realised this.

"I'm confusing you, I apologise," he said before leaving to the door, but Clover was unable to look away from the wall where he used to be.

If Aster *was* planning on attacking them, they always had their one secret weapon. A tactic so hidden, even the strongest soldier would be left stumped: hitting him with one of his books. Without his boots, Aster was the same height as Clover, but he was so frail that one hit to his shin would make him topple over like a stack of cards. He was the least intimidating person in the house, by far.

They began to hatch a plan. The next day, Clover would search for clues on how to leave the moment they were left unsupervised. Any suspicious notes, textiles, animals– or better yet, help from the strange mice– could aid in their escape, if they needed it.

They barely noticed when another voice began to speak to Aster at the other side of the room, an empty voice that Clover recognized as Dorothy's. And amidst the hushed whispers, Clover found themself growing overwhelmed.

Dorothy's voice grew louder and more agitated the longer she spoke with Aster.

They heard Rose's voice among the commotion, which was higher than the other two, and the way she spoke rang out a terrified hush.

"Stay with the guest, I'm taking Rose to town," Dorothy told Aster after Rose spoke, and Clover threw their head in their hands.

"Now?"

"There may be trouble."

When Dorothy led them back to their room, they almost didn't notice the missing balcony door. They fell asleep without a second thought.

The manor was beautiful (or any word that meant more than beautiful.) It was a world unknown to Clover. There were dark wooden doors with stained glass indents, flowers carved into every piece of furniture, and long-winding hallways lined with wallpaper. Clover wondered if there was anything more captivating. Grand staircases were at every corner and were met with dark red carpet. After mere hours amidst the house, they had already given up their quest to escape. The manor was safe.

After some time, however, they began to grow bored. The excitement of doors appearing when they turned their head was beginning to fade, and the silence of the manor was becoming more apparent. It was a constant, unbearable ringing in Clover's ears, like an insect.

The strange stuffed animal butler was nowhere to be seen, and they hadn't spotted Aster since he said goodbye to Rose and Dorothy. Loneliness crept closer and closer to Clover with every step they took. It seeped into their veins, causing a cold chill to go down their spine and their breath to grow shallow.

As if to answer their call, at the end of a long hall was a pair of glass-centred double doors, the light revealing dust in its rays. They smelled dust and smoke.

It was a library so expansive Clover could not see the tops of its bookshelves. Grey rocky walls hid behind hundreds of shelves and desks. Every book was bound in cloth with gold lettering delicately written on each spine. Clover's eyes were drawn to one specific cover which read *Rogue's Voyage*. It was a beautiful shade of red, with a built-in bookmark. With it and a few other books, they decided to retire from the room. However, as they turned to leave a quiet squeak interrupted the silence of the room. It was the sort of frequency that disturbed the dust around it. *Shrill*. What an interesting word that was.

Clover was unable to find a cause of the noise, not a window was open, nor was a floorboard loose. Yet, the squeaking continued. It rang like a bell throughout the room. Finally, at the very corner of the shelves, far in the back of the library, was an insect. So small it could hardly be seen. It was trapped beneath a book, and screeching for help. Clover moved the book– silencing the creature– and watched as it hopped away, deeper into the house.

Near the creature's almost-tomb was a desk covered in papers. Clover could not help themself, reaching for a paper. Unfortunately for Clover, the handwriting was illegible, as if written by a child. Beneath the desk was a makeshift bed, and they recognized the white-and-gold quilt as the twin to the one in their bed. *Dorothy's* bed, they corrected in their mind. They felt their brow lower, and their stomach cramp. They felt guilty, it was their fault Dorothy was forced to sleep in the library forthwith. Forthwith? They still did not understand what that word meant.

After the library, they decided to set their sights on the kitchen. After many twists and turns (and a strange bump-in with a particularly large mouse,) Clover found another large door with a window in the centre. Through the window, Clover could see a large kitchen with old mahogany counters cluttered with loaves of bread and spilt jams. Entering the kitchen, they were overwhelmed with the smell of freshly baked bread and the sound of scurrying.

At Clover's feet sat a small cat-like creature identical to the stuffed animal; except this one was a real animal. Its hands were leathery until it met with the fur of their arms, and dark circles covered their eyes. It was a cat bandit!

"Dear!" Clover exclaimed, almost dropping a book from their arms. The creature scurried near the oven before looking at Clover, beckoning them to follow. A voice bled through their thoughts.

"Not a deer, not one at all!" The animal's mouth did not move as it spoke.

Perhaps Clover's injury was worse than they thought.

Clover watched as the creature pulled a small string attached to the door of the oven, which revealed more bread inside. After the animal hoisted the door down, it made a distinct sound, not unlike a chirp.

When they first walked into the room, they did not notice the small doors on the wall behind the oven, nor did they notice the minuscule stairs leading down to the counter. However, after the animal made their call, the doors opened with a swiftness not unlike the way Clover flung open the doors of the manor.

Large mice appeared from behind the doors, walking just as a person would. The mice marched down the staircases in what seemed to be insulated suits down to the opened oven. They took turns in groups hauling the bread onto a large metal pan on the counter nearest to the oven, before breaking the last one into many pieces and carrying them back into the doors, which shut behind them forcefully.

Clover was stunned, but before they could react to what

had happened, the cat-like creature jumped onto the counter and began rolling the loaves of bread into paper wrappings with its nose, if Clover knew any better, they would've been concerned with disease. But they did not know any better, so there was no problem.

Gently, the creature wrapped every loaf of bread before rolling almost all of them into an opened cabinet. Clover looked at the two left on the counter and then at the creature as it jumped back onto the counter. It crept closer to the two packages and nudged one closer to Clover.

"Are these for me?" They asked, and the creature continued to push it closer. Clover nodded, "Thank you."

They walked upstairs to the hallway that their room— technically Dorothy's room— resided in until they heard something peculiar. Soft sobs flew around the hall, riding on dust until it hit Clover's ears. Their hand hovered over the door handle as they tried to listen closer, until... *SLAM!*

A book fell from Clover's arms, and the crying stopped.

Clover had quite a lovely night, everything considered. Two of the three books they read were wonderful, and the bread was mostly edible. When they woke, they felt warm sunshine on their face, engulfing the whole room in its rays. Calm was not the correct word to describe how they felt, but it was the only one they knew that came close.

There was a beautiful wonderment in the written word that they had not known before. It was easy to learn in a house such as the one they were staying in, but they feared collapse if they read anymore. They had learned so many things about humankind that they had not known before, metaphors, words, different worlds.

Now fully awake, their mind was happy to finally have words to describe all which they saw and felt; it was its own sort of magic.

Walking out of the room, waiting for their eyes to become accustomed to the light, they looked at the hallway before them. Light swam through the windows, making the wooden floors golden. The number of bookshelves next to each window became denser the farther they walked. As they approached a familiar shelf of dolls, they were forced to hold back an astonished gasp.

Sunlight hit the dolls' eyes perfectly, that must've been why they were placed there, in that specific spot. Clover smiled at them, their own eyes widening as they took in the light reflecting off of each glass eye. One of the dolls in particular had eyes that were so large and glittering that Clover wondered if it was reflected onto their face. Wide, sparkling, green eyes looked back into Clover's own, and it reminded them that they were not the only person in the house.

Clover looked down the hallway with a newfound hunger. Mr Williams could refuse to speak to them, but he could not cure Clover of their curiosity. That was– of course– until Clover heard more quiet sobs coming from the door next to them. Their determination left as quickly as it had come. Dejected, they sat in front of the door as quietly as they could without disturbing him. He must've been worried for his sister. That was the only explanation Clover could think of. The more they thought about it, the more they were worried for her too, and Dorothy as well, to an extent. There was no reason for them to be, as they were still unsure on whether they were kidnapped, but they could not help it.

They stretched, letting their entire back touch the door, and looked at the paintings that covered the rare bits of shelf-less wall. A few, in particular, caught their attention. One of them was a portrait of a clown, but it was not like any clown Clover could imagine. The clown was portrayed in large, textured lines, and was in front of a window attempting to reflect its happy face, except there was no reflection. Clover found it tacky.

Near it was an ethereal painting, the sort that latched onto the deep, visceral part of the mind and spread until there was nothing to think of but its strokes of paint and abstract lines. The figure of a barn owl blended into the cascading lines of illustrated winds, tawny and luscious. It was almost offensively two-dimensional in nature, with no attempt at a realistic depiction, but it was still stunningly charming, a new dimension in itself. It was like the sight of a goddess, with her wings outstretched to the heavens, pleading with the painter to make it as beautiful as she felt, as she deserved. Above it, in gold lettering, was a single word: *Verania*.

Below it was another, a simple family portrait of Rose and Aster, with both looking very young and wounded. In a wooden chair sat a juvenile Rose with her hair grown over her eyes. She was wearing a long evergreen gown that looked old but unworn. It was accented with beautiful white lace that matched the visible petticoat. The chair she sat in looked old and rotted, and Clover was disgusted at the thought of sitting in a chair like that with such a beautiful dress on, they were sure it would stain. Aster stood next to her wearing round spectacles, his eyes painted sloppily. He looked much younger, but even in painting form he held the same expressionless face; not a frown, but not a smile.

Underneath it was a portrait of Dorothy, separate from the family. She wore a green vest, seemingly the same one Aster wore in the painting above. She couldn't have been a butler, but she didn't feel like family either. Curious.

Clover admired the portraits until their eyes glazed over.

There was a soft *thud* at the other side of the door, and the sound was so quiet they almost couldn't hear it. They didn't wish to speak, but luckily they did not have to.

"I am lackadaisical," Aster's voice said from the other side of the door. Clover let out a snarky noise, their throat not yet used to the action. They tried to wrap their mind around what that word could've possibly meant.

"I see."

It was silent, the walls echoed their ever-knowing groans at Clover's feeble attempt to keep up whatever it was they were doing.

"I worry for her."

"Dorothy's with her," Clover said in a feeble attempt to help. It must've worked, as a laugh erupted from the other side of the door. They didn't know what was so funny about that statement, but it felt nice to make someone laugh, they wondered if they should look into becoming a comic. "Does she have the same magic you have?"

They heard Aster take a deep breath, and they prayed he would answer. They were excited to hear more of his magic. Clover, despite having almost nothing to work with, understood that they did not have magic. Perhaps that was why they found it all the more fascinating.

"Not quite, she's more of a psychic than a healer." He said. "Her vision is not from her eyes, but from her mind. She can see everything I cannot, except– confusingly– you."

"Is that why they had to leave?"

"Yes." He was silent for a moment. "We wish to help you, detective."

The title did not feel like theirs, but they did not wish to correct him.

"Call me Clover, Mr Williams."

He laughed from the other side of the door, "Only if you call me Aster."

They huffed out an awkward laugh before almost being crushed by the opening door. Aster dashed out of it, looking almost hysterical.

He wore a long black cloak that was held together at his neck with a wooden brooch resembling a yellow flower. His hair was hastily put up into a thick braid, curly strands falling around his thin face. While grabbing his cane from the cupboard across from the door he looked down at Clover in their nightgown.

"Would you walk with me, Clover?" His eyes were wide behind his glasses in such a way that Clover worried what he would do if they declined. They instead asked him to wait as they rushed to their room to change into their vest and trousers.

The grounds of the estate (which Aster referred to as a castle,) were as enchanting during the day as they were at night. The house stood on a cliff overlooking the ocean, its stained glass windows reflecting in the direct sunlight. It was a windy day, and the forest opposite the ocean echoed a song of birds and rustling leaves. Walking with Aster seemed like the best time to ask the questions Clover still had, however, they couldn't seem to get a word in. He did answer some questions, like where they were ("Palmond Cliff, near Dolston,") what it was like being a wanted criminal ("Much more pleasant than you'd think,") and how far the nearest town was ("About a day and a half by carriage, not including the time it'd take to get back,) but he never answered anything else, not including the plant identifications.

Clover, like anyone else, knew Aster Williams was an important name, but could not remember exactly why. However, they did not question Aster more after the first few times they were shut down. Clover may have been conversing with a criminal, but they were still polite.

Aster was smiling throughout the whole walk, pointing out his favourite flowers and stopping every time a gust of wind went by. His cheeks and lips were as rosy as the flowers around him. The air smelled like the ocean and despite Clover trying to seem annoyed, they were ecstatic to be outside.

"Aster?"

"Yes?"

"What exactly is Rose looking for?"

Aster's benign expression changed into one of confusion, but it soon resolved itself.

"Follow me." He said excitedly.

Inside the library, Clover watched as Aster looked at the shelves, pulling out random tomes and flipping through a few pages before shutting them loudly. Once again, Aster wore the same blank expression as he did in the portrait in the hallway. Clover wondered if the smile he wore in the gardens was rare, perhaps even Rose had not seen it recently. Their eyes shut as they sat at one of the desks and waited until Aster slammed a book down. It was large, the largest book

Clover had ever seen by far; it must've been one thousand pages long, at least.

"What is this?" Clover asked, tracing the words carved into the cover in a language they did not understand as Aster pulled out more identical books.

"Rose's journals for the past week. Flip to the last page." He said, adding the last part in a more direct voice.

The page was not filled in but was instead *being filled in*. Words appeared on it like magic because– Clover assumed– it was. They flew upon the page, written in by an invisible hand.

Clover tried to read it the best they could as the words appeared, but they weren't capable of wrapping their mind around it. The words large and the sentences choppy, it read as one string of consciousness going on and on for millions of words.

"Aster, I'm sorry, but I don't understand," Clover said genuinely, eyes transfixed on the page.

"I thought journaling would help Rose's health." He replied, waiting beside the shelf. "Is the page almost completed?"

"Almost, there are two lines left." Clover hoped the confusion in their voice was well hidden; they didn't wish to ruin whatever Aster was doing. They watched as the last sentence appeared, but it did not end with a period. Like clockwork, a loud sound came from the bookshelf Aster was standing next to, and a book almost identical to the one Clover was reading appeared on the shelf and was snatched by Aster.

He laid the new book on the desk and pulled a fountain pen from one of the drawers. He flipped to the first page, and in purple ink wrote in large letters,

"Rose."

Clover waited silently as the words stopped. The page was filled with a white emptiness as if Rose had stopped thinking entirely. Clover heard Aster hold his breath in the quiet echo of the library. The dust lingered and made their throat itch, but they hoped Aster wouldn't notice.

"I found it!" The words appeared.

Clover watched as the two communicated in the journal.

"What is it?"

"Meet us in Dolston, bring the carriage."

Aster paused for a few seconds.

"Is anything the matter?"

Now it was Rose's turn to pause, and silence filled the room once again.

"I cannot say."

"Rose, please," he scrawled.

"I can't see it entirely, only bits and pieces."

"The vision?"

Clover laughed despite their better judgement, but the situation was so *absurd* that they couldn't help but realise that they had been waiting patiently for a book to answer. They wondered for a moment if this was all a strange elaborate dream, or if they were going crazy. Thankfully that thought was interrupted by Rose's answer.

"Clover's future."

Aster stilled and peered over his glasses at their anxious face.

"I'll pack for a long trip, just stay put. Go to an inn if need be, and go to Devan Earl if it isn't safe."

Aster began to close the book with a crack of its spine, but he opened it once more when he realised Rose was still there and words were still appearing.

"Dorothy says hello." She wrote. Aster smiled, before writing one last thing.

"Give us a few days, we shall be there soon."

Later, after Aster left them to their own devices, Clover decided to wander around the main room. It was easy to pretend they were back home there, wherever home was. Clover found that it was easy to remember things about themself, what they liked and disliked about people (they liked most people,) and what music they preferred (high-energy songs with lots of woodwind and harp, they found it enchanting,) but whenever they thought about specific events of their past it all went blank.

They knew they should feel upset, or uncomfortable, but much like the space where their memories should've been, they were empty.

Clover's attentions were diverted when the front door opened, releasing a cold chill into the house. At the door stood Aster, walking out of the house wearing his wool coat and an old hat. He stood there for a moment before setting down his cane, closing the door, and opening the one next to it after a long struggle.

This door revealed a long corridor full of clocks, each one ticking at different intervals.

Remind me to never enter that room, Clover thought. Aster stood in front of a large clock in the centre of the corridor before turning around, noticing Clover in the process.

"Where are you going?" Clover asked, helping Aster close the large door, it was heavier than they had expected.

"Visiting. A. Friend," Aster said, pausing between each word to slam his body into the door and force it in place. They both let out a sigh as it finally shut. Aster rubbed his shoulder with his free hand, the pain must've been common for him.

"A watch would be a good investment," Clover said to their host, which in hindsight was not the most polite thing to say, but it seemed Aster didn't take offence.

"That would be easier, wouldn't it?" He scoffed before pausing at the front door for a second time. Aster squinted in deep thought. "Would you like to come with me, Clover?"

Once again– as they had nothing better to do– they obliged.

The walk was slow and pleasant, and the trees rustled an ancient song with their leaves. There were many flowers around. Rose bushes bloomed, honeysuckles wrapped around every branch, and wildflowers of all kinds grew around the old dirt path. Clover tried their best not to stop too many times to look at the scenery, but most of the time could not help themself. It was too beautiful.

Something about Aster made Clover believe he was a fabrication, that he was merely hiding his secret nature. He seemed scared, yet self-respecting. Exactly how old Aster was, Clover could not decipher. They hoped he wasn't *too* old.

Clover was distracted by the thought of what it would be like to wear spectacles; their eyes felt fine, but perhaps a little sore from the sunlight. The bridge of their nose felt heavy when they thought about it. It suited Aster's whole haunted-yet-charming attitude, although Clover was not sure what the state of themself would be if they were to have told him that, it was difficult to tell.

"Do you need those?" They asked him, pointing at his face.

"What?" He gave them a questionable look, "My eyeglasses?"

Clover nodded.

71

"If I wish to see, yes."

They thought about it for some time, as they walked beside him.

"Do you think..." They struggled to word their question. "Do you think I need glasses?"

Aster hummed in apparent thought. "If so, it doesn't seem as if you need them now, unless you are seeing me through a mist."

"I don't think I am." They realised how strange it sounded after they said it, but Aster only smiled.

"That's good, then."

After about an hour of walking in the forest, the same colour began to pop up more and more. The green leaves were consumed by purple flowering vines, growing everywhere from the tops of trees to the shrubs nearing the ground. It was the most enchanting thing Clover had ever seen, and they felt their eyes grow wider the more they looked at it, drinking in every flower they could see. Soon they reached a split in the path, with two roads, one going north, to the town, and one going south, deeper into the forest. In the middle of the two roads was an enormous tree covered in the same wisteria, reaching out and covering the whole area with its branches and vines. The flowers were so dense that no light was able to get through them, resulting in the whole area emitting a faint violet glow, the ground covered in fallen purple petals. At the base of the tree were small purple mushrooms emerging from the wisteria petals all around. Clover allowed Aster to lead the way, going deeper into the woods, where more flora and fauna awaited through the portal to purple-autumn.

"Aster, those mushrooms were glowing!" Clover said excitedly, catching up to him so they could walk side-by-side.

"Quite right," Aster's eyes twinkled in the darkness of the forest.

"This is a fairytale, I can't believe it!" Clover added, "That's a compliment, by the bye," Aster's face twitched with that same strange expression.

"It isn't as wonderful as you believe it to be," He said. Clover was silent, afraid they had hit a nerve, Aster continued, "The forest respects me, and you by extension. Take care not to ruin that respect."

Clover felt like a child caught doing something they weren't supposed to. As they opened their mouth to apologise, a great sound bellowed from the centre of the forest. It sounded like every animal screaming, and with it came waves of singing birds and rushing wind. Aster turned around once before pointing to one side of the path.

It was a deer larger than a house– twice as large as Clover at least– with bone-white skin and thick fur gathering at its legs, mixing with patches of moss. Its mouth was not small like most deer, but as great as a wolf's in size and fatality. Its mouth opened as it finished its call, and sharp teeth were presented with light which escaped through the smallest cracks of the forest. It had two sets of antlers, one stronger than the other, which matched its two sets of eyes, one gold and one red.

"A eudel," Aster whispered to them, his past anger seemingly forgotten, "An ancient deer, barely found beyond this forest."

Its beauty was beyond words, it was incomparable. With the tail and teeth of a wolf, the antlers of a moose, and the body of a stag, it was a terrifyingly inutterable sight.

The two watched in silence as the eudel closed its mouth, and– with only a single glance spared to its audience– disappeared into the woods, purple-furred animals trailing behind.

"The king of the forest," Clover said.

"One of them, I've seen quite a few. They never stand long enough for me to draw them."

"Are they a family?"

Aster hummed, pondering the question.

"I suppose they could be, I've never seen a young one before."

Clover felt pride in the thought of bringing a new idea to him.

They came to the end of the path as it entered a large clearing, and in it sat a small cottage engulfed in wisteria, the wooden boards barely visible. No smoke left the broken chimney, and it did not look like it had for a long while.

Aster stopped in front of the large green door.

"If you tell anyone about what you see here, I'll kill you myself."

Clover froze. They hoped they were good at keeping secrets.

"Of course."

Inside the cottage was a sight as incomparable as the eudel. The first thing they noticed was a hole in the ceiling, wisteria swallowing the inside of the house. The cottage was cluttered with everything imaginable, jars, bones, books, it was all there on lopsided shelves.

For a moment, when they first looked at the centre of the house, they could've sworn they had seen something terrifying, but they could not remember it. Only the memory of its terror remained.

Sat in an old rocking chair in the centre was an old woman. She was taller than Aster even as she sat, and her curly purple hair was beginning to turn grey. On top of such hair grew two antlers, exactly as they would on a deer. Her skin a deep sepia, her gown extravagant; she looked like the statue of a queen long lost.

Clover wondered if she had ever stood from the chair, or if she was stuck to the moss and wisteria that grew around her. After seeing her face– covered by thick hair, her eyes closed limply– they began to wonder if she was dead.

Aster left Clover in the doorway and kneeled near the rocking chair, setting down the covered basket he brought and his cane next to him. He grabbed the woman's hand with his own and closed his eyes.

They waited in that position for some time, before the beautiful emerald light seeped from Aster's fingers. As the light reached her arm, she proved to Clover that she was– somehow– alive. Her fingers, once limp, wrapped around Aster's hand and gave it a light squeeze before opening her eyes.

She paid no attention to Aster, despite having her life saved by him, and instead looked at Clover with violet eyes. Clover didn't know if she was staring *at* them or *through* them, but they were frozen with fear. She began to move towards them, moss ripping from the bottom of her dress like grasping hands, and Clover worried if Aster had brought them here as a sacrifice, but she stopped in front of them, the two separated by a small tree growing through the floor. She was taller than Dorothy, almost as tall as the eudel. She extended her hand, and Clover took it.

"Now, who are you?" She said, moving as close as she could while still being attached to the ground, a honeysuckle vine growing around her antlers falling before her eyes.

"My name is Clover."

"The Detective, I see." Her voice trailed off with a tilt of her head, like an owl, "It is a pleasure to meet you. You may call me Esme."

Her voice was clear and respectful, speaking with a faint accent Clover could not recognize. She led Clover to a small overgrown table in the back, dragging many plants up by the roots the more she walked, but it seemed as if she didn't notice. Aster was in the kitchen next to it, pulling up weeds from between the cupboards and dusting off dishes. His hair fell in front of his face before looking up, making eye contact with Clover and giving them an awkward smile.

"Has it really only been a year since you last visited, Teddy?" Esme asked, making Clover jump.

"I'm quite sure of it, a storm must've come through while you were asleep."

"Asleep?" Clover asked.

Esme looked at Clover with kind eyes before glancing at Aster, asking him permission to speak.

"How old are you, Clover?" She asked them.

Clover did not know. They didn't know if they were supposed to.

"Teddy, how old are you?" Esme corrected.

Aster bumped his head on the cabinet he was cleaning, and Clover didn't know if he was surprised by being spoken to or by the sudden noise that resulted from it.

"Oh, well–"

"Early thirties, correct?"

He whipped around, bewildered.

"I turn twenty this summer, Esme!"

Both Clover and Esme stared at Aster in shock. He sat at the table with them, eyes widened more than usual. He was nineteen? That was a shock.

"Do I really look *that* old?"

Clover and Esme sat in silence, and it was enough of an answer to make Aster put his head in his hands. Clover watched as he ran his hands through his hair before looking at them exasperatedly.

"I need to get more sleep, don't I?"

Clover tried their best to convince him that eyebags were very popular this season, but it didn't seem to work.

"Might you fix my roof now, Teddy?" Esme asked, and as he turned to leave with a huff she gave Clover a discreet wink.

"I'll be returning shortly, I hope," he said to Clover. The moment he was out of sight, Esme turned to them.

"Would you like to know your age, Clover?"

Their eyes grew wide in pleasant surprise at her excitement, before remembering that the question was very strange, and they should not have been pleased by it.

"Oh, yes! I really would."

Esme smiled so greatly, it was overwhelming. She stood from her chair and took a scroll of paper from one of the bookshelves. Clover followed, cautiously, to the small fireplace at the end of the room. She unrolled the parchment and grabbed a fountain pen out of a mug on the floor. With a flourish, she handed off the paper and pen to Clover with the same air as if she were passing down a sword.

"Write down all of the questions you have in your mind."

"Yeah, all right. Of course." They didn't dare attempt to find out what Esme was about to do. They assumed that it would be something both terrifying and perplexing. "Is there a reason why Rose can't tell me?"

"Rose? Miss Williams?" She questioned, and Clover nodded.

The "W." in the initials from their nightgown couldn't have meant anything else.

"Yes, I believe. I'm not too sure of anything right now."

"Don't worry, dear, I understand." She picked at a patch of moss growing from her antlers. "Roselinda can see everything known, and everything unknown. Some see her as a psychic. I see her as an omen."

It was almost exactly how Aster explained it, but Clover wished to know the extent of her strange abilities or how it played into their condition. Perhaps they could write that down.

"I see." They answered, and they opened their mouth to ask another question, but Esme was not done speaking.

"The farther she searches for something the further she strays from this world. No one person should know those things. I believe she has begun to block it out," She wiped some dust off the top of a bookshelf. "One day she will go too far and be lost forever. Lost sight, lost vision. They are two different things, Clover."

Their vision began to glide as their conscience swayed with her words. Clover's eyelids sank until darkness was their only company. But in an instant, she was done speaking, and Clover was back as if nothing had happened.

In the end, Clover could only come up with six questions. They wondered if Esme was some sort of psychic, but her antlers were so stunningly real, it confused them. They weren't sure if their questions were good enough, but they let their doubt sink into the ground, watering the moss with their uncertainty.

"I'm ready, I think," Clover said.

"Hang on, just a second, please," Esme said from the table, looking up at the roof. Clover looked at it as well. It seemed that Aster had patched the broken ceiling.

"I do apologise for the mess," she said softly.

"It's quite all right, I'm becoming used to it," Clover replied, smiling at Esme, she began to laugh, they were both aware of the state of the manor. She had a lovely laugh, full and hearty.

Esme went to the fireplace once more and opened its door. Bright purple flames licked at the walls voraciously. Clover wondered if burning the plants outside created such a colour. She threw the paper into the fire in one movement.

The hearth started to rumble, and roars erupted up the chimney. Clover could hear Aster fall off of the roof with a loud yelp, not unlike the kind a cat would make when stepped on. The fireplace looked close to exploding, and after looking to Esme for reassurance, they realised that she, too, had not expected this.

Her hands grasped the handle with a harsh noise before she attempted to push it closed but to no avail. The flames were just too strong.

But as quickly as the roaring came, so too did it stop. Clover began to wonder if they had imagined it all, and started to believe it too, until a loud voice erupted from above.

"You who live in the light have found those of darkness. Those who come from abundance will always seek it once lost. Go to the House of Opulence. Return what was once yours."

The house stood still for a moment, but in a blink, Clover's paper came back out with one last roar. And with that, it was silent.

The singed paper read, *"Newly twenty-two."*

"Well," Esme started, "I believe my connection was interrupted," she spoke with shaky uncertainty.

Aster ran in through the front door with sticks in his hair and yelled the most respectful yell Clover had ever heard,

"Esme, what happened? What's going on?"

Esme didn't say a word.

Clover was unsure of many things. Where did the voice come from? What did it all mean? Did Aster also have a brain injury now?

"Clover," Esme said slowly, ignoring Aster, "They have your memories."

"What?" Clover's mind reeled, "What do you mean?"

The colour of her eyes changed from deep purple to a bright yellow, then settled at a crystalline blue.

"They are magic users in Avindre, stealing memories of those in a weakened state of mind, and challenging them to a game to get them back."

"Where in Avindre?" Aster asked. Esme looked to be in another world. She did not face Clover, but once again through them, to Beyond.

"The House of Opulence, Cherin."

Clover felt bumps against their wrist where their hands held each other.

"And, do we..." Clover stuttered. "Do I have to leave now?"

"Yes. It's good you woke me before this trip, Williams," Esme said, with a strange masquerade of depersonalization in her voice, as if deciding if she liked being in their presence. Her eyes were purple once again. "You have to go, as well."

She put her hand over Clover's head. As she did, the feeling they had felt at first sight of her returned. Her face; old yet young. Feminine yet masculine. The magnificence of a woman mixed with the prominence of a man. The lines of her face melted and morphed within a blink, and Clover's eyes burned as if they had gazed into the sun, but in another blink– quick with pain– she was normal again. Their terror did not subside.

"You are a charming detective, I have decided to help you. This will give you information to help beat the Olliryes. There are two, Dionysus and Olliver, but you will forget them." Clover could feel their mind clear for the first time.

"Remember your dreams, Clover. They are all you have." In a blink, she was gone, leaving behind a small fire and an empty chair.

"Does she do that often, Aster?" Clover asked, still staring into the space that used to be Esme.

"Yes," Aster said, and once again, Clover was not shocked. They had started to accept that this was how their life was going to be.

Chapter VI: The Legend of Juno and Dahlia

Daisy

Long ago, there lived a kingdom of creatures who could grant the greatest of wishes. They helped as many people as they could, for it was their job. The creatures went by many names, but the one used the most was *fairies*.

Fairies came before all other creatures, before humans, before fish, before cats and dogs. It was unclear what or who created fairies, but many tried their hand at guessing. Whatever differences there were in the history of fairies, there were two things that they all had in common: one, that fairies had magic, and two, that they had an obligation to share it.

One of the fairies who loved it the most was named Juno. Juno lived in a small house on the north branch of the largest tree in the world, although he didn't spend much time there. Juno would spend every day adventuring the world. Realistically, this world was most likely a few human paces around the tree at most, but for a fairy of common stature– about five acorns high– it was a great feat.

One day, Juno was exploring outside the forests of the

modern-day Dahlia Empire. On the outskirts of one, he found something peculiar, something he had never seen before: a giant. He was aware of giants, of course, all fairies were, and they were among the creatures that fairies granted wishes to. However, this giant was strange, they looked nothing like how Juno had been told. Most giants were covered in fur, like wolves or bears.

Speaking of bears, Juno remembered that he still needed to find a certain bear who had given his wish to another, a very kind act that Juno thought should be awarded, but that wasn't important right now.

The giant was wearing many layers, with the top being a thin woven cloth that moved like water as the creature walked around the forest clearing, picking berries and placing them into a basket larger than Juno's neighbourhood. He was extremely confused, why was this giant acting like a fairy? They seemed so strange, like Juno's sister if she had grown much taller.

Juno flew to the giant with caution and stood on a berry at the bush they were foraging from.

"Hello, giant."

The giant seemed baffled when Juno spoke, which made sense, as most didn't speak the languages that fairies did, he was relieved, perhaps this wasn't as weird as he had thought. That was until the giant spoke back.

"Who are you?" Juno had felt his heart drop to his pointy shoes. The giant looked at Juno, confused. Almost as if they had never seen a fairy before, which would've been out of the question five seconds ago before it proved it could understand the language of fairies.

"Who are *you?*" Juno replied.

The giant stared at him for a long time.

"I'm Dahlia."

"Well, *Dahlia*, I'm not sure if you were aware, but you're not supposed to understand me, and where is your fur?" Juno flew around her face, noticing that the only fur she had was on the top of her head, which seemed very stupid to Juno as it was going to be winter in only twenty moons. He decided that he would give a gift to Dahlia: fur like the rest of her kind. It must've been embarrassing being the only one without it.

"What do you mean fur?"

It was important at this point to know that Juno had never actually seen a giant, fairies each lived for around 300 years and still, no fairies in the past few generations had met any giants. Juno just assumed that *somebody* must've got their wishes.

"Don't giants have fur? Like bears?"

"Giant? No, I am not a giant, I'm a person." Dahlia laughed at him.

"A person? No, no, you are a giant, I've heard many stories of them, so you must be one, and they are all covered in fur, but you aren't."

"I look like everyone else in my village, no one has any fur; what are you, if you are not a strange butterfly?"

"What do you mean? Have you never seen a fairy before?"

"A fairy? No, I've never heard of them."

It was Juno's turn to look baffled. It was almost a rule that every creature got at least one wish granted by a fairy. If not, then they weren't doing their jobs. The more that Juno thought about it, the more he realised that he hadn't been granting wishes for a long time. What if this village was assigned to him and he didn't realise it? He hadn't been to his house in a long time, perhaps he was sent a letter explaining it. He began to fear the future of his career. He had to make it up, posthaste!

"Well, dear giant," he began to say, "I have a very special gift to befall you, one that will let you help many people."

Dahlia was intrigued at this proposition, for her village had been struck with a plague that killed all of the cattle in their area. If this gift could help her bring the cows back, she could save both her family and her town.

So she shook hands with the fairy, be it awkwardly because of the difference in size, but nonetheless, the agreement was made. Juno tried his best to concentrate on giving Dahlia an important but sensible gift, but couldn't stop worrying about whether or not he was in trouble. Juno's magic became more unstable, and he began to draw power from the newly revealed full moon.

Juno pulled the moon's light closer and closer to Dahlia without realising, and with a single movement of his small hand, accidentally gave her the greatest gift in human history: magic.

In those times fairies were the only ones with magic, for it was their life source, just as blood was to humans. The shining blue liquid coursed through their veins giving them larger eyes and hearts, and colourful pigments to the skin. It was forbidden for a fairy to give magic to any other creature, it was said to be very dangerous.

The magic from both Juno and the moon went into Dahlia, and she began to transform. Not into a fairy, but into something else entirely. Her eyes became larger, and her skin gained a bluish tinge, her fingers grew longer and she shrank ever-so-slightly. She doubled over as her lungs shrank to accommodate less oxygen. Her body now included something new to humans, a new chamber of the heart.

When Juno realised what he had done he was greatly embarrassed. How could a high-ranking fairy like himself make such a mistake? Looking at the moon he realised that it had gone from a full moon to a crescent. What a fool, he was!

Dahlia looked at herself in the reflection of a nearby pond, and she saw how her cheeks flushed the shade of blueberries, and how her eyes bulged. She was– though she lacked the words to clearly express it– extremely angry.

"How could you? You tricked me!" Dahlia shouted. At that point, it was important to state that Juno did not like admitting to mistakes. So, as he did many times before, Juno doubled down.

"That's how you thank the fae who gave you magic?" Juno said to her, pointing to the grass beneath Dahlia's feet. Around her stood beautiful wildflowers of every colour, and the grass had gone from brown to green. In Dahlia's village, they did not speak of magic, and if it wasn't for the sight of her reflection Dahlia would not have believed it. Like that, the fairy was gone, most likely off to frantically ask his boss what had happened to the giants, or perhaps even to search out a certain bear in need.

When she returned the next night to investigate, no light permeated the forest's natural defences. It was the first time Dahlia was alone with the forest. Where had the moon gone off to? Would it ever come back? There was no way for her to know, but that was not the only thing she pondered.

"Juno?" She called out to the darkness, but there was no response. No response from the fairy who made her unrecognisable to her family. "Juno!"

She shouted until she could no longer, going deeper into the forest.

Below her feet, she felt grass, then dirt, then cool sand, but never did she regain light. Branches scraped against her legs and face as she ran, but no matter how far she went, she could not see.

She did not notice when the sand she ran upon became nothing at all, nor did she notice the general lack of feeling her body began to experience. Dahlia was in a pond of sleep. One she couldn't understand, one beyond the concepts of time and reality that had only just recently begun. Her heart shattered in her senseless swim, taking her final breaths away with it. There was no transition between panic and stupor in her pond of dreams.

In a moment, almost as quickly as she had arrived, she returned to the forest. Water beading from her hair and down her face.

Dahlia was in a pond– a real one– with a large, golden moon shimmering above her head like fresh butter. She was colder than she had ever been in her life as she sat in the pond's sediment. Without any noise or warning, the moon began to *grow*. And it continued, even as she blinked awake.

"Juno?" She whispered to no one.

A strange humming noise began to reverberate throughout the trees as the sky parted for the moon, and with a suddenness like no other, a crack appeared in its centre. Dahlia couldn't think, she wasn't sure what to do, she didn't know the words to explain what she was witnessing. She was in the forest, there was no one to help her.

The crack in the moon grew, and so did the strange sound's

volume, it was like the screeching of hundreds of animals all at once.

When it shattered, she shut her eyes and braced for impact, but all that came was a soft tickle of light upon her face, glittering throughout the world.

That was the night the moon exploded, giving its magic to the sky, the plants, and the people. The monsters which terrorised the human race perished in a single moment. Forever gone were days separate, forever gone were nights afraid.

At least, that was what they assumed.

Chapter VII: Avindre

Datura

At the centre of the room was a table with ten chairs placed with the care most would expect from someone being paid to place chairs around a table. And although the chairs were placed with intricacy, it was interrupted every night, making the room smell of lavender and smoke: a herbalist's shop in flames.

In the chairs tonight sat a group of people in their gambling coats, eyes sunken and spirits dead. All spirits, apart from one. A man sat with an expression that looked blank to the untrained eye. One who was accustomed to the game, however, could tell it was the face of someone certain he was going to win.

As the others continued to bet, the man looked up from his cards, uncovering the fractals beneath his mask. The dealer looked at him, waiting for the inevitable. He revealed his hand– the scar reaching even his fingers– and won his fourth game of the day.

The manager walked out of the gambling room with the same scent of poisonous pride he had felt after every game, the sense of knowing that he was the only one leaving with his spirits intact. He took off his mask, the scar's branches reaching his eyes and forehead. When the scars got to his head of long black hair they became light streaks, like lightning.

As the others walked out, masks still hiding their despairing faces, the man watched them. He knew they were forever changed. He entered the main room of the gambling house richer than all others. Nothing new to him.

The man wondered whether it was all worth it, if creating an environment of such war and despair was what he wished to do with his life. Those thoughts were soon replaced with ones of triumph; he knew better than to think like that. He decided to be proud of his accomplishments, afraid of what would happen if he wasn't.

"Dionysus!"

It was Niamh, his secretary. She stumbled out of the western hallway, her chatelaine rattling against the silver buttons of her cycling skirt.

"Good evening, Miss Petrov!" He replied before walking in the other direction with haste. He could hear her huff across the hallway.

The gambling house was nothing short of lavish, the pillars embellished with real gold figures of mythology. The king of the land stood tall, keeping it safe. As world history went, Dionysus was proud to live in the one nation most accepting of his work. He had heard of Terra Florens's new statements which hinted at their sudden shift against magic. They stalked their siblings in hopes of complete and total control, unknowing that they were one of the targets. Dionysus did not know much else of Terra Florens, as he did not care for politics that did not relate to his own.

This said King of Avindre was a wonderful leader, no war,

revolt, or assassination attempt stopped her from keeping her people safe. However, she did not have the greatest reputation with the lower class, be it of her religious stance (which was none,) or her tendency to indulge in commissioning hundreds of artworks at a time. King Juno, (named after the fairy who created magical humans in mythology) ruled with a sophisticated but ruthless fist, one built from years of training to protect the nation. Avindre stood proud, bordered by their allies, Highland and the Dahlia Empire. Across the water lay a land shrouded in mystery and ruin. Terra Florens was once a large trade centre, doing business with both Avindre and the whole world. This all changed when their king died and was replaced by his brother, a perfidious person of dreadful constitution, Valentijn.

Since Valentijn was the king's brother, no one was surprised that he was the next in line, no one except King Augustus's daughter, Octavian. There were rumours that she was supposed to be first in line for the crown, but after her disappearance, there was no one to ask for proof of that claim. The princess was gone; like her younger sibling, who had died hours after their birth two weeks before the death of the king. The only people not scandalised were those in Terra Florens themselves. If it weren't for his secretary being so infused with royal relations, he wouldn't know the first thing about Florien politics. Truly, Dionysus was not one to gossip.

Avindre was not like that, Avindre was beautiful. There was nothing to fear there. Dionysus told himself that every day as he walked through the long halls of his family's gambling house. There was nothing to be worried about.

He sat at a small table in the corner of a room and watched the people around him, all giving him the money he deserved.

91

At least that was what he was told. The voice rang in his mind like a bell that never ceased ringing, and the person across the table gave him a disgusted look. The voice got closer to him, it always did, but he could never escape it. His hands itched for the flask in his coat pocket. He didn't look scared, and he didn't feel scared, but the voice told him the same thing nonetheless.

"There is nothing to fear in the House of Opulence."

Aster and Clover packed all they could into an old wagon with the help of the strange cat creature (whose name was Thimble.) The wagon was old, as much of an artefact as the house itself. It made Clover wonder just how old everything was, how old the world was. *Lethe–* their mind filled in automatically– *the world is named Lethe.*

Clover was in charge of getting books, as they assured Aster that they were more than capable. In reality, they didn't believe he was able to carry a single box of books, much less four. They weren't sure why they needed so many books, but Aster kept bringing more, assuring them that they were necessary. When they finished cleaning out half of the library, Clover waited outside for imminent danger (or the sudden realisation that they were a hatmaker with two kids, whichever came first.)

The land outside of the manor was lush and green, and while one side of the cliff peered over the ocean, the other faced the forest, which grew from green to purple.

They had almost fallen asleep, head in the clouds, when a noise startled them.

Aster had thrown a bag into the far back of the wagon and was in the process of covering it with a quilt when he realised that Clover was awake. They felt toasted by both the sun and the blanket of sleep.

"What's in that, Aster?" They asked drowsily.

"Just some of Rose and Dorothy's clothes, it would be a shame if it got ruined in the rain."

Clover hummed in reply before noticing the cane that leaned stately against the wagon, waiting for Aster when he finished sitting on the wagon floor, fastening the various boxes and bags into place. Clover was aware of how little work they had done getting the wagon ready. In their defence, they were recovering from a head injury, but it still didn't feel right to them.

They thought about putting it aside and continuing to nap until Aster's arm jerked, and he went limp for a moment.

"Are you all right, Teddy?" Clover asked him. They moved closer to him. Aster was massaging his hand. He stopped when Clover got near and attempted to appear well, leaning against the short wall of the wagon, but while doing so his eyes closed, trying to hide a wince.

"I'm fine, a bit dizzy."

"Right," Clover didn't believe him. They looked around and added, "May I help with anything else?" Aster paused, too embarrassed to answer.

"Well there's a few things I need to get from my room, but I can do that on my own…"

Clover did not wait for Aster to finish his sentence before running into the house. They ignored the nagging paranoia that wanted nothing more than to run away from the house and never come back. They had a choice to make, either run hopeless, or stay and hope to learn of their past. As they took the final step up to the manor's second floor, they understood that they had made their choice.

Walking into Aster's room for the first time felt like walking into a gallery. Beautiful trim framed the walls, which were covered in hand-painted murals, assumedly of Aster's creation. They depicted many different things: people with long pearlescent wings, floating eyes of every colour, and different animals. Clover was overwhelmed with how beautiful it was. Like the rest of the house, there were many bookshelves, but the dust that accumulated throughout the home was not present in Aster's room.

Three desks surrounded a comfortable chair in one corner of the room, each covered with many sorts of things. Books without covers, dolls, paint, paper, small sculptures, ink pots, the sorts of things that were naturally enchanting. A jar of sea glass glimmered atop the windowsill, and beside it was a dusty chessboard. The bookshelf nearest the desks had little pictures carved into the wood, and Clover imagined Aster doing them while waiting for paint to dry. It was within range of the desk chair.

On said bookshelf were many dollhouses, each made with such detail they looked identical to life-sized rooms. Miniature desks, pens, libraries, rugs, kitchens, and anything Clover could think of were sitting on the shelf.

Across from the desks was a large, comfortable-looking bed with thick quilts spread over it, the most prevalent being a large green one with visible stitches. Upon it sat pillows of different patterns and sizes, and settled on those pillows was an old teddy bear wearing a dress no doubt sewn by a child. Next to it was a bedside table which looked like it hadn't been cleaned for a very long time, as it was covered with old plates and glasses.

Looking back at the shelf, Clover noticed a certain miniature that they hadn't seen at first glance. It was in the back corner, pushed behind a miniature kitchen. Clover walked over to it cautiously, almost fearful, and attempted to see it without touching anything. They were stumped on what it was supposed to be due to the darkness of the shelf until they noticed familiar carvings etched on a miniature bookshelf. They pushed the kitchen to the back of the shelf, where there was extra room.

It was as Clover had assumed. There, hidden behind the kitchen, was a perfect replica of the very room in which they stood. The very same murals, shelves, and desks were there in miniature form. Sitting in the chair in the centre of the three desks was a doll, hunched over, its body glued into the seat. The doll had long, thick, white hair made of yarn that covered the face of the doll, however, it was easy to figure out who it was supposed to be. Next to the doll was a replica of Aster's cane, the silver embellishments and the carved head of a bird Clover couldn't distinguish were perfect to scale.

There was something else as well, something hidden even farther back. It was not a doll, but a piece of paper folded away. It was pressed against the wall of the bookshelf, purposeful and intriguing. As Clover carefully pulled it out from its space, they wondered not if Aster was near, only of the paper's contents.

Perhaps it was nothing, but Clover had begun to understand that their curiosity was a familiar friend. They opened the paper to reveal with shaking hands the likeness of another familiarity, a very old friend. For on the paper was a drawing of a person with dark curls and intense eyes, forever looking forward. It was very familiar, yes, for it was them.

Their skin was coloured deep and flushed, and for some strange reason, they were wearing spectacles. In the sombre light of the room, Clover inspected their face. It wasn't a perfect recreation, but it was comforting. It was what they saw in the reflections of water and windows. Their straight, official nose, their strong chin, and even the subtle freckles upon their cheeks were drawn with gentle precision. They looked into their own dark eyes with a smile, felt the natural ringlets their hair created with a skip of their heart. They were not scared by it. They suspected Rose had drawn it during a premonition. They wondered if premonition was a word she liked; they wondered why they weren't more concerned.

The door opened behind them, and Clover turned to see Aster– life-sized this time– holding his cane, identical to the one in the diorama. They were once again petrified.

"I never told you what to find," he said sheepishly. He began to rummage through his dresser, pulling out wool coats and vests, cane lying against the wall. They hurriedly slipped the paper back in its place as his back was turned.

Ignoring the embarrassment of both forgetting to ask what to get and also being caught staring at something they were never meant to see, Clover prodded.

"Is Avindre cold?" They asked Aster, taking a few of the coats from his bursting hands.

"Oh, yes, very much so, *terribly*, especially this time of the year," Aster replied, his eyes widening for dramatic effect. He paused, staring at the mural on the wall in front of him. This area of the mural depicted a field of flowers. Aster's bright eyes lit up.

"Do you know anything about floriography, Clover?" He said suddenly.

"No, not at the moment," Aster looked perplexed until Clover gestured to their head.

"Ah, right, of course. Remind me to check your injury before we leave." Aster's voice returned to sounding serious, which vexed Clover, "Maybe some of your memories will come back if I heal you again."

"What does floriography mean?"

Aster seemed very glad to answer that question.

"Well, do you see the yellow flowers on the wall, the ones with the cup?"

Clover looked closer at the mural.

"They're wonderful."

"Those are daffodils, floriography means the language of flowers, daffodils represent chivalry and unrequited love."

Clover hummed in response, not understanding the importance but wanting Aster to think they did.

"So do all flowers have secret meanings?" Clover scanned the mural before landing on another yellow flower, one they recognized. "What about this one?"

Aster grinned as he rolled up the coats from his dresser, now sitting on his bed. Behind the stack of clothes was the teddy bear, hiding from Clover's sight.

"That is a yellow rose, it stands for friendship."

Clover stared at it for some time, thinking of what to say without it coming out strange.

"So that would be our flower?"

Aster made a polite but confused noise in response.

"To represent our friendship," Clover clarified. Aster looked up at them, eyes widened, before laughing a quiet, breathy laugh. The kindest laugh Clover had ever heard. Granted, they had not heard many.

"Yes, I suppose."

Outside, Clover took a breath of warm, sleepy air. The weird cat sat asleep on the large stuffed animal that they had last seen at breakfast days before.

"What a strange cat you have."

Aster paused and stared at Clover with doe-like eyes.

"Clover, do you mean Thimble?" Aster said slowly. Thimble chirped at the mention of his name.

"Yes?" Clover replied, setting down the heavy bag of coats onto the wagon. Aster continued to stare in shock.

"Clover."

"Aster?" Clover began to get worried.

"Clover, Thimble is a raccoon."

"And that is a?"

"Animal."

"Oh."

Aster ran his hand through his hair with obvious stress, and Clover could do nothing but stand and wait for Aster to speak again.

"Perhaps your injury was worse than I thought."

Clover paused.

"Perhaps it's my magical amnesia," they joked.

"Perhaps," Aster replied with full seriousness.

Aster healed their wounds once more.

An ocean of green waved at them as they departed, each strand of grass forming into one along the overstretching horizon. Wildflowers peeked out of the current, and foxes jumped over small streams far away. Small, fluttering creatures danced around like stars above their head, and Clover wondered if the rest of the world held the same beauty. It would not have surprised them.

Falling asleep in a carriage driven by someone of dubious relation was not a part of their plan. They already planted the seeds of trusting him, with the flowers, and even if that was not purposeful, it didn't mean the action wasn't useful to them. But, even still, it seemed like their sense of self-preservation had been lost with their mind. They kept repeating a phrase over and over, *"I'm not dead yet."* They said it under their breath before they could stop themself.

They gave in to sleep as the wagon rumbled along the worn dirt road, away to Dolston, to the north. The warmth of the sun lulled them into a comfortable slumber.

When they woke, they were in front of the large gates of a castle, and they could hear a baby crying. A woman whispered amidst the seeming emptiness. Clover closed their eyes to hear it better.

"Good night, my love," she whispered, and the kindness of it made Clover smile. "I need you to be good while I'm gone."

When they opened their eyes, they were in a beautiful hallway of sleek marble and gold; the walls reflected as if they were mirrors. In front of them sat a door with a brass label with the name scratched out. The baby's crying continued throughout the castle. Clover slowly turned the doorknob, clouded with their disillusion.

Inside the room stood an empty crib with a young girl next to it, weeping softly. Her hair was black and curly, like Clover's own. Her small hands curled around the bars of the crib, she couldn't have been more than ten years old. The windows reflected in the warm light of dawn. Music crept in through the cracks of the door. Turning away from the crib, Clover felt their feet sink through the floor heart-first.

They were falling through a tunnel, going further and further into the depths of the castle. Spinning around and around. The tunnel of brick turned quickly to stone, and then to dirt. Clover felt their hair fall out of their head, and with that, the tunnel began to stir. The walls twisted and turned into unidentifiable shapes, warping around Clover's mind and making their head hurt. Suddenly, they were falling endlessly down a tunnel of books, all-consuming darkness looming below. The darkness grew closer and closer until their heart dropped completely, shooting their hand upward to grab anything for support.

They were in complete and utter darkness, apart from a small red dot in the centre of their vision. Clover tried to blink, but they could not find their eyelids. The red dot began to grow, shooting out red tendrils throughout the darkness. The dot grew more and more until it was a pupil. The eye opened, and Clover felt the feeling of terror mix with the sudden dropping of their stomach. There was an echo; someone coughed. Once, twice, until there was nothing else to be heard but the hacking. The eye evolved once more into a strange, beating flame that consumed everything.

Suddenly, they heard the sweet melodies of bluebirds, and the screams of crows just out of sight. Wind rustled groaning trees with bursts of sudden affection. It was an otherwise empty forest, and the rock beneath Clover's head cooled the headache between their ears. It felt like spring, but the trees had not yet regained their life, so it couldn't have been far in the season. Not a single flower bloomed on the forest floor.

The world whirred around them, even as they continued to

sit unmoving, but there was an unnatural frequency behind the wind's voice. It created dissonant sounds in the forest unlike any Clover could recall.

From ground to air, they lifted themself. It was a grey wood, damp and dreary, like an illustration. They walked until they reached the tree closest to their rock, and placed their hand against its rough skin. Cracked and whistling, the tree leaned against Clover's hand in the wind.

A soft fluttering of wings approached their ears, and upon one of the tree branches did a bird of brown-and-grey plumage perch. A hooked beak turned with its head, and Clover could not help but mimic the movement with their own. It was a shrike, the butcher of the woods.

It flew to the bush at the tree's roots, which Clover leaned over. It was an interesting creature. Without thought, they plucked a small branch off of the bush.

Blood swelled where the bush was wounded, and as if they had disturbed an ancient land, the surrounding trees all began to whistle and groan, the sounds eerily similar to a person's. The bush screamed in pain, its branches shaking in natural fear.

Where bark emerged into knots and lumps, the trees creaked and morphed until the knots looked like eyes, and the lumps were a nose, and a gash of a mouth appeared beneath them. The screams grew louder.

"Wherefore tear'st me thus? Wherefore tear'st me thus?" The forest demanded.

And all at once, they understood just how large the world truly was, how great and shocking the very nature of existence could be. From the smallest grain to the largest creature, millions of choices and paths determined their end. But how useless their end was in the grand scheme of life! Worms eaten by fish; fish eaten by man; man eaten by worms. They were the slightest experience experiencing many other experiences. They were nothing, but simultaneously they were all. Once the worms died, they would return again, and again, and again, until they were spread around the world, into the very core of Lethe.

They returned the stick to its bush, and listened to the cries of its soul echo through the forest. Bloody and raw, like the people beneath the soil. The people beneath their feet.

Waking up, it took Clover many seconds to realise they were conscious. It was daunting, and they still thought they were asleep for many moments. They felt drained and exhausted, as if they had been running for hours.

The sun overwhelmed their bleary, itchy eyes behind the safety of their eyelids, which were now exactly where they remembered them to be.

"Clover?" A voice repeated, incredulously. "Clover?"

They opened their eyes, and saw Dorothy holding a package covered in brown paper. Clover did not speak as they looked around, their eyes aching in the terrible brightness. Rose was in the carriage as well, waving her hands around Dorothy's face until one of her nails caught on her hair, ripping out a strand.

"Ack-! Have you no touch of mercy, Rose?" She yelled, swiping at Rose's still-extended hand.

"It's very bright in Dolston during the evening. I was only trying to find you." Rose's voice lifted from the back of the wagon musically.

"We're already there? I thought— Isn't Dolston two days

away?" They stuttered. Looking around, they saw the large street of a cramped town. The grey brick road was overgrown with moss, and large lamp posts towered above as other carriages rattled to and fro. Smoke emerged from chimneys like long-reaching spiderwebs decorating the sky. Citizens raced through the streets with an insatiable hunger to arrive wherever they were going. Automobiles were sprinkled throughout the crowd, their drivers wearing fine uniforms embroidered with the words: *The King's Police.* Strange yellow trees grew at every corner, and Clover could almost see spores radiating off of them. People in dark coats lingered outside of shops advertising "Sir Calcifer's Cogent Cure-All" and "Harretson's Pink Pills for Pesky Problems."

A young boy tripped on a loose brick in the street, tossing the contents of his old satchel onto the dusty road. Everything seemed to be covered in the dusty ash, and Clover felt their throat close up subconsciously, as if the mere thought of breathing in the town's fumes made them susceptible. The boy looked up from the crash, and even from Clover's place at the carriage, they had the strangest feeling that they had seen him before. In the last second before the boy might've been able to see where Clover sat, they slumped back against the wooden bench and stared at their shoes.

Aster walked out of the tailor's shop's front with a package underneath his arm, Clover watched as he and Dorothy lifted it into the back of the wagon. His hand shook as he looked around. When Clover followed his line of sight they saw that the boy had run off.

"You're awake," Aster exclaimed as he tied the packages down, "Good, very good."

As he hoisted himself into the seat, Clover was bombarded

with the site of the silliest shoes they had ever seen. His boots ended in a sharp point, curving mildly upward. Like a fairy's.

"How long was I asleep?"

"The whole trip," he replied, now inspecting his coin purse. "It's normal to sleep a lot after your body heals at a rapid pace."

Clover now understood why they felt so hungry, but something else made their stomach churn.

"You haven't slept in two days."

Aster nodded and gave them a straight-lined smile. Clover looked to the back of the wagon again where Dorothy and Rose sat. Dorothy was fluffing a lumpy pillow beneath Rose's head.

"I feel like I am in the past," Rose chirped merrily, "This wagon makes me feel so historical."

The wagon began to move as the horses trotted once more. Clover, still very disillusioned, did not know where they were going. As if reading their mind, Aster began to speak.

"It isn't old enough to be conspicuous," he told Clover, "Rose's magic reacted to a large concentration of people at the docks, which we realised means they are sending out Marianne."

"Who's Marianne?"

Aster cracked his knuckles and sighed with exhaustion before answering their question.

"The Marianne is the only boat that leaves the nation with passengers, only the king's men and the wealthy are allowed on. If you pay enough you're able to skip the blood tests, which we'll have to do due to Rose and I's high junolian concentration."

"Junolian...What?" It sounded familiar, the definition on the tip of their tongue. It was something they had said many times before.

"We have magic."

"Right, of course."

"And I *found* a badge!" Rose giggled quietly, and her voice enunciated the word found in such a way that made Clover anxious. They were sure she did *not* find it. Her fingers fumbled the badge into Clover's hand, it was made of silver metal and read, "Official Officer of Sir Majesty the King."

"Very wordy," they muttered.

"With that badge, we can get the documentation from an old friend of mine," Aster said quietly, so no soul on the street could hear, "Iris."

Chapter VIII: The Lavender Archive

Iris

The following notes were found in a series of journals published anonymously under the pseudonym "Antigone Dubois" to an underground archive in Terra Florens, which was founded to ethically study magical powers in a nation that had ended all research. The sentences were written in loopy black ink, and most were unable to read it due to the penmanship and overall mediocre sentence structure. In terms of a textbook, it was far too opinionated. The last paragraphs seem to have been pasted in much later.

There are many sorts of powers in the world, each defined by the amount of magic flowing through the person's veins through the Junarian filter on the left side of the heart.

Magic does not act the same as human blood, it's too unpredictable. Because of this, sometimes magic concentrates in one part of the body, and in rare cases, more than one.

Magic cannot be taught or earned, however, it can be given if the person is ready for the consequences of such a thing, and should make sure that they have a person with magic capable of healing on standby. Magic can also be further harnessed with proper schooling.

The two most common places for magic to positively concentrate are the mind and the hands. Here are some examples of mind-related powers:

Mind reading: The act of connecting to another human's brain waves via magical interception. Different from brain-washing as the magic user cannot change the thoughts of the other person.

Brainwashing: The act of connecting to another human's brain waves to persuade them in some way, the only kind of power to be used in the Florien government.

Knowledge-based powers: These are powers that cause the magic user to learn things in ways that would otherwise be impossible.

Hand-based powers are very different and have been less researched due to their lack of use in the Florien government. Healing powers go under this category, however that is an umbrella term for the many ways someone can be healed.

Illusion: Is, in most cases, a mind-based power. Allows the user to control the sight of others temporarily.

Giving life: The ability to give life using magic can also make the body heal itself faster, dangerous to do for those whose hearts cannot slow down easily.

Plant/Biology related powers: Those who can control animals or biological material may be able to speed up the healing process. In most cases, Plant and Healing magic can be harnessed by the same person. These people are still respected in most Verian circles, despite their government's opinions. (Note: Those with this power are unable to quicken the growing process of fane due to the closeness needed.)

There are many others but not enough information, see

more in *The Types of Flowers by Antigone Dubois.*

Those with large junolian concentrations (a trait passed down from the parents) have been known to be born with unnatural hair and eye colours. These traits can also be passed down to non-magic descendants.

There is a phenomenon that those who suppress their powers can have a variety of symptoms due to it such as changing physical traits such as hair colour, eye colour, skin pigmentation, and most importantly magical build-ups.

A magic build-up happens when someone with a high junolian concentration suppresses their magic ability by either not using it or covering up the part of the body holding the concentration, such as wearing gloves for a hand-related power. Magic build-ups can be fatal, and, in the case that they aren't, can cause the magic to grow restless and essentially do the exact opposite of the person's magical nature. Those who can read minds might instead allow people to hear their thoughts for as long as the symptoms last, sometimes never-ending.

Doctor Zinnia Stricken conducted experiments on dead brain tissue and found that there is an electric current which runs through the human brain, and as a magic user herself, suggested that it is in these electric waves which allow humans to manipulate the outside world with their magic. If the same electricity which runs through humans runs through the air and world as well, it could be the reason why magic can move from inside the body to outside. Zinnia worked at the Royal Infirmary as head physician for ten years before teaching at the School of Anatomy in Palperroth.

Ethical experiments have been done to find the scientific reasons why humans can use magic the same way they would use an appendage. Surgeons such as Dr Jasper Dellia (1825-1872) of the former Liston College of Magical Persons (shut down in 1872) thought that magic was able to leave the body through the skin, just as sweat would.

Long in the past, those without magic in Terra Florens were called *acosmists*, however, the term is rarely used now. Those with magic– or high junolian concentrations– were called aeternists.

It is very rare to find someone with no magic at all, with the majority of the population having a small quantity unable to be controlled. It is why bright eye colours still are common with acosmists. Most of Lethe does not care about magic or no magic, it is another part of life, but it seems that human beings need to have something to hate, they need something to feel superior over. Despite years of history stating otherwise, there will always be something for people to complain about, something to hurt others over.

If there is one thing that humans love almost as much as superiority, it would be the act of explaining things. They long for something to turn to when they are afraid. They long for science to tell them why something happens. With magic, this cannot be done. Some simple laws of magic can be observed, but anything more is currently not possible.

Creation of Life: Related to healing and giving life. It is not a type of magic but instead a particular effect of some healing magics. When mixed with a malfunctioned (or backfiring) mind control magic, it can create a state of being between life and death. Results in long comas and on some occasions those experiencing it can temporarily gain personality traits from the healer that gives back their life. This includes the usage of words not before in their vocabulary and false memories.

Can also occur if healed after death.

The wagon stopped far after the path turned from brick to stone, and from stone to dirt. It stopped outside of an abandoned building with vines eating the wooden walls. A sloppily-painted sign hung over the door, "Devan Earl Apothecary."

"Water the horses, Dorothy. The rest of you stay put," Aster said, and Rose groaned from the back seat in boredom.

"Me as well?" Clover asked between bites of a meat pie Aster had bought in town. In reality, they did not desire to enter the dilapidated building, but they felt annoying was better than silence. The shop was located on the outskirts of the city, where the air was clean and the sky free from ash. They longed to stretch their legs, but not if it meant breathing in dust.

"Yes, you as well," Aster replied as he shut the door of the apothecary, leaving the three in silence. Probably for the best.

Aster entered the dingy apothecary, dust and mildew floating about. Holding a hand up to cover his mouth from the incoming dust cloud, he rang the counter-bound bell twice. Old herbs moulded themselves to the walls; spiders worked their webs in the darkness.

Behind the counter was an all-too-familiar rug. He wondered if he would be welcome still, his thoughts spiralling, until he kicked the rug to the corner, revealing the trapdoor.

It had been months since he had last seen them. Had he ruined his only chance at changing something in this kingdom? Had they forgotten him already? But thoughts of rebellion swirled with reminders of the orphanage, and he knew nothing else but the rage that lived inside him. He would always have a chance for revenge, even if he had to achieve it alone.

Aster didn't want to admit his hesitation for taking the trip, he could very easily stay home as he had done for years, but he knew he wouldn't be able to live with himself if he did. When looking into the eyes of a problem, it was impossible to ignore his desire to fix it.

The trapdoor creaked eerily as it opened, and he climbed the rickety ladder below, only mildly terrified for his well-being. A familiar door waited at the end with a conspicuous lock in the mud next to it. This was when Aster remembered that he did not bring the key.

"Curses!" He muttered, feeling his pockets for a key he knew was not there. But through his panic, he wondered if he was overestimating the level of security held by the most successful rebellion of Terra Florens. In their defence, they hadn't been getting much business the last few months.

The doorknob turned without objection, and Aster was both thankful and disappointed. The room under the apothecary was a large and haunting library: The Lavender Archive.

Lavender represented elegance and grace, something that King Valentijn heavily believed he embodied, it was what he gave his police and guard to use as kindling as they lit the houses of 'wrong-doers' on fire. He stated to the Florien Periodical that he chose it, quote, "Because I want its influence to linger in the town for hours, so the stench of flame and flora could mingle." The way he spoke with such dramatic flamboyance as if he was speaking about a new pair of boots and not the lives of his people made Aster's blood boil. If Terra Florens had a competition in magniloquence no one would dare suggest Valentijn a loser, for while he did not understand what the word meant, he would feel entitled to win it. That was how the king was, always the winner of games he created.

It took fifteen years of death for The Lavender Syndicate to be officially created by Aster and Iris.

After taking a book from one of the tall shelves, Aster turned it over in his hands, noticing that one of his aliases was written on the title. He allowed himself to smile at how sloppily the book was stitched together. How hopeful he was in his youth. He longed for a reconnection.

He dropped the book briskly and watched as it fell to the floor with a loud clatter, and listened closely to the resulting shuffle of footsteps in the back of the library.

"Who goes there?" He heard a voice shout, it was prominent and boomed throughout the library.

"Guess," he said flatly, picking up the book and placing it back on the shelf. Whispers erupted around him and quickly Iris appeared at the end of the aisle.

Iris Webbleton, the leader of the Lavender Syndicate.

"Aster," she said respectfully. Her braids went to her shoulders, coils emerging where her hair came loose. Aster wondered how long it had been since she last did her hair. He also momentarily reminisced about the two of them in their youth, braiding each other's hair before going to town. Iris always had red hair, but ever since she left the orphanage, it seemed to get brighter with every sighting of her.

She wore a vest in a masculine cut over her puffy-sleeved blouse, with large muddy boots peeking beneath her skirt. She wore no corset because she believed one should be able to choose what they wore and how they wore it. Aster agreed, but was conflicted with his personal sense of romanticism. She was welcome to make a statement, but Aster wasn't as eager to empty his wardrobe for one.

Ever since the orphanage, he was seen as a hero to the underground magical communities in Palperroth, Dolston, and Solle. Aster did not feel like himself when he was surrounded by so many people from his past, he felt too vulnerable, too prone to dramatics.

"I have something to ask of you, Iris," he said slowly, trying hard not to breathe in more dust than needed. He lifted the badge Rose "found" from his pocket, "I do not come empty-handed."

"You never do," Iris grabbed the badge with a sly grin, "Don't know what we'd do without you, Aster."

"Perhaps this will help you do another public stunt sometime in the future?" Aster asked with a charade of innocence. Iris lifted the badge close to her eye, inspecting every groove. Her eyes darted from the badge to Aster.

"Yes. Yes of course," She hid the badge in her skirt pocket, and with a sigh she added, "Will help *me* do a public stunt."

He was reminded of how she spoke back when the orphanage still had her, it was as if she were miles away.

"I will be back to lead after this. This is important to the rebellion, to the Syndicate."

"I understand."

Aster could tell what was wrong but chose not to bring it up. Iris began to walk into the back of the library, and he followed, making sure to keep his distance.

"Rose stole it." He grinned, and Iris snorted despite her better judgement.

"Always eager, that one."

His head sank, for now he was forced to further ignite her spirit.

"I need to get onto the Marianne."

Iris stopped in her tracks, and Aster tried his best to hide that he almost ran into her back. She turned with haste, and he felt her breath hit his nose, she was never good with personal space.

"Marianne!" She exhaled, "Isn't it a bit late to leave the nation?"

"I am not ashamed of my crimes."

"I know, of course, I know."

"I need to help a friend."

"The guard? The one who's been in the paper?" She accused..

"Detective," Aster corrected, "Private investigator, separate from the crown."

"If you're sure," She took the badge out of her pocket once more, as if debating whether its value was worth the trouble, "I can telegram Hyacinth, she'll get you the documents, how many do you need?"

"Four."

"Rich Florien family, very lucky,"

"Indeed," Aster felt his lips curl into a smile, revelling in the irony. "We are."

She took a piece of paper from a desk and ripped a long strip before leading Aster down a familiar hallway. Iris said nothing, but her braids glowed like the embers of a fireplace. A small wooden door was hidden in the shadows of the dusty library, she stilled before it. Aster could hardly hear her.

"Where have you been, Aster?"

Aster's heart dropped, and he felt his vision begin to blur the way it always did when he was surprised. It was a symptom of his condition after the orphanage. The disgusting, horrific, mortifying orphanage. He began to wonder if the plan was a mistake. Iris was blunt sometimes, but that was because she had to. She too had raised most of the people in the Syndicate, even lending a bed to Aster when he had to go to town before he owned a horse. It was not fair of him to latibulate.

"I'm sorry for leaving without telling you."

"I still don't know where you live."

"I'll be back after this trip," he tried not to react when she turned to him, "I promise."

"Do you know what I've had to do since you've left? I have had to help Anthony with the barriers *you* made twice, find another to stand in as healer *and* head librarian, handle the aftermath of what happened at the Dolston Library, continue communications with General Wesley, *as well as* train the new recruits. Do you understand how little I have slept in the past three months?"

Aster stood silent as she reprimanded him, and he was somewhat relieved that she was. Disappointed Iris he could handle, and even Taciturn Iris was manageable, but it was Sad Iris he feared. She pinched the bridge of her nose.

Iris held the piece of ripped paper she grabbed up to her lips, and turned to the door. She blew a line of air onto it, and Aster watched as a small flame grew between the fibres, eating it in a cloud of smoke. The embers were blown onto the handleless door and landed on the wood, burning a pattern onto it. The pattern grew into a crest, one that Aster knew very well, he made it with a vial of blood and wisteria. It was the same thing he had done outside the house long ago.

The door burned away with the crest and revealed a large, even dustier room than the last. It smelt the same as Aster remembered, like sweat and mildew with the soft overlay of soil. It looked the same as well, grey walls apart from one papered one that he always stared at in deep thought. Many people sat on the beds strewn about, children in one room and adults in the other. It was a bare-bones living quarters, but it was still leagues greater than the orphanage, where many of the children were from.

Magic users of all kinds lived in the bunker. Healers, ignitors, electrifiers, mind controllers, defenders, empathizers, transporters; any sort of power imaginable lived underneath the noses of the royal guard. Most were recognizable, the entire group from Dolston's school sat by a smokeless fire playing cards. They were still very young, but their eyes held the same hollowness that Aster knew all too well. They looked at him with their empty faces when he entered, some smiled, but most simply nodded. Aster still was not used to being respected.

Anthony Griffin (a last name he chose for himself, as he was unable to remember his one from birth) had magic which specialised in his ears. It allowed him to be able to hear even the slightest disturbance in the airwaves, but after an infection during his childhood left him without the use of his left ear, he was unable to use the full range of his power. That wasn't to say that he was useless. Anthony was a very important part of the Syndicate due to his charismatic strength, which was one of the many strengths Aster lacked.

"He's back everyone!" Anthony shouted when he saw him, "Your saviour has returned from the depths of the most dangerous lands!"

"Actually, I've just been at home," Aster replied quietly, Iris scoffed, "And sadly must leave again, Anthony, don't get their hopes up."

"If I don't, then who will?" His mellifluous tone was so familiar to Aster that for a second it was like nothing had changed. They hadn't forgotten him after all. He stifled a silly grin.

"They should be grateful enough they're alive," Iris said as she sat at an old desk, one that Aster had dragged in years ago from one of the manor's rooms. Thinking about his home made his shoulders slump with fatigue and his legs ache with longing. He hadn't slept in days.

"Have you no hope, Iris!" Anthony collapsed onto a bed with his hand over his heart as if he had been shot, and the children giggled at his antics. Aster sat on the floor beside the bed and watched the group by the fire play cards. The sound of Iris rapping at the typewriter made Aster's temples ache.

"What are they playing?" He asked one of the younger kids. He noticed that the groups of older children never played with the younger ones, despite their desperate pleas to be included. It reminded him of the groups at the orphanage, how the older, mature ones acted as another set of adults, leaving the young ones to fend for themselves. The more rambunctious ones tried to fight it, but the same situation was born in every orphanage; it was how they were designed.

"Snap!" The young girl shouted into his ear. He thanked her, but he also regretted ever asking. As soon as he turned, Iris's hand shot in front of his face, papers waving frantically.

"Bring this to Hyacinth," she told him.

"I don't mean to sound ungrateful by any means, Iris," he attempted to speak in a light tone, "but what happened to the electric telegraph?"

"I forgot Anthony broke it."

Anthony looked to be fearing for his life when Aster turned

back to him. Aster was glad for that.

"The sun looks like a marigold flower," Rose droned in the heat of the empty field, "Doesn't it, Clover?"

"What?" Clover was not paying attention.

"Doesn't the sun look like a marigold flower? Tell me it does."

"I don't know Rose, no one can look at the sun," Clover explained, "It'll burn your eyes."

"Oh, I know that, I could see once," she whispered, and Clover could tell she was agitated that they assumed she didn't know, but then, in another hushed whisper she pleaded once more, "Can't you try?"

"I'll go blind, Rose."

"Being blind isn't all that bad."

Clover did not respond, the heat sweltering on their face.

"I quite like living in Terra Florens for a good few reasons," Rose began again, ignoring Clover's silence. "Dyed clothes feel better than plain ones, we have lots of dye here."

"Can't you find out what the sun looks like?" Dorothy interrupted, her voice more hollow than usual, "With your eerie mind powers?"

"That ruins the fun of it," Rose groaned, "Just try once, please?"

"All right, all right," Clover complied.

When Clover looked up, their eyes began to burn in an instant. They settled on staring at a cloud nearby.

"I suppose it does look a bit like a marigold," they lied. Rose gasped softly at the thought.

"I knew it," her voice was quiet, sleepy.

Clover inhaled and looked for the hundredth time at the

grass rolling in waves with the wind, watching the wildflowers flutter. They clumsily leaned down to pick one, almost falling off of the carriage as they did. When they fell back, they saw something most peculiar in the shop's window that was not visible at standing height. It was a mask, one identical to the one Aster wore that night at the balcony. Lavender stitches cascaded down the curve of the beak. *Interesting*, they thought, *Fascinating!*

"Hold out your hand," Clover told Rose, attempting to ignore the mask, and when she complied, they dropped it into her open hands. She felt for it, and gasped when she realised what it was.

"Is it a marigold?"

"I'm not sure," replied Clover, "You should ask your brother."

Rose hummed and spun the flower between her fingers.

"Isn't it just lovely how we are all named after flowers? Or plants?" She said, Dorothy cleared her throat in frustration.

"There isn't a Dorothy flower."

"Yes, there is! Haven't you seen one?" Rose lifted the flower in her hand upward to the sky, "Here's one right here!"

"I thought you said it was a marigold."

"I'm quite sure it's just a weed," Clover mumbled.

"Well, it's a flower to me, and that's all that matters."

Dorothy leaned over to look at the flower with closer detail and said quietly,

"It is pretty, I suppose."

Everyone was silent.

"I want to eat the sun," Rose said. Dorothy and Clover stared at her with abject dismay.

They were interrupted by the slamming of a door. Aster held up a collection of official-looking envelopes with a tired smile, and Dorothy cheered from the carriage floor.

"Did you get the papers?"

"Not quite," His voice lifted and his tiredness seemed much more apparent. "You'll have to drive, Dorothy. We have to go back south, across the Split."

"Again?" Rose yelled.

"The Split?" Clover exasperated under their breath.

"It's what they call the river that lays in the middle of Dolston, you were asleep the last time we went over it." Aster lifted himself out of the carriage so Dorothy could replace him in the front seat. She sat straight and stable, where he was anxious and trembling.

"Rich people live South, poor people live North. There's more fane near the rich. Sodding things," Rose said. It sounded as if she was reciting something.

"Fane? The yellow things?"

"They smother magical ability, and if you have enough of it in your lungs it can cause fatigue, it makes it very easy to catch you if they see you are affected."

"How did you get past it the first time?" Clover asked when Aster was done explaining and looking over the papers in his hand. The words on the page were in a language Clover couldn't understand. "Did you wear masks?"

"We held our breath."

Clover was unaffected by fane, they realised as the wagon rumbled over the bridge. They were able to see many more spores in the air, yellow dusted every surface like a coating of flour over a baked good. Aster and Rose seldom moved and reserved their energy for holding their breath. Clover counted the number of breaths Aster took next to them from when they crossed the bridge until they left Main Street: five.

It made their head spin when they thought of it.

The carriage rattled on until they approached a well-off home that looked to have been recently cared for, at least judging by the state of the lawn. Thick purple flowers curved their vines around the brick walls of the home. Smoke from the chimney rose to meet the clouds with yellow fumes.

"Is she burning...?" Dorothy asked, her voice trailing off.

"Turmeric," Aster answered. Clover suspected that he scrunched his nose for a reason other than the risk of fane, the spice wafted through the air in thick waves.

"Who is this, Teddy?" Rose asked from the back of the carriage, and Clover was unable to understand why she bothered asking, it seemed redundant in her condition.

"Her name is Hyacinth, I've only met her twice, but she's trustworthy. She provided sanctuary to..." He paused. "Our non-magical allies, some time ago."

Rose was silent. Clover too heard the hesitation in Aster's words, and became all the more confused when he glanced at them from the back of the carriage.

He left once more, but not before giving the horses a pat. It was far enough from fane, so Rose and Dorothy's following silence was caused by something unrelated to the conservation of air. Clover assumed that it had something to do with the number of people populating the road. Boredom was a heavy feeling, they realised. A heavy, bittersweet nothing. They tilted their head back to the sky and awaited Aster's return, for there was nothing else to do but count birds on the metal roof of Lady Hyacinth's house.

Chapter IX: Counterfeit Castle

Sunflower

Aster would have to have a talk with Iris about making him do her dirty work. *Hyacinth? Really?* He couldn't believe it.

Hyacinth's estate was built by a wealthy late guardian and was bequeathed to their nonsensical daughter. And that meant a lot, as Aster's own home had much to answer for in terms of sensicality. The metal gate swung behind him with a loud crash, making Aster cover his ears momentarily. He was in her domain now.

Hyacinth was the kind of person that Aster couldn't stand. She couldn't have been much older than Rose, but the way she spoke of magic– while she herself did not possess it– was nothing less than disturbing. She preached of a magic greater than the physical kind, of a spiritual magic that she alone possessed. Her home was always densely populated with clueless individuals who believed her to be the daughter of a fairy. It made Aster squeamish, but he could not ignore the benefits that an alliance with her brought. She had connections everywhere.

He knocked on the large circular door five times, each one

evenly spaced out. It was how Hyacinth would know it was one of the Syndicate. The paint on the door was peeling at the edges of the panels; it was like it understood its fake promises.

The door was opened three seconds after the last knock by a servant, a short man with fake pointed ears and green speckled across his cheeks. Aster tried his best not to turn up his nose.

The man led him through the house in silence, and as he did Aster noticed a peculiarity in the home. Gone were the paper decorations, elaborate golden statues, and bustling crowds. It was all empty. In a large desolate room, which Aster recognized as an old sitting room, he saw Hyacinth on the floor poking the drowning embers in her fireplace. She had her hair made into a bow atop her head, and she sniffled into a handkerchief Aster could barely see.

She was a mousey, freckled girl. Always speaking, and always having something to add to the conversation, but it seemed that something had taken away her security.

"Miss Hyacinth, one of your people is here," the servant said, and when he spoke she jumped from her spot on the floor and turned to Aster with a wide-eyed stare. She had something on her face, a third eye on her forehead painted in ash.

"Crowden!" She gasped. Aster cringed at the codename Anthony chose for him when they first met Hyacinth. She wiped ash onto her striped day dress and walked to him on the other side of the room. "You can't be here."

"Excuse me?"

"I have the papers, just leave, quickly, don't turn back," she shoved him back into the hallway after snatching a stack of papers from the floor and handing them to him. When he looked around the servant was nowhere to be seen. It wasn't possible! How could she have known about the documents?

"Miss Hyacinth, what's going on? I can help you."

She fell to the ground and held onto the hem of his coat and began to weep.

"It's too late…" Tears gathered around her eyes and muddied the whites.

"Hyacinth?"

She looked at him, and when she did he could see that it was not the same person as before. He saw his face reflected back to him in a sea of yellow in her abstruse eyes. What had her eyes been before? Brown, hazel? He scrambled away, but she did not chase after him.

She wiped the ash from her forehead and began to speak.

"How long do you think you can keep this up, Aster?" It was her voice, but he knew he had never told her his name. He knew he should run, but there was a force, perhaps an extra sense, that stopped him from moving. "You are not the nice man you pretend to be."

"What?"

"You speak of peace and of kindness, but you are a child born of violence, of treachery," Aster remembered the existence of the dagger at his belt, and although his reflexes wanted to abandon it for his magic instead, his brain wouldn't allow it. Despite his hatred for the girl, he had no desire to kill Hyacinth. His cane was also thrown across the room, so that too was unable to aid him. "You have scorned the gods, Aster Williams, what will you tell your family? You are a family man, I know."

"Don't call me *man*," Aster whispered, he didn't know exactly why as it wasn't exactly incorrect, but he couldn't think straight. She leaned forward. "Who are you?"

"You don't know who I am?" The thing said through Hyacinth. "How strange, for I know exactly who *you* are. But that would make sense, wouldn't it? As you are the one who created me."

"I couldn't have created you." He replied, "I may be a monster, but I do not create monsters."

Hyacinth looked down at him, "You created her."

"She is her own creation, do you shame a mother for her child?"

"No. I don't shame anyone."

"You shame me."

"You aren't real." The shadow said.

It was mere hallucination, Aster tried to convince himself of that. It was a hallucination born from his sleep deprivation, and nothing more. Still, Aster could not fathom how his brain could conjure such a terrible sight.

"I am as real as you are," Aster looked into the eyes of the monster. It picked up the papers on the floor and placed them on Aster's leg where he had fallen.

"The longer you run away from your problems, the more real I become, Aster Williams. We are all throughout the piece of rock you have named *Terra Florens*, we lurk in every crevice of your man-made machines and pierce through the flesh of your sacred home. With every monstrous act committed we grow stronger. We are just behind your eyes, impossible to be found or removed, but seeing all."

He, unable to hold back his violence, attempted to punch the monster, but the moment his fist made contact, its stolen face fell away into a cloud of smoke and shadow. Only the echo of its past words survived. *We are just behind your eyes, impossible to be found or removed, but seeing all.*

"Follow me through all of Lethe, it won't matter," Aster said to nothing as he stood. "You are as real as I allow you to be."

"Do you want to know the horses' names, Clover?" Rose said, once more in an attempt to make time pass by faster, no doubt. Clover couldn't feel much, but boredom seemed to be a feeling well-known to their injured brain.

"If you'd like to tell me, I am willing to know."

"Well, the mare– the one with the white splotches and furry hooves– is Sorrel, and the one Dorothy and I took here is Basil."

"Very sweet," Clover said, their eyes shut.

"They are married."

Could horses get married? *No*, obviously not, it was a joke!

"What a beautiful mind you have, Rose."

Aster returned sooner than Clover expected, but later than they preferred. When he came into sight Clover noticed signs of ageing. Not truly, but his fatigue was far more visible than before, and his face had never been so shallow. Clover somewhat enjoyed how he looked so disgruntled.

He held a new stack of papers in his hand, along with the ones Iris gave him. Or at least Clover was quite sure Iris was her name, they struggled to keep up with Aster's quick-worded explanations.

"Teddy?" Rose gasped.

"She had them quicker than expected." He replied with an airy laugh. Without Rose's eyes covered by bandages, it was much easier to see how her brow furrowed. He must've done something wrong. It was also easier to see the deep scars that ripped through the skin around her eyes, despite being long healed.

The air changed as they drove further away, past the smoking bakery, past the back-end doctor's office, and past the second-hand fabric store. The open carriage clunked back onto the grey stone road of Main Street, where Clover noticed Dorothy turning her head from a particular store.

It was an undergarments store, and while Dorothy turned for politeness, Clover looked closer with great interest. The carriage slowed to allow a long line of schoolchildren to pass the road, and Clover found it to be the perfect opportunity to read the signs outside the store.

"Whale-bone corsets, cotton shifts, magnetic corsets... Fine Garments for Sensible Persons!"

"From Boarders to Lords, From Ladiesmaids to the King, Everyone is in need of the new Amaryllis Style Athletic Corset!"

"Canary & Cassandra's All-Cotton Bust-Binding Corsets... Flexible Design... Comfortable Construction..."

Clover hoped no one had noticed their eyes linger on the advertisements. It was enlightening to see life away from the manor, a life they had known forever (a few days.) The mystical pandemonium of the city's Main Street was enough to distract them from Aster's breathless purple tinge. There were candy shops filled to bursting with sticky-fingered school-children with their light blue uniforms and tired eyes. Bookstores lined the corners of the street, and pawnbrokers held small domains between the general stores and apothecaries. People with long dresses and large sleeves gallivanted to and fro, walking small dogs. A large yellow tree loomed out of the city walls in the corner of their eye.

Clover's heart was set alight with all of the beautiful, terrible things the world had to offer them. There was a childlike wonderment born the same day as their long-slumbering pessimism. Like a child, they were unabashedly curious, but like an adult, they were overcome with a strange sort of fear. They wished to see it all, every blossom and every thorn.

Chapter X: The Marianne

Cornflower

Dolston's docks were great, not in regards to looks or the general morality of the people, but in its sheer size. It took up the entirety of Dolston's coast. At least, that was what Clover's map told them. They had spent the past two days preparing for the departure of the Marianne, and Clover often found themself asleep on the floor of the carriage, map in hand. There wasn't much else to do, any thoughts past the shape of the land made their head spin.

At the dock, large ships prepared for the worst of the oceans beyond, and families huddled beneath ragged blankets, hoping to see the boat's departure. Far off, in the mist, sat a decrepit lighthouse on a small rocky island. Rose told them that, despite its appearance, it was less than twenty years old.

The dock was built of thick stones first placed hundreds of years ago, and was composed of two branches. One which connected to the south part of Dolston, the side below the Split, and the other which connected to the north, atop it. It left a sickly feeling in Clover, but as it mixed with their other strange feelings, the sickness's location was difficult to pinpoint.

They stood at the dock, above where the Split's maw met the sea, and felt the rumble of the supports as they were hit by quick waves. Clover was reminded once more of just how small they were.

It was easy to find the Marianne. A steamship bigger than the sky, larger than anything Clover could comprehend. Slick black walls of rock stood before them, blocking light. They didn't think mankind would've been allowed such an accomplishment. Something so large, so terrifying. It almost brought them to tears, as if they had come into contact with a god.

Clover couldn't stop moving, whether they were making sure everyone had their trunks, reminding Rose to tie the ribbons on her hat, or even readjusting Aster's braid, they felt like an old maid with a particularly dubious bout of hysterics.

After only a fortnight on the vessel, they would arrive in Cherin, Avindre, home of the House of Opulence, a high-end gambling house, the place where Clover would have to win back their memories. The alibi was simple enough: they were a rich family of four travelling to Avindre to visit their cousins.

For the two weeks, they would no longer be Clover Page-Bettencourt, but instead the esteemed Sinclair Bronte travelling with their husband and two daughters. Pretending to be someone they were not was not as daunting as they first thought, and it also helped to know that Aster was in no position to shame Clover for it. They were just relieved they didn't have to pretend to be something too far-fetched, like an old man.

Although those from Terra Florens were scared of the dangers that resided on the other side of the ocean, there was a force drawing the rich to leave just because they knew they could. The Marianne no longer brought things to trade with Avindre due to their cut relations, but as long as Avindre allowed Valentijn to do what he liked, he would stop throwing public tantrums. At least, that was how Rose described it. To Clover, it sounded like the beginnings of war.

At the front of the dock was a small table where a group of people accumulated beside a large sign which read,

"No quacks, no unspeaking Plicitarian, no hankering compounds, stimulating liquors, or narcotics. No one without passing port or certificate of birth from the years 1830 to 1884. No hypnotised persons nor people with dirt on face."

A woman stood with a carpet bag and an old book while someone in a government uniform shouted at her for violation of the rules.

"Probably one of the quacks," Dorothy whispered to Rose. She hid a giggle behind her hand. Clover didn't laugh.

"Bronte?" The docksman called out into the bustling crowd. Clover's head snapped up,

"That's us," they whispered, then once more to the docksman, "that's us!"

Pushing through the crowd, Clover spouted a variety of "Excuse me!" and "Pardon me!" Which didn't help in soothing their nerves in the slightest. Before they reached the boat, they were stopped in front of the ladder by a woman in one of the government-official uniforms, bird mask and all, dyed with the magnificent flowers of Terra Florens. It looked similar to the crow masks from the manor and Devon Earl , but while Aster's was embroidered with silvery-purple threaded stalks of lavender, the officials donned small yellow flowers. Clover understood it to be fane.

131

"Jonathan Bronte?"

"That's me," Aster replied sheepishly, Clover wanted to elbow him but realised it would've been far more suspicious than an anxious tone of voice. They were thankful that their instincts stopped them from ploughing their elbow through Aster's purple coat and hoped the official didn't notice their grimace. She paused for a bit before tilting her head and saying,

"Your documentation please, sir."

"Yes! Of course!" Aster scrambled to pull the papers out of his bag, his hand getting caught on the clasps, very inconspicuous. "Of course," he said one last time.

After the documents were placed in the official's hand, all four parts of the family watched as she went through them, and when she nodded at the last page they all let out a silent breath of relief.

"Sinclair... Natalia... Sophia..." She muttered under her breath, looking through the documents once again whilst also looking at the people the paper described, "You're all here, enter."

Behind her stood another official, but this one wore a mask resembling a heart-faced owl.

"Pray you will be spared," the owl said with a sweet voice.

They were hurried away, but Dorothy whispered to them as they walked.

"That was the Church of Vera, some low-ranking Veranth."

Clover pretended to understand.

Chariot Cross was getting old, he knew that. By the time his father was his age, he had already met his mother in the beautiful town of Greystone, Highland. Because of this,

Chariot was determined to do the same, to find the man of his dreams.

That was how Chariot came to be on The Marianne, a ship going from Dolston, Terra Florens to Cherin, Avindre on a two-week trip. He had been in Terra Florens for the past five years after he had been hired by the king as an expeditionist.

The Highland border was only two trains away from Cherin, and the taste of home was still ripe on Chariot's tongue.

Oh, how he longed for the mountains! Each crowded room and rumble of the boat connecting with the depths below further fueled Chariot's wanting to finally go back home. Terra Florens served him well– until it didn't– and now, the only thing in his mind was the sound of water and the promise of love in his future.

Opening the door to his chambers he quickly realised he would not be spending it on his lonesome, three bunk beds stood in front of him. The wooden posts of each matching the panelling on the walls. It was a very comfortable room, with bookshelves and bedside tables. Sitting on one of the beds he hoped that he would be lucky enough to be the only one assigned to this room. That was until a family entered.

Through the door came a family of four.

There were two adults and two young women, although one did not look the part, she towered over the rest. Chariot stood straight and held out his hand as a sign of respect. A person with dark curly hair, one of the adults, took it.

"Hello, what is your name?" The stranger asked him with a curious look, they spoke with a confident and charismatic tone, one that Chariot envied. He was never the greatest at communication.

"Cross." The group paused, as if waiting for more, "Chariot

Cross of Highland."

"Highland you say?" Another spoke, this one resembled more of an egret than a human, but was otherwise quite striking in appearance. His lips were rosy as a summer night, and his hair was pale, but Chariot refused to go after a married man. Looking at the rest of the family, Chariot wondered how magical their genes must be, as the daughters did not look alike at all!

One of the young girls was very finely dressed. Her puff sleeves, fur coat, and even her gloves were unlike anything Chariot was used to, they must've been extremely wealthy to be able to afford such things. That was not to say all people from Highland are poor– Chariot would always clarify to his friends– it was that *he* was, poor, that is. The girl's eyes were grey and presumably unwell by the way the blond girl led her into the room. It made Chariot almost wish he had a sibling so caring. He was an only child.

The blond girl was the opposite of her sister, it seemed. Wearing a cycling skirt and a plain blouse, she looked very odd indeed. And that was without mentioning the monocle, or the fact that she was a giant. Chariot tried not to stare anymore, it would be rude to make any further observations. The fancy girl spoke.

"Oh, do ignore my brother, he does not mean any harm." *Brother?* More questions began to bubble up. On closer inspection, the two he assumed to be married did not wear wedding bands, nor did the charismatic one give a second glance to the beautiful man next to them. How tragic!

He nodded to the room with a polite smile, but Chariot said one last thing before leaving.

"Well I'm going to go tour the ship, I'll try not to stay in your hair." And with his head high, Chariot left the room.

He was to transfer chambers, of course, but he wanted to leave an impression.

Rose held her face in her hands, attempting to hide her embarrassed laughter as Aster paced around the room muttering things such as "Our cover!" and "It was so simple!" However, he never quite finished any of the statements before beginning another. Clover watched the scene, shaking with fear and amusement. Dorothy sat on one of the bunk beds, reading as if nothing had happened at all.

"I am sorry, Teddy, I didn't mean to!" Rose giggled before feeling for the brooch on her fur coat, staring off into the general vicinity of Clover, who sprung up to help her when no one else did.

"Rose, you have to understand the severity of this situation! Do you know what would've happened if someone with our documents heard that? We would both get caught."

"So would we," Clover chimed in, "You know, for helping criminals."

"You would be fine, Clover," Dorothy said from behind her book, and Rose and Aster ceased their bickering temporarily. Clover too was caught off guard by the statement. They were confused since they thought it was very clear the reason they were on the boat, it wasn't like they weren't profiting from it, the only reason they were helping was so that they would be helped in return. They wondered if Dorothy only bickered for the sake of bickering.

She continued with her nose up, "You don't have magic, you could run and plead manipulation."

"You all helped me, this is the least I could do to pay you back for your kindness after my accident," Clover answered, and Aster looked at them with a strange expression, like he was surprised they would even answer Dorothy's foolish question.

"By helping us commit a crime?" Dorothy berated.

"You forget that Clover is the reason we are here, Dorothy," Aster interrupted, and suddenly Clover felt like they had walked in on a parent speaking to their child. One of his hands held onto the room's small table loosely.

"If that's what it takes," Clover said nonetheless.

She flipped a page and said, "That doesn't sound like you." Clover paused, their anger rising like the waves outside.

"And how would you know what I sound like?" They spouted abruptly, the words coming out like venom, "Not even I know."

No one moved. Tears welled in their eyes but Clover hoped no one noticed, and they knew they shouldn't be upset by it, but the wound was still fresh. They couldn't help giving in to the urge to fight back.

"Sorry," Dorothy said quietly, not as genuinely as Clover would've liked.

Clover shrugged, despite still feeling infuriated.

Dorothy stayed silent. As did Rose and Aster, who wore sour expressions on their faces. It seemed the unpleasantness of their bickering wasn't stronger than the subconscious ability that all siblings had, which was the ability to make each other laugh at inopportune times. That was not to say that there was anything funny about the situation. It was simply the fact that Aster found Rose's uncomfortable face hilarious. And as she heard his suppressed laughter, almost laughed herself. Thankfully, Dorothy spoke before either of them broke.

"Wait."

"Hm?" Rose replied, confused.

"It never said Natalia and Sophia were sisters, right? Just that they had the same last name?"

Aster nodded.

"Could be Sophia's aunt," Dorothy said simply with a shrug, Rose clapped her hands together with glee.

"Why hadn't I thought of that?"

"For someone with all knowledge you certainly are quite dumb." Dorothy smiled despite her words.

Clover wondered if Rose would take offence from this, but as the others continued to get settled in the room, they accepted that it was the end of the conflict.

"Quite a nice fellow we are stuck with," Rose said apathetically as if the words she said didn't matter. She sat on the bottom bunk of the bed, closest to the door, "He sounds kind."

"*Is* he kind?" Aster asked whilst searching through the bookshelves. "If there's a storm the books shall fall," he added with a pout, muttering as if the decorators of the Marianne were listening.

Rose sat for a few moments, pondering the soul of Chariot Cross, looking into all he had done in his life, before saying quietly,

"Yes, he is."

Aster nodded in response, taking books off the shelf and putting them in his bedside cabinet (Clover hoped– for Aster's nerves– that it was nailed to the floor.)

"Do you want to know what he thinks of *you*?"

"Me? Why me?" He said absentmindedly, no doubt still thinking about the state of the bookshelf.

"Yes, you in particular," Rose replied with a grin, Clover

realised what she meant.

"Rose, do you mean?" Clover gasped. Aster turned to the two of them.

"What? What do you mean?" Aster said.

"I believe you know," giggled Rose.

"I don't! That's precisely why I'm asking!" Aster leaned forward, spewing out playful confusion. Clover looked at Dorothy, who continued to read on the top bunk across the room, pretending they did not exist, but in the corner of her mouth, her lips twitched with an affectionate smirk.

"May I tell him?" Clover asked, feeling more like an old maid than a grown adult at the moment.

"Tell him what?" Aster sounded genuinely worried now.

"Oh, go on," Rose giggled. Clover waved Aster over, whispering in his ear between laughs. Aster's eyes went wider than usual. He was unaware of Chariot's stares, or how he bowed specifically to him before he had left.

"He can't– He couldn't– I'm married!" His sentences raced hysterically, which made even Dorothy laugh.

"Perhaps Highland is in your future, Aster," Dorothy teased sophisticatedly.

"I always did like those sweet cows, the hox," Rose said with a dreamy sigh. "The only ones left here are stuck in Tambury."

Clover came back to reality, as if a switch had turned on, and once again they felt out of place. A deep emptiness of the soul struck their heart. They were suddenly reminded of the terrible situation they were in. It was a miasma of melancholia.

It'll be fine, they reassured themself. They would find a way to get it back, their memories, their childhood. It was very simple, nothing to write home about (not that Clover knew where that was,) a few magic users had taken advantage of Clover's mild coma. It would all be okay soon.

Clover watched as Aster went to leave the room, and they had the sudden need to assure him that they appreciated him and meant no disrespect. What if he changed his mind on helping them? They quickly caught the door.

"I am sorry for teasing you," They said in the door frame.

"Oh, it's all right," Aster smiled and went to leave once more. Panicking to keep his attention, Clover grabbed the sliver of skin uncovered by his sleeve or glove, his skin was warmer than Clover had expected. Clover understood the implications of the act, but they assumed Aster was mature enough not to overthink it.

Aster's eyes went wide and looked back into Clover's. He had *overthink*'ed it.

"Thank you for all you've done," Clover said to him, Aster's eyes glimmered in the candlelight of the hallway, and Clover's foot slipped from the door, closing it fully. The sudden silence of the hallway made Clover's ears ring, and they released his wrist. "I don't know all of what you've done, but thank you."

"You would've done the same," Aster said, and Clover began to feel a strange subgenre of discomfort. With a laugh, he said, "If this is about pretending to be married to you I really don't mind, I don't find it improper."

Clover tried to laugh, but it got stuck in their throat. The conversation was already far too awkward.

"The issue is," Clover sighed, unable to find the right words. "The issue is I don't know if I would've done the same, I don't know how I would've done anything. I recognize things, and I can make observations, but I do not know where they come from."

139

Aster leaned against the wall next to them, and what a strange sight it would've been, had anyone seen it. Clover hoped he would tell them it was nothing, that Rose could now see their future, but he said nothing of the sort. Clover was suddenly reminded of what appeared on the strip of paper at Esme's house.

"I'm twenty-two."

Aster laughed, "Older than I. I turn twenty next month."

Clover counted in their head with haste. When were they born? *Newly twenty-two* is different from just *twenty-two*. So perhaps April? Or May? They could not do the maths quick enough to figure out what month it was currently, and they were too embarrassed to ask Aster.

"I am three years older than you?" They recounted. "No, only two?"

"Two is not so bad. There have been worse matches in history." *Matches?* Clover's brain struggled to understand what that could mean. Was he trying to build a fire? That would not make any sense.

"Matches?" They could not deny the chill they felt.

You are being purposefully stupid, Clover. The mean voice in their head said. *You know he isn't trying to build a fire. A man as high and mighty as he would have another build it for him. Probably why he keeps Dorothy around.*

"What's your favourite colour?" He said as Clover argued with their brain.

"I beg your pardon?"

"What's your favourite colour?" He repeated. Clover was dumbfounded for a moment. They had never thought about it.

"Yellow." It was the colour of candlelight and flowers.

Daffodils and fire. They looked down at their bow tie. Yellow.

"See?" Aster grinned, "You know some things."

"But what if it wasn't my favourite before? What if everything I think now is completely different from who I truly am?"

Aster thought about this for a long time.

"When I was young my favourite colour was blue," He said slowly.

"What is it now?" Clover replied, taking the hint.

"Green. It's not wise to fear change."

They sat in silence, but Clover did not mind it. Clover began to wonder if Aster ever had a photograph taken of him, or his family. Maybe he had, a long time ago. He had this air to him that was inhuman, but Clover shook away the idea as quickly as it had come. The last thing they wanted to do was to turn to deification.

It made sense that Aster's favourite colour would be green. He loved nature, and it was the colour of his eyes. Clover knew he was holding things from them, but they couldn't bring themself to hold it against him. Not because they didn't want to, but because they simply *couldn't*. It was not in their nature, whatever their nature was.

"Your situation is not new, people have made it through what you're going through."

"That is good to hear."

Aster turned to them quickly, and after opening his mouth to speak once, twice, then three times, he said, "How should I refer to Sinclair?"

"Sinclair? Oh, I see, what do you mean?"

"Who is Sinclair to Jonathan? For the alibi's sake. Friend? Fiance? Husband or wife?"

141

Clover thought for a few moments before stating quietly,

"I believe Sinclair is Jonathan's husband. At least, that was what it was before."

Aster nodded slowly, and once again Clover began to feel unwell.

"Do you remember anything about your family?" He asked. "Has it come back to you yet?"

Clover wished to sink into the wooden floor and never return.

"No," it was said like a death sentence.

Aster's smile didn't grow, but it didn't shrink. He must've done something different with his eyes, or maybe his eyebrows. It was a strange smile, and Clover began to wonder how many expressions Aster had to fabricate for him to get so good at lying. He turned away from Clover.

"Don't lose hope," Aster said softly, "with want, it is all we have."

"Thank you, Aster."

"Now my dear *husband*, would you like to tour the ship with me?" He asked jubilantly as he offered Clover his arm. Clover accepted it after getting past the shock.

"Of course, Jonathan," they responded, almost exasperated. Clover learned that they did not like being teased, especially not when they had magically-induced amnesia.

Chapter XI: Setting Sail

Holly

The exact procedure done on Rose as a child was one called a "Necromantic Extraction" which was done by Florien Orphanages for Magical Children to experiment on the biological nature of magic. Due to the Juvenile Magic Act of 1872, all information on magic had disappeared, however, it never stated that scientists could not start experiments over again, and thus started a series of experiments called the "Supernatural Juvenile Ability Experiments." or the "S.V. A. Experiments." Rose was one of such experiments, specifically number eight, the last experiment of the Solle orphanage.

The hypothesis of this experiment was simple; they wished to find out what would happen to a child with no magic if they replaced the magic part of the brain with that of a magic-bearing child. The way the experiment was flawed, however, was that there was no *magic part of the brain*. In the future, scientists would pinpoint that magic comes from a filter in the heart, allowing magic to flow through veins in a more concentrated state.

That wasn't to say that nothing happened to Rose after

the experiment. Since blood was the true carrier of magical power, a large organ (such as the brain) could hold high levels of magic. When they gave her morphine, mildly lobotomized her, and replaced her frontal lobe, it was assumed by the doctors that she would not survive, but she was saved by inebri.

When Rose lost her parents and became a guinea pig, her new frontal lobe emitted magical hormones, allowing the body to both accept the new organ and have it grow to be exactly as it was before. Because of her tragedy, Rose was able to not only survive but trigger something never seen before. Technically, Rose was part inebri. A dark, shadowy ball of magic.

The brain of the magic user used in the experiment was from a child named Penny-Jane Grey, who was able to see the future. Back in that time, cleaning medical tools was not common practice, so the blood of many others entered Rose's own, and caused a magic infection. She was permanently blinded, but she also had access to the knowledge of the entire world, even others.

Rose Williams was a young girl with expensive tastes and a loyalty to her routines, and she was shaken knowing that it would not bode well with the fact that she would be on a boat for two weeks.

On most nights, she would take her hair out of the style it was in– let it breathe– and massage her scalp with a hair tonic. After it dried, she would use a pomade that smelled of jasmine and run it through her hair. Because of the unnatural amounts of magic in her veins, her hair grew at an unnatural speed. So, before bed, she had it cut right under her chin.

Her favourite part of her nighttime routine was reading, and every night she would do her "lovely reading ritual" as she so called it.

The aforementioned ritual consisted of walking to the where carpet ended and the wooden floor began, as that was where her mirror was. Then, she would pray. She did not pray to a god, but instead to Penny-Jane Grey, the girl who died for the Necromantic Extraction all those years ago. She decided to do it whenever she felt she had used her power for something foolish. Once she spoke to Penny-Jane, she would open her eyes, revealing her grey, cloud-like pupils. She didn't know it was possible to stretch the muscles in her eyes until she was forced to learn the importance of it.

One of her favourite things to do with her power was to read, she could see the words in her mind so clearly, it was as if they had been printed on the backs of her eyelids. She could see any book she wished, not only ones that were already written, but ones that were going *to be* written. Her current favourite was one with fire swords and living statues. It made Rose emotional, but wasn't that the sign of a good book? She was also in the middle of one about cowboys in space by the time she arrived in the boat.

On the Marianne it would be difficult to do any of those things, the layout of the room was not memorised yet, and there must've been a new law that *forbade* anyone from putting door labels in Braille. Safe to say, Aster was not the only one with critiques on the ship's interior.

She knew she was very lucky to see to some regard, but it was like being farsighted. On one hand, she could see how the world ended if she tried hard enough, but on the other hand, she was unable to see the walls in front of her. It was that balance in life that made everyone speak to her as if they were walking on eggshells. Rose did not feel as if she were walking on eggshells, more as if she were playing a game of bullet pudding with no bullet, digging around in flour for metal that was not there.

Flinging herself onto the bottom bunk (and thankfully succeeding,) Rose felt the soft blanket beneath her. Teddy and Clover were probably touring the ship, and she knew Chariot was currently asking to switch to another room.

"Going to sleep?" Dorothy said from somewhere across the room.

"Maybe," Rose replied, a yawn interrupting the word. She would look to see where Dorothy was exactly if she weren't so tired.

"You shouldn't," Dorothy stated, somewhere near the door. Rose could hear rustling, perhaps the rummaging of a bag. She sat up with a scoff.

"What's going on?" Rose felt Dorothy put her fur coat back on her, and she decided to *see* what was the matter. Reaching forward into her mind, she pulled out the reason. People gathered on deck to watch the boat set sail. Rose groaned in frustration. She could hear the crowd already.

Dorothy took that as enough of an answer and began to lead Rose from their room to the upper deck. It took them quite some time as a hatred of stairs ran in the family. She felt the presence of her brother and the Detective close by, they were most likely the two awkwardly shivering by the rail.

When they reached the railing of the boat, Rose was able to feel the ocean breeze, the gusts of wind blowing her fallen strands of hair into her face and making it tickle. Going from the stuffy air of the bellows to the deck above was like taking a breath with new lungs. Rose reached her hand over the railing and felt the wind break.

"It's happening." Clover, the detective, said excitedly. Rose liked remembering Clover's occupation for the sole reason that they seemed to always state the obvious, it was a nice change of pace from the way her brother spoke. Quiet, not unlike a sphinx's riddles three.

She felt bad for Clover, and if helping them gave her an excuse to finally leave the house, then it was helpful to everyone. Rose shuddered to think of how Dorothy would be after more time by herself. Rose also appreciated that Aster finally had someone his age to talk to instead of being cooped up with two young sisters. She wasn't lying when she told Clover she hoped they would stay, even if it was for a mildly selfish reason.

Settling her palms against the cool metal railing, her hands brushed against Clover's sleeve, velvet. Rose was not one for velvet, and it seemed that Clover wasn't either. They rolled up their sleeves after the contact. It must've been one of Aster's coats they were wearing, or Dorothy's.

"I have never been to Avindre," Rose said to Clover.

"Perhaps I have," They replied, and she began to wish for the boat to go much faster, she hated how people spoke when they were burdened, it hurt her soul.

"We will find out soon!" She yelped with sudden joviality that made Teddy flinch next to Clover. She fumbled out an apology before deciding that speaking was not her strength, knowing very well that she would start talking again the moment they got back to the room.

She heard the shuffling of footsteps and knew that people had already lost interest in the departure of the boat. Fine by her.

"We're going back now," Teddy told her.

Rose appreciated when Aster led her through unknown places as Dorothy tended not to warn her before moving, which was daunting at best. Next to her– in the hallway most likely– she heard a conversation between two academics on the accuracy of phrenology.

"You don't understand, it has been proven many times! It can be tremendously accurate with the right studies!"

"Oh come off it, church bell."

"Church-bell! Well, I see where your loyalties lie!"

Rose tried her best to hold back a giggle. Oh, how excited she was about this trip!

Mr Cross did not return after his departure, Clover noted. Perhaps he had changed his mind on leaving Terra Florens.

It seemed as if the sleeping arrangements were settled telepathically, as everyone else seemed to settle immediately, Rose on the bottom bunk of one with Dorothy at the top, most likely because it made her feel even taller. That was what Clover assumed, at least.

Aster was in distress over which bed to take, and Clover was preparing to sleep on the floor. Instead, to save Aster another twenty minutes of decision-making, Clover wordlessly went to the top bunk of the middle bed, hoping to everything that there wouldn't be a storm during the night.

Storm it did not, but Clover's mind was plagued with another sort of horror, a dream.

Long ago, the city of Palperroth– and many other areas of northern Terra Florens– was plagued by the most terrible storm to date. It had been raining for so long that the crops began to drown, and lightning brought down unsinkable ships. The streets flooded with Vera's tears, wreaking havoc on the capital. No one dared to breathe, much less leave their homes.

Despite this, a detective was marching down Main Street, weaponless and drenched in a spring shower. The cries of a baby mixed with the sounds of water pelting the brick road, so it was only as he approached the drowning basket that he recognized it for what it was. With a gasp, he collected it and took off for the nearest church.

Years later, the same detective walked the streets in search of a serial thief. Behind them marched a small child, the apprentice.

The apprentice was found years ago on the same street, shivering in the cold. The baby had grown into a healthy child with a deep curiosity for all things. Being raised by a detective, they had become a natural problem solver and a very observant apprentice. The rain waltzed around them as they searched, this storm not as awful as the one years ago.

Two voices delicately sang with the wind. One deeper voice, harsh and short, and one higher one, with elongated notes and delicate endings. While the words entered the child's ears, they also saw a rabbit, sitting at the corner of the street. They decided to chase it, abandoning their father momentarily. Running through waves of water they pursued it, going further and further away from the heart of the city.

The rabbit disappeared in front of their eyes, into the corridor of their dreams. In its place stood a large, magnificent animal with furred hooves and antlers reaching out to the broken moon. Reaching, taking, stealing the sky away.

Clover was drowning. Suffocated by green liquid, which sat heavily on their lungs. They fell into a deeper body of water, but it was far too dark to see what was touching their arms. Like a fish on land, they were claustrophobic. It was a large space not created for their body, which tried desperately to remind their mind of it; their stomach roared and their heart leapt. Their arms and legs tried to cling to their surroundings, but the things around them slipped out of their fingers, as if they were liquid too.

They desperately needed help, screamed for it, thrashed in the water like they were trying to kill, but to no avail. They were completely alone. They had been forgotten, like an abandoned child.

Clover woke up at midnight in a cold sweat, the room dark and dusty. They heard waves whipping against the wooden hull of the Marianne, as if the ocean was angry that it dared to attempt the trip. Thankfully, it was not rocking so much as to knock over anything (or anyone, in Clover's case.) They attempted to climb down the wooden ladder.

Esme couldn't have picked a worse way to help Clover, they already had trouble sleeping.

With their foot still on one of the bars of the ladder, they decided to go back up, head hitting the pillow with a muffled thump. They felt excruciatingly awake. Inspecting the ceiling, they noticed every lump and line of the paint. It was hard to remember that it was not merely yellow ochre on those walls, but also hide glue, mixed and mulled into the streaks. They wondered what animal the hide glue was made of, maybe a cow, or an elk, maybe something more magical like a callon, or a hox. Clover was reminded of the conversation earlier that day, and they wished they could understand why it irked them so.

They felt a sudden hatred towards Chariot, as if he had attempted to take something that Clover had already claimed. Jealousy was a painful parasite, one that took the food from their stomach and made them squeamish. It was a shadow over their identity, it was the vindictive part of their brain magnified. They wished they could cut it out. Clover felt guilt, and shame, and every awful feeling put together.

Perhaps Rose didn't like Clover, that could've been the case as well, perhaps she found Clover annoying, boring, and too much work. It wasn't difficult to imagine in Clover's mind, it was not the first time they had convinced themself of awful things. It was as if their pride had been crushed between her long nails, and like sand, they felt it crumble to the floor.

Clover couldn't be surprised in any regard, they knew that if Rose, Aster, and Dorothy didn't feel pity for them, then they wouldn't have helped them at all. It was pathetic to think of it in any other way. Clover would always be one thing to them, an act of kindness. Perhaps it would be best if Chariot took them all away to Highland, leaving Clover alone in Avindre. They shook their head against the pillow, perhaps too forcefully, as they heard Aster stir. Clover sat still until they were sure he was not awake.

How inappropriate to even think of marriages at such a time! And about a friend so newly found, even! Clover couldn't believe how quickly their mind spiralled into such thoughts. Inappropriate, indeed.

Sweltering in the heat of their self-hatred, Clover began to play with the strings of their nightcap; it smelled of chamomile. Taking a deep breath, they felt their eyes droop down, asking for their permission to finally rest, which they accepted with kindness.

Before falling asleep, however, Clover caught themself staring at the back of Rose's head, jet-black wefts flowing off the bed like a wave of ink. They realised how heavily her opinions mattered to them. How foolish that she– a teenage girl– had made Clover– an adult detective– feel utterly worthless. The thought made them feel even worse. With their eyes shut, Clover swam through the darkness between their eyelids, swimming, swimming, swimming, until, at last, they found a land of wonderless stupor.

Clover woke up to the bustle of everyone getting ready for the day. Sounds of clatter and sleepy conversation. They were too tired for communication, and only caught pieces of speech through closed eyes, still feigning sleep.

"Wake up," they heard Dorothy demand, but they did not move.

"Let them rest," Aster told her, "They were up late last night."

Oh. Clover no longer found it amusing to pretend to be asleep. The thought of Aster witnessing their breakdown the night before made them sick. Sitting up, they found that Dorothy and Rose were already out the door, having left Aster to grab his cane.

"You didn't use it yesterday," Clover said after yawning. Aster hummed.

"Well, I didn't need it yesterday," he explained with a smile, Clover nodded, still much too tired to understand anything.

"So it just," Clover's sentence was interrupted by another one of their yawns, "It just goes away sometimes?"

"Not quite," Aster was now apparently very busy surveying

the doorknob, "Some days it is easier to cope without."

Clover nodded once more, but this time because they understood.

"Where are we going?"

"Breakfast," Aster did not seem pleased.

"Not a fan of it?"

"Not a fan of people, more like."

"People?"

Aster let out a sigh, "We should be keeping appearances, but I could tell everyone you aren't feeling well if that's what you'd like."

Clover touched their hand to their chin to mimic thinking.

"Would you bring me something back?" they said, Aster laughed so suddenly that an old lady walking in the hallway gave him a dirty look, which he returned with a small apology.

"Of course, Clover."

Clover let out a long dramatic sigh.

"I suppose I'll go." They put on a disgruntled expression until Aster shut the door with a chuckle. They didn't know why they acted in such a childish manner, but that was something they would worry about later.

"How dramatic this trip has made you!" Aster laughed from the other side of the door. Clover was glad he could not see their face.

Walking into the large dining room in a new dark blue coat, Clover's delusions of the Marianne being a boat for all were thrown out of the elaborately designed window. The Marianne was a vessel to transport only the finest. Doctors, adventurers, and even the king's men were dining in the very room in which they stood. Clover began to wonder if that was Aster's idea all along, to be able to be so close to those searching for them and leave them none the wiser. It was a miracle he hadn't been caught already, there were only so many people around with white hair.

Catching Dorothy's eye across the room, they went to her with almost a hundred faces following. Settling in the chair beside Aster, they hoped their face could communicate their anxiety, but– in Aster's defence– he didn't look much better.

It did not take long for them to become distracted by the feast prepared. It was better than anything Clover could've ever dreamed of, and they could tell the rest of their "family" were trying to tone down their shock as well.

Fluffy pancakes were covered in pine-smelling honey and sweet elderberry syrup, thick slices of bread were lathered in blackberry jelly, and sparkling elderflower cordial decorated the lips of patrons with small, white flowers. In an ornate bowl at the centre of the table were pickled dandelion leaves, which produced a smell so bitter and foul-tasting that Clover could feel it on their tongue across the room.

It was a lucky breakfast, and apparently one all Floriens ate after the beginning of a seafare. Dandelions represented divination, and the more someone ate, the closer they would be to Vera, making their wish destined to come true. The flowers were scattered around the table in the forms of jellies, syrups, candied flowers, and were also infused in the baked goods.

Something crashed onto the floor next to them. The clanging of metal rang in Clover's skull. The woman to their right had dropped her fork and– without thinking– Clover picked it up for her.

"Oh, dear, aren't you just darling," The older woman said

cheerfully with a great laugh, and once looking at Clover gasped, "Oh, my. Do I know you?"

Clover felt as if they had been stabbed.

"Well, I would hope not, as I do not know you." They said with a charm they were not aware they had, and it was less of a joke than they were allowed to admit at the moment. The woman laughed once again.

"Must be my brain acting up again, you know how it is with age," Clover knew how it was *now*. "What is your name?"

"Ah, Sinclair Bronte," they could feel Aster's eyes on the back of their head and cringed at how hard they failed at keeping a low profile. "And this was– is– my husband, Jonathan."

Aster gave her a nod, to which she chuckled again.

"Newly married I assume? I can tell from the blush upon your faces. You are both so young, you remind me of my sister."

If she noticed the awkward looks Clover and Aster gave each other, she did not bring it up. After giving her another smile, Clover turned back to their plate.

"Oh!" She shouted, making both Aster and Clover jump in their seats as they turned back to her with haste.

"Oh?" Clover repeated, concerned and embarrassed.

"Are you two going to the ball tonight? It is said that if everyone goes, the trip will be successful!" Her smile fought for space on her face, she was all teeth and no emotion.

"Oh, I don't know…" Aster began at the same time Clover said,

"The girls would love that!"

They turned to Aster with a sheepish grin and shrugged. The woman did not notice the disagreement, and took Clover's hand into her own,

155

"You must come! You absolutely must!" She spouted, dedicating the last statement to Aster, the circles of his eyes growing deeper than ever before. He was quickly exhausted by her excitement.

"You will see us there," he said finally, holding his hand out, she swatted at it.

"Ah, I can't wait! I simply can't!"

"Did someone say there's a dance?" Rose chirped from down the table, and Clover began to wish that their chair would swallow them whole to hide from the conversation.

"Yes, Natalia, there is," Aster said through gritted teeth.

"Can we go? Say we can go!" Rose remained charmingly hysterical, Clover turned to the woman, leaving Aster to calm Rose down.

"And what is your name?" They said to her out of politeness.

"Countess Rivera." They shook hands. There was a second where her eyes faltered to Rose and Dorothy, and her face contorted into something of a grimace.

After crossing the drastic bridge that was learning which fork to use (or how to use a fork in general,) Clover was full of both food and conversation. At the end of the meal, Clover noticed other passengers taking a bit of pickled dandelion leaf from the bowl in the centre. When it was passed to them, they hesitated.

"They expect it," Aster whispered to them, and without another moment of debate they placed a small mound on their plate. Clover took a hesitant bite of the greenery. It tasted even more bitter than it smelled. The taste reminded them of what wet metal smelled like. If this was what luck tasted like, they weren't sure they wanted it.

After returning to the room, they noticed that all of Chariot's things had been moved, and Chariot himself was still nowhere to be seen.

"He moved rooms, didn't want to infringe on a family," Dorothy said with a familiar emptiness, her nose in a book on manners.

"Are you learning anything there?" Clover asked, allowing some teasing to fill their words and awaited a stifling glare, but it never came.

"I am learning that I should always start conversations, but never end them." She said quietly.

"I see," Clover was taken aback, "and who shall end them?"

"Boys," she said sadly, "Boys I am courting."

"Ah."

Dorothy balanced the book on her face and groaned, causing Aster and Rose (who were still unpacking Rose's many bags of clothing) to turn and look at the both of them.

"Are you courting anyone, Dorothy?" Clover said cautiously, as if trying not to step on a wolf's tail in fear of it waking up.

Clover's eyes darted around the room, wondering why they were the one to give this talk to Dorothy, they felt that this particular conversation was better suited for a parent. Aster and Rose had disappeared, to Clover's chagrin. Dorothy flopped on Rose's bed and once more made a disgruntled noise.

"No, I despise men," She replied sadly. Clover nodded in understanding. Settling down beside her, Clover began to wish they were someplace safer, places such as a dragon's lair, or a pit of wolves, but those thoughts were overcome by sympathy. "I despise everyone."

"I suppose that makes sense," they replied, thinking about

157

Aster's obnoxious shoes.

"You're married to one," Dorothy said, pushing her head up against the headboard and squishing her done-up hair. Clover scoffed.

"Not in reality."

"Does it matter?" Dorothy looked down at her house boots for a moment, as if they had suddenly disgusted her. Shoes on the bed, *really*, Dorothy? "Do you feel fine?"

"Fine?" Clover repeated nervously. It seemed that Aster and Rose had conveniently left the room, leaving Clover and Dorothy to their conversation. "Dorothy, you don't have to get married, you know. Not to a man, not to anyone."

"Don't I?" She looked as if she were going to cry. "I don't want to burden Aster anymore, I'm not family like Rose is, so I have to get married, it's the only way. Who would marry me, though? I'm so strange and unnatural in my manners, I will never be like Rose or the other girls. I'm no good." Dorothy's dark, empty eyes shimmered with tears, filling up full to bursting. Clover placed their hand on her shoulder, and unsure of what else to do, took to surveying the empty wall. "Aster hates me, I'm sure of it," Dorothy continued, turning away. "Rose too. They all wish they could push me back into whatever ditch they found me in. That's why it is essential that I become engaged the moment I turn of age."

Clover thought for a moment.

"I'm sure Aster and Rose are more than happy enough to live with you for as long as you'd like. I've seen how they treat you, you are as much family to them as they are to each other."

Dorothy was silent, playing with the strands of her bright hair (Clover was still unsure of how it came to be that colour, perhaps she ate too much turmeric as a child.) They felt a strange moment of contentment sitting there with her. She seemed so small, so fragile. It was as if Clover had a destined responsibility to be there at that exact moment and allow her to speak her mind. Clover heard a piano playing in their mind, a slow, steady tune of bittersweet melancholy, they allowed the music to enter their lungs with every breath.

"I've treated you unfairly, and I feel dreadful for it," Dorothy said between a jarring silence.

"Dorothy." Clover wrapped their arms around her in hopes of hiding their awkward expression. They weren't sure what they expected, but they were shocked to hear that she lacked the rapid heartbeat which they heard each time they were overwhelmed. Were they dramatic in their reactions? "You have nothing to feel sorry for."

"I have been so unkind to you for no good reason, don't tell me I shouldn't apologise." She let go of Clover and pulled away, leaning back against the headboard, "You've been nothing but kind to me."

While this was true, Clover did not blame her for it. It seemed unfair to do. Holding out their hand, Clover gave the both of them a new start.

"Let's be friends," Clover proclaimed. "I, Clover Page-Bettencourt, am hereby asking you if you would like my friend, Dorothy." Their name felt good to say, natural.

Her eyes lit up like the sun after a stormy night. Grasping Clover's hand with her own, she shook it viciously back and forth.

"Really?"

"But–" Clover held their finger up officially, "You have to agree to some terms."

"Terms?" Dorothy giggled, but despite the humour, she still

went tense. "What terms?"

Clover hummed in intricate but false thought.

"Number one, may you ever again refer to me starkly again, and on your head be it," they told her, and they noticed Dorothy's cheeks inflate. "Number two, never speak on the state of my romantic connections again, even if it is false."

Dorothy nodded greatly for dramatic effect.

"Number three, the last one, let's see…" Clover pretended to think, "If you are to cry, make sure to give me a warning so I may prepare myself."

"Yes, yes, I agree to your terms," she finished the proposal, "from here on we shall be friends."

Clover's chest swelled with pride when they heard that; it was nice to be called someone's friend.

Getting Past
Guilt

Embracing God's Forgiveness

HC
A D
New York

ur purpose at Howard Books is to:

Increase faith in the hearts of growing Christians

Inspire holiness in the lives of believers

Instill hope in the hearts of struggling people everywhere

Because He's coming again!

Published by Howard Books, a division of Simon & Schuster, Inc.
1230 Avenue of the Americas, New York, NY 10020
www.howardpublishing.com

RD
s

Getting Past Guilt © 2003 by Joe Beam

Library of Congress Cataloging-in-Publication Data

oe.
ing past guilt : embracing God's forgiveness / Joe Beam.
. cm.
ides bibliographical references (p.).
)igit ISBN: 978-1-58229-294-6

juilt—Religious aspects—Christianity. 2. Forgiveness—Religious
ts—Christianity. I. Title.

2.B43 2003
5—dc21

2003049902

9 8 7 6 5 4

RD colophon is a registered trademark of Simon & Schuster, Inc.

ctured in the United States of America

rmation regarding special discounts for bulk purchases, please contact: Simon
ster Special Sales at 1-800-456-6798 or business@simonandschuster.com.

by Philis Boultinghouse and Kay Marshall Strom
design by John Luke
oncept by Ken Fox
esign by Stephanie Denney and LinDee Loveland

treatment of words in quoted Scripture was added by the author for emphasis.

e quotations not otherwise marked are taken from the HOLY BIBLE, NEW
NATIONAL VERSION®. Copyright © 1973, 1978, 1984 by International
ociety. Used by permission of Zondervan. All rights reserved. Scripture quota-
arked NASB are taken from the NEW AMERICAN STANDARD BIBLE ®

Chapter XII: The Dance of The Florien Elite

Olive

Everyone temporarily residing on the Marianne took great excitement in the idea of ballroom dancing, as only the finest were allowed to attend. Not a single person slipped through the cracks. Not a *single* person, but four.

Clover Page-Bettencourt stared at their outfit with satisfaction. It was the outfit Aster had bought in Dolston. A fine dark green suit jacket, pants, and black waistcoat perfect to put their silver pocket watch in. Clover stared at the shining metal, it made them feel something strange. Sadness, they presumed. Nonetheless, they tied their yellow bow tie proudly.

Spinning around once more, they felt fit to leave the washroom attached to the suite. Rose was– as always– sporting the most elaborate gown Clover had ever seen, no doubt sewn by her brother. Clover could imagine how she must've begged him to add more lace to the already exquisite cobalt-blue dress. She was the type of person one had a responsibility to stay civil with; she made Clover feel as if all of their troubles would melt away as long as she had a good opinion of them.

Aster had on a blood-red coat of velvet, matching the pin cushion tied to his wrist. He was hemming Dorothy's ball gown, as she had changed her mind about not wearing it last minute. His hair was up halfway.

"Aster, this dress looks old," Dorothy complained with a steady, bored voice.

"Of course it does," he said with pins held between his teeth, "You're wearing a caged crinoline."

"Aster, please." Dorothy pleaded. Aster looked up at her from his sewing for a split second as if to say *"That wasn't an insult."*

He caught Clover's eye and winked, making Clover look away. They didn't know when their friendship with the family had crossed into inside-joke territory, but lost all focus in the glint of Aster's teeth around a pin.

"I personally love this style, I find it much prettier than the current dresses," Aster said comfortingly, and Rose, who was currently sitting at the room's lone vanity, scoffed. She wore an evening dress newer than Dorothy's. Unlike Dorothy's long sleeves and full skirt, Rose's arms were bare and her dress was thinner and more triangular in shape. Rose spoke to Clover.

"Can you tell that this dress was made for a corset?" She sighed, toying with the loose pieces of fabric where her arm met her torso. "If only I could…"

"Next year, Rose, must we repeat this discussion?" Aster groaned. "You know you're too young, you're just trying to make Clover uncomfortable."

"But they can tell the dress is made for one! Can't you, Clover?"

162

"I suppose, but would you be in pain?" Clover replied, not entirely sure what a corset was or did. Rose guffawed.

"Oh, please Clover, not you too." Rose teased, and Clover heard Aster laugh quietly behind them. Clover was not entirely sure what they had said wrong. "It has nothing to do with pain, there is no pain involved."

"Perhaps for the average person, yes, but you know why you cannot." Aster reprimanded.

"You wear them."

"Rose."

"I'm a bit nervous about dancing in front of all of those people," Dorothy said after clearing her throat. When she crossed her arms, there came a loud ripping noise, which made both her and Aster's eyes grow wide. "That did not sound good."

Aster sighed and held his hands over the rip, Clover watched as it repaired itself in a faint green light.

"I don't think I will ever get used to that," they admitted, mouth agape. Aster shook his hand once as if to shake off the excessive magic.

"You flatter him too much, Clover, soon he'll start caring about the way he looks," Rose declared. "Braiding flowers in his hair and running about."

Aster laughed and shook his head.

"And…" Aster said with triumph, stepping back from his work, "You're done."

"Spin, Dorothy!" Rose said, clapping her hands together. "Those dresses are so lovely to spin in!"

Dorothy feigned displeasure at the request but spun anyway. The light blue dress was different enough from Rose's to make her stand out, but plain enough to allow her to hide in the shadows if she so chose. When she spun, the fabric rippled slightly at the bottom from the lack of petticoats and a surplus of thin steel creating the structure underneath.

As Dorothy went on to help Rose style her hair, Aster turned to Clover and whispered, making sure the girls did not hear him.

"I'll be on the lookout for anyone suspicious," he began, his voice so quiet Clover had to lean in to hear him, "so you may have fun with the rest."

Clover was transported back to reality, back to the land where magic was used for more than fixing dresses.

"Will you at least leave the last dance for me?" Clover asked, they felt that it was unfair for Aster to spend all night stressed while everyone else celebrated. "I'm sure Dorothy could be on the lookout, I bet by then Rose would be overwhelmed by it all."

Aster's face screwed again into that strange expression, which Clover began to realise was the one he did when he was thinking. He tilted his head and stared at Clover, as if he were trying to find any ulterior motive in their face. It made Clover self-conscious, the motion being so close to Esme's eerie body language.

"If you would look out at the beginning, it would seem less suspicious, that way I could dance with Rose."

"She would love that." It wasn't as if Rose could dance with anyone else, it was less about the steps and more about the experience. "And we may dance at the end?"

Clover hoped it didn't seem as if they were pleading, they wanted to make sure everyone had a good time, that was all. They had been restless for far too long, and if they were to die soon they might as well go all out.

"I would like that very much, Clover." With that, he walked away as if they had just made a confidential business agreement. Clover watched him fix the braid Rose had attempted to put in Dorothy's hair.

A bell rang out throughout the vessel. The ball was about to begin. Dorothy sprung out of her seat, hair half-done.

"I don't think I can do this, Rose," Dorothy uttered, voice bordering the line of shaking.

"Don't worry! No one will be looking at you," Rose replied, and Clover wondered if that was supposed to be comforting.

"Because they'll be busy admiring you?"

"No, because they'll be too busy looking at the person they're dancing with," Rose announced as Aster helped her up from the vanity chair.

"You'll be all right, and if you get overwhelmed you can always sit with me," he said, keeping one arm stable on the vanity.

"You won't be dancing?" Rose said, and both she and Dorothy equated themselves in levels of petulance. "Then who am I to dance with?"

"I will dance with you first, then perhaps you can dance with Dorothy," the girls seemed happier with that proclamation, and Rose's pout healed. "I will have Clover for my last dance."

Once more the bell rang out through the boat's unsinkable body, sending a cold reminder to everyone that they were going to be late. Clover brushed off their coat. Dorothy turned so fast she almost hit them with her elbow.

"Clover."

"Yes, Dorothy?" Despite agreeing to be her friend, they could not help but feel anxious in her presence.

"Will you dance with me? If no one else will?" Her stone

face seemed on the verge of collapse. Clover attempted to embody the essence of Sinclair Bronte, noble and refined.

"I would even if the whole room was asking for your dance card." They said, and the sweetness on their tongue was so uncommon they weren't sure if it had come off as polite as they had hoped, but Dorothy looked happy enough. They had that, at least.

Aster gave Clover a quick, recognizing nod as he held the door open for them all. The group walked out into the hallway with their dresses and coats, ready for a night of dancing and sitting; laughing and crying.

Entering the ballroom made Clover's head spin. They had seen the ballroom the day before as they toured the ship, but that was when it was empty. Beautiful flowers of all kinds bloomed at the front of the room in baskets, all for the guests to choose from. A man took their coats and placed them in a large room to the side– the coat room, a sign said.

Aster took the unstated pleasure of picking flowers for each of them, perhaps by whether he thought they would like them, or (what Clover thought was the case,) by meaning. For some flowers, like the stem of wallflowers (as told by the label) he gave Dorothy, or the red aster he put in his coat pocket, the meaning was quite obvious, but for the white gardenia he placed in Rose's braid, Clover wasn't sure.

Clover waited for their flower patiently as Aster perused the many baskets, and watched as other guests quickly selected their own, usually something red.

Suddenly a flower was tucked into Clover's breast pocket, and all their vision was clouded with his hair. The plant had small white and red flowers, and matched the ones in the vase labelled "white heather." Aster stepped back and readjusted Clover's bow tie as if they were not human and instead an elaborate mannequin. They found it strange. However, it seemed that Aster wasn't done, as he also placed a daffodil beside it.

"Chivalry," Clover said, looking at Aster for confirmation. He nodded.

"For our friendship."

"But, wasn't that a rose?"

"A rose is too vague, and if not for our friendship, let it represent you. A daffodil can also mean *new beginnings*."

They could not hide their smile, but they were not afraid of looking silly.

"And what does white heather mean?" Clover asked.

"In Kivet they use it as a symbol of protection before the first snow."

"Thank you," Clover was once again overwhelmed. "Thank you, Jonathan."

When Aster went to fix Rose's braid, Clover saw Dorothy eyeing them from where she stood, but she turned her nose up when they looked back. In silence, they lifted one brow, but they were once again dismissed. So much for being friends.

They still didn't understand who Dorothy was to Rose and Aster.

"Now we are all ready," Aster said simply, leading Rose to the main room. Clover and Dorothy followed, one observing and one zoning out respectively. Flower petals decorated the elaborate tile flooring, dancing around in the wind with every swift, distinct motion from the guests, forming a pattern of lines going all about.

Clover was surprised by the sudden appearance of Countess

Rivera. It was not that her company was unwanted, but the largeness of her personality overwhelmed Clover in ways that they did not expect. They all bowed their heads in greeting after taking sight of her.

"Bronte, Mr Bronte, Miss and Miss Bronte," she sang, giving each of them a polished curtsey in her jovial dark orange gown decorated with embroidered plants. Her sleeves puffed and pleated at the shoulder seam and a long train trailed behind her.

Her body language had changed since breakfast that same day. Countess Rivera had an air of innate wisdom about her before, but it had not come off as haughty at the time. Then, perhaps because of the large collection of party-goers around her, her nose seemed to have begun to favour the ceiling more than the people she was speaking to.

Countess Rivera's party gave the "Brontes" a large variety of greetings, some bowed, some curtseyed, and some gave just a nod. To all of which they responded in turn.

"Lovely to see you all, your outfits are very... unique." Her eyes darted from the gowns to the man standing next to her.

"Why, thank you," Aster said decorously, either completely ignoring the passive aggressiveness or entirely unaware of its presence.

"It is nice to meet you all." The man beside her said.

When the Countess realised there was nothing else for her with them, she moseyed to the other side of the room. As she left their sight, the band began to play and a symphony of violins, harpsichords, and flutes filled Clover's ears.

Clover sat with Dorothy as Aster and Rose danced the first set. Clover did not understand all of the moves to this one– or any of them– so they were glad that they had an excuse to sit it out.

People asked them to dance a surprising number of times during it, but Clover gave the excuse that they "did not know this one," not that they needed a reason to decline. One said person was Chariot Cross, whom they had not seen since their first exchange. They were at first inclined to accept out of sheer politeness and the fact that he was not an entire stranger, but remembered they were supposed to be keeping watch. He then asked Dorothy, who seemed very excited at the proposal, but looked to Clover for guidance. They gave her a nod, knowing that there wasn't any commitment to it. Clover held the greatest respect for him, despite their not-so-hidden envy.

"Not dancing with your…?" Chariot's voice trailed off in apparent hope.

"Husband? No, not this set." Clover did not make eye contact, in hopes of further concealing their lie.

"I see," Chariot smiled. He bowed to Dorothy and took her hand, leading her to the floor next to Aster and Rose. He nodded to both, but bowed his head longer to Rose, overcompensating.

As the dancing started once more, Clover tried to look out for any strange interactions or whispers, but they were quickly distracted by the sound of Rose laughing.

She was spinning around in such a way that Clover was sure she would knock into someone else, but it seemed as if no one paid any attention to her. Aster met her in the middle and gave a small bow, accidentally bumping their heads together. She raised a silk hand to her mouth to hide her laughter. They were not the best by any means, and the act was borderline offensive, but Clover could not help but feel happy for her.

When the dance came to a part where they had to move away from each other Aster led her back to where she was supposed to go.

Aster spun around in time with the others, making sure not to leave Rose out of sight for too long. His red flower blended in with his waistcoat in the low candlelight. He looked much younger than usual, and Clover was glad the moves weren't too physical. They caught him slowing down at the end.

When it was over everyone participating bowed and Aster raced Rose over to the table, sitting down with a loud sigh. Rose plopped onto the seat beside him and set her head in her hand sleepily.

"That was exhausting," Aster remarked.

"That was *fun*," Rose corrected.

"I should've brought my cane."

"'Tis' your fault you didn't."

"Do you want me to get it?" Clover asked, but Aster brushed them off.

"No, no, don't worry about it."

Clover shrugged until they saw Dorothy standing alone. Clover waved her over. Her eyes drooped, and her rosy cheeks seemed paler than usual.

"Where did Chariot go?"

"I don't know, I think he left after the dance, it's all right," she said, overwhelmed. Clover sat her down. "I'm just a bit shaken by it all."

"Breathe, Dorothy." They told her, keeping her real name a whisper. Her fingers tugged absentmindedly at the braid which created a yellow halo around her head.

"I am always breathing."

The next set, they all sat out.

People continued to dance with joy and gaiety throughout the night. In the fourth set, Clover danced with Dorothy and was very glad to do so. Although they were not the best at it, the smiles around them were more than enough encouragement to continue.

For the fifth and sixth sets, Clover danced with a young debutante and a soldier respectively, who both had much higher standards for knowledge of the steps, and grimaced every time Clover stepped out of line. The moment the sixth ended they realised that people were speaking of leaving. The next dance would be the last.

Clover walked towards their table after bidding farewell to the soldier. Aster's gloves lay unattended on the table, forgotten.

They held out a hand to him, which he stared up at expectantly.

"Have you changed your mind?"

Aster took it with a melancholic smile, his hand shockingly cold.

"Not yet."

If Clover didn't know better, they would've asked how he was so cold, but even Clover knew that it would've breached some unsaid code of conduct. Rose had fallen asleep at this point, her white gardenia mere moments from falling out of her hair. Even Dorothy seemed too out of it to dance another.

"Let's do one last set!" A man from Countess Rivera's party shouted to the band. "A waltz, perhaps?"

"Oh, dear." How convenient. The band began, and Clover realised that they were once again in way over their head.

"The Cherian Waltz," Aster said softly, looking at Clover, who knew he was waiting for them to change their mind.

171

They almost did.

"Is it difficult?" Clover asked. Aster tilted his head, half shrugging in response.

"I've done it once or twice, you may follow my lead."

Aster led them to the centre of the room where people were congregating into two rows where they each went, facing each other. Clover watched as Aster bowed deeply, hand over his heart, unblinking. Clover nodded in response. The music was slow and quiet. Those in the left row (Aster's) moved forward, in time with the music. Those on Clover's side stuck out their hand, which Clover mimicked. Aster moved Clover's hand from one hand to the next, and he placed his other hand on Clover's back. Turning around, Clover made sure that all other pairs were doing the same, as they had the sudden urge to believe that they were embarrassing themself.

They turned, walking in time with the other pairs, Aster leaned down ever-so-slightly to whisper into Clover's ear.

"I have a secret I have always wanted to confess," they spun.

"What?" Clover had to wait for an answer as the dance pulled them away from each other. Aster let free the hand on Clover's back to turn towards the back of the room. He then pulled Clover back in as the dance demanded. With full seriousness, he spoke, their faces close enough so that no one else could hear.

"I have always wanted to dance with a detective."

Clover was so distracted by their nerves that they almost didn't catch his grin. The music picked up pace. Turning around each other in three/fourths time, Clover kept their focus centred on the young soldier next to them in hopes of copying her movements.

The dresses were both beautiful and unexplainable. One

person had their hair done in the shape of a cat, with a black speckled dress to match. Another had a large ruffled collar which extended in the back to reveal the head of a swan. The sleeves ranged from huge to tapered, and the inspiration for the looks came from all parts of nature.

They were content enough spinning in time with their row and pausing when the music slowed. Once again Aster bowed, his eyes locked on Clover with a smile unlike Clover had ever seen before. Clover bowed their head like at the beginning and held out their hand, meeting Aster's in the middle. Aster spun them, turned around, and spun them once more. He then spun them a third time, this one slower. Clover's other hand rested on his waist. They could feel the velvet of his jacket against their fingers, they hated velvet. They wanted to throw up.

With one note from the tuba, they moved, turning around. On the next note, they turned once more, and at the last Aster pulled them closer, his hand still secure on their back. His eyes stared back into Clover's, and for a while, they could no longer hear the music. His eyes seemed to get larger by the second.

Aster let go, his breaths shallow near Clover's face.

"I'm sorry," he said, and he sounded as if he were going to cry. The music continued, and Aster spoke no more. His hands shook, and the whites of his eyes looked on the brink of spilling.

Aster made it to Rose and Dorothy first and took off towards the coat room. Clover found it pleasant enough to sit and wait for him to emerge until Rose spoke, her cheek against the table.

"A lady mustn't get her own coat."

"I believe Jonathan can handle that on his own," they did not mean to be rude, but their patience had begun to bleed. Rose spat back the same passive aggression.

"Well, I believe he needs help."

Dorothy looked at the both of them with large eyes, unsure of what to do. The last of the party-goers were all but crawling to the door in austere drunkenness.

"Of course, Natalia."

Clover stood, brushing off the dread which lay fresh in their stomach, and turned to the coatroom. Their arm was grabbed with a suddenness that almost made them jump. Rose held on weakly, and they weren't sure they had the forbearance to listen to what she was going to say.

"My brother, he–" she whispered, "He is a perfectionist in his own politeness. He is incredibly sensitive."

"He sounds like quite the gentleman." When they replied she leaned closer.

"He's been this way ever since our childhood, he can wrong others in so many ways without knowing, but even the slightest disturbance in politeness will send him spiralling. Please, Clover." Dorothy did not make eye contact as Rose spoke. "He thinks he can escape fate."

They stared at her for some time, attempting to find the reason for her sudden outburst or why *they* had to be the one to help Aster, but accepted defeat when they saw the exhaustion in her eyes.

They opened the door to the near-empty coatroom to find Aster sitting on a short cabinet, shrouded by lamplight. His head dipped to the floor and his hair split out from his hands which held up his slowly tipping skull.

"Please don't stare," he said, quiet as a mouse, "I can't bear it."

Clover felt a blush creep up their face, and their humiliation began to dawn on them. Did *they* do this? Grabbing the girls' coats, Clover had half a mind to leave Aster in the room, but the half which pleaded otherwise won the battle. They sat beside him– or tried to, without any help from the dusty coats which hung forgotten and crowded Clover's face uncomfortably– and held their breath. They hoped to refrain from breathing in too much dust.

"Are you all right?" They asked him, holding back a grimace. Clover tried, with great difficulty, not to stare.

"I have pushed myself too far, I should've sat out longer," his voice did not shake, it was spoken as a fact. "I have been foolish."

Clover now understood. The reason why Aster apologised was not disgust, but instead pain.

They assumed it was something that Clover did subconsciously, perhaps the way they spun or the way they smiled, but that was not the case. *Don't worry, Clover! He isn't mad at you, he's only in great bouts of pain and anguish! Huzzah!*

Clover was suddenly swarmed with guilt. They took a deep breath and half-heartedly swatted at the coat nearing their nose. Aster's hands lingered on his knees.

"Do your legs hurt?"

When he laughed, it was alike the wind ringing through the cracks of an old house. Pained. He was the personification of his home.

"Yes, they do."

Clover didn't know how to help, but they knew at that

175

moment that they despised the feeling. They looked around at the cramped room as if a solution would fall in front of them. They looked down at their bow tie, and they wondered if it was usual to feel breathless with one on. It made them focus on their breathing pattern, and when they began it was impossible to stop. Before the cycle of forced breathing began, however, Clover hatched a magnificent plan upon the sight of their pocket.

Aster continued to stare at the floor, and Clover noticed that his spectacles were beside him, on the cabinet.

As nonchalantly as they could, they placed their hand on his shoulder and tried not to bring attention to Aster's resulting flinch. They realised just how large his eyes were without his spectacles. His eyelashes were light, as if frosted.

"Clover?" He asked, and whether he was sanguine from activity or nerves, Clover couldn't tell. They didn't want to know. They attempted to make the next movement of their arm swift, but as their hand got caught on a strand of Aster's hair they were forced to stifle a wince. Aster's eyes looked around with a hilarious franticality when they pushed his bangs back out of his face.

Then, keeping one hand pressed against his hair, and moving the one on his shoulder to retrieve the flowers displayed in their pocket, Clover carefully placed the daffodil behind Aster's ear. They kept the stalk of white heather to themself, as they feared the white petals would get lost in his hair. It would be hard to clean.

Aster opened his mouth to speak multiple times, but evidently failed. His hair had the texture of brushed-out yarn, the kind Clover had found in his room. They felt sick. But it was a good sickness. The kind Clover imagined they would feel after reading the conclusion of a book.

"Will you sit with me for a moment?" Aster asked with a glance at Clover's shaking hand, which they removed from his hair with haste.

"If that's what you want."

"This has all been very difficult for you, I'd assume."

"No, I like dancing."

Aster laughed, "I meant the part where you lost your memory, or the part when we committed treason."

Clover was humiliated at their utter lack of understanding or, to a greater extent, their lack of agency.

"I'm all right with it; like I said before," Clover muttered. "There isn't much else I can do."

"Yes." He stated. "Yes, I suppose so."

There was a pause.

"Will you give me some assurance?" They felt a lightness in their stomach.

He turned, facing them, "Yes, of course, whatever you need."

They thought of what they should ask. There were so many things they *could* ask.

"Are you sure there is a basis for this trip? You aren't going to leave me there?" They asked after thinking for some time. Then, a most shocking thing happened, Aster *giggled*, there was no other word to describe it. It placed Clover under a strange degree of terror.

"Leave you? Goodness, Clover, who do you think me to be?"

Clover couldn't help but feel embarrassed.

"I'm not sure, if I am to be honest, and I would like to be honest with you." His smile faded, and he sat with a look of contemplation.

"There are some things I cannot be honest about, but I say in full earnest that you will know all of them by the end of this trip. I have known Esme since I moved to Palmond Cliff, and I can say with every logical piece of my brain that she is trustworthy. If I– or Dorothy, or Rose, or anyone– make you uncomfortable, tell me, and with no further questions I will put a stop to whatever behaviour you prohibit. Ask me any question I am at mercy to answer, and I shall do it happily."

"Why can't you be honest, Aster?" As soon as the words left their lips they felt the air change. His eyelids drooped in a manner so wounded even Clover could tell that he was hurt by it. "Please."

They listened to him breathe in the newly-changed air.

"There are bigger things at play, Clover. Rose won't even tell me."

Clover wanted to ask him why he let her speak to him in such a way, why he allowed himself to be a tool, but they could not bring themself to. The air was thick with dust and perfume.

"Did you know of me? Before the crash?" They asked. Aster ran his hand through his hair, careful not to touch the daffodil.

"I did know *of you*, yes. You had a good life, a very popular one. A good father as well, I used to read about him in old papers." When Aster spoke his eyes began to glaze over, and he had a faraway look in his features. He spoke as if he were telling a bedtime story. *A father?* They had a father!

"Did I know of you?" Clover asked, and they knew they had only asked the questions Aster hoped they wouldn't. His expression changed from humour to melancholy multiple times before he answered.

"I believe you did." The silence deafened even the noise on

the other side of the door. Clover hummed.

"Can you not heal yourself?" Their confidence was being questioned the longer they spoke.

"No, I've tried."

"How does it work? Your ailment." Clover asked, and they hoped it was not too personal a question.

"Do you truly want to hear about it?" He squinted, holding onto his arm.

"Truly, I would like to understand it."

"Well, I suppose it's like fatigue, or deprivation in a way," he started, "I've had it since I was a child, and no matter how many times I try to heal it, it never goes away. It is like a curse that is constantly branded on every muscle. I can't run, and while some days I can walk without any trouble, it can change the very next day."

"And nothing helps?"

"Nothing."

They sat without a word. It was difficult to comfort someone, but from what Clover already knew of Aster they didn't think he would accept it if they tried. When they opened their mouth to speak, Aster stood with a suddenness so unlike him, Clover feared they had offended.

He held his hand to his ear to fix the daffodil which dangled from his hair, and placed his spectacles back on the bridge of his nose. He grabbed Dorothy and Rose's coats from where Clover had left them, and exited with a quick bow. It happened so fast, that when he shut the door, they were still processing their conversation, hand frozen in an attempt to reach him.

Chapter XIII: Vera and Chrysos

Carnation

Lady Vera, Veranium, Lady of Light, the Great Mother, the One to Lead us to the Light. She was called many names, but in Terra Florens, she was Vera. She was the most known and beloved deity in Andromeda, the more temperate continent. Seraphine, the continent closely north– which contained countries such as Avindre, Highland, Dahlia Empire, and Ogyin– did not show much support to her. The first sightings of her followers were found on graves in Old Carovela, Terra Florens. Carved and cared for by the hands of mankind when they still feared the shadows.

It started with drawings of a young girl– or sometimes an old woman– with long hair and the face of an owl. Those features would stay with her for the rest of her existence. She held, in a cavity in her chest, a skinny candle forever alight. To some, she was so large they believed the moon to be her heart. To others, she could've been any woman walking the streets.

Vera was to never open her eyes, some said. They believed that if she were to do so, horrible things would befall humanity. Others said that she didn't require sight.

There were rules in the religion, and due to the religion being so strongly tied to the creation of Terra Florens, there were compromises to be made in order to respect the ancestors. For example, the three sacred forests were not to be touched under any circumstances. When Tambury was built in the middle of one of the forests, violence began.

Similar rules existed for burials. When an important figure engaged in the religion died– or if they died in Old Carovela, or any of the cities or parishes in a sacred forest– the burial was done atop the dirt using tombs of mud and flower petal bricks. Because the living were created by Vera, those under her believed that they should return to her as well, so the burning, dissection, or preservation of bodies was prohibited as well.

There was a historical fear of water, as it was widely believed that Vera could not see them if they were away from her light. Because of such, Terra Florens was one of the last economically sound nations to adopt the use of boats and sea travel.

In history, the beginning of Terra Florens started in a small town called Carovela, which was built in the centre of a field. In mythology, a dark forest surrounded Carovela, keeping them trapped and away from Vera's candle.

The candle was as much a part of Vera as her hair was, or her whiskers. It was the light that allowed humans to see, she held the candle in place for them while they worked. When she thought they deserved rest, she would blow out the candle. It was not her fault she was unable to see the monsters lurking in the shadows without her light, and humanity could not bear to tell her.

When Vera learned of the monsters lurking in the shadows,

she understood that her children needed a piece of her flame, so she decided to keep the candle alight.

Humanity cheered for many hours, until long into what should have been the night, when the flame began to set again. Vera was unable to keep the candle alight with the nighttime winds.

After the longest day, she decided to search for a creature to help her humans and called upon the fairies. Fairies had been her favourite creation. They were excellent problem-solvers and her most dutiful helpers. She called upon one fairy in particular, Chrysos. Chrysos had been known for their distaste for wish-making, and Vera hoped that if she gave them another task, they would find comfort in humanity once again.

From the land, she took a branch and lit an eternal flame with her candle. Vera gave it to Chrysos and told them to protect the match and bring it to the people in Carovela.

Chrysos was so enraptured with Vera that they did not listen to what was being asked of them, and were unable to recall what their quest was. They were not subtle with their dislike for humanity and its never-ending list of wishes and decided that– until they were able to remember their quest– the match would be kept in a box far from humans.

Long ago, before the twin towns of Dolston and Carovela, before the royal city of Palperroth and the no-man's-land of South Rosamund– and even before the building of Carovela– there lived the three forests of Chrysos. One in the east, Tambury; one in the west, all land above the Red River; and one in the southeast, Palmond Cliff. The three forests stood long before the beginning of civilization, and in the case of the eastern forest, the Pharaen Forest, it also marked the end.

The forests were the cause of the Great Florien Civil Wars, a series of battles between the followers of Vera and the crown, which resulted in the assassination of the queen and the banning of firearms in Terra Florens.

The forests were known for the unique colouring of the plants and animals in the respective forests they inhabited. The Pharaen Forest– the one in the east– homed thousands of hox in the plains between great hills (*Hox: magical bovines with a single eye capable of predicting the weather.*)

Trees of fane grew abundant, and everything was the colour of the sun. Fane, also known as "witch's poison," was capable of weakening even the most powerful magic user.

In the rocky, mountainous land of modern-day Palmond Cliff, dense purple foliage was king. The Cherean Forest was known for its fungi, such as the glowing hen, the spotted witch, and the king's gold. The mushrooms of the forest were said to produce natural light.

The Colean forest was the most elusive with large, crystalline caves unexplored by even the most daring of expeditionists. The blue colouring of the plants and gems was Chrysos's home for many of their more violent myths.

Chrysos was said to change between three forms depending on the location. In the Cherean Forest, they were seen as a tall woman with the antlers of eudel and purple eyes; her hair was long, dark, and enchanted with her magic.

In the Pharaen Forest, their form greatly differed, for there they took the form of a man with fluffy hair the colour of hox fur– yellow– and markings of fane vines along his arms. He also had the horns of a bull.

In the Colean Forest, they were seen as something between, with blue hair and the antenna of the giant crystos beetle.

183

Despite the Cherean Forest having the most fungi, it was during their time in the Pharaen Forest that they grew to appreciate poisons.

Chrysos could only be described as magnificent. Every turn of head, every strike of the match given by Vera. Every movement was a blessing to any living creature fortunate enough to see it. The heart of the three forests would beat for them alone. The dead took one last breath to breathe in the essence of their magic.

They were a limitless creature, unable to be described. Fairies did not work in the same ways that humans did, they did not have the same emotional machinations that could relate to human systems like currency or gender. However, many historians liked to believe that *they* understood Chrysos in a way that no other was able to see before, and that the gender of Chrysos was– in actuality– really quite simple. Their claims were only able to be understood when everyone took into account the fact that they were evidenceless chauvinists.

But Chrysos had been angry for far too long in the Pharaen Forest, and the further mankind dug into its soil the worse their anger became. Nature had reclaimed Tambury, the town north of Dolston. Built in the heart of the Pharaen Forest, Tambury was able to harvest the power of the fane trees in order to subdue the magic of those with high junolian concentrations.

Some believed that Chrysos was not, in fact, a single deity, but instead three very similar ones. The theory was quickly shut down by the general public, as they did not enjoy being called wrong, so the majority of people believed it to be only one fairy. Whether they were a fairy, a god, or both was not agreed upon either. However, Chrysos (in their Cherean form) once told a fox that they were very happy with the label of fairy, as long as they weren't forced to grant wishes.

Since the behaviour of Chrysos changed drastically depending on their form, most myths made it very clear on the location in which it took place. One, however, was not only vague on the location, but also included animals seen in each forest. It also lacked a large aspect of Chrysos in most myths, which was that their Cherean form did not have a right arm, which was lost mysteriously and replaced with a branch. The myth's author wasn't known, as it was passed only by word of mouth, and only written down hundreds of years later. Because of the game of telephone which the story was told through, the vocabulary was changed to be read by more modern eyes. Some said that the story traced back to the ancestors of the Dianthus family, but not many people took it seriously due to their past cons with the circus.

Long after the story of Chrysos and the War of Lightfall was born, many stories began to circulate about a new deity which was the foil to Vera. Heard first in 1692, it was said that Sir Crowden of Hydrangea House had a terrible curse placed upon him in Doveport, back when it was the home of all trade. Despite the story originating in Terra Florens, it was very popular in the two small kingdoms below it, Plicitar and Eleuthero. The story found the kingdoms before the civil war had split Plicitar into two.

Chrysos and the War of Lightfall

One day, not long after Chrysos received the match from Vera, a war broke out among the human civilisation in the centre of the land. The civilisation was called "Carovela" and was attacked day and night by the monsters that traversed the area. Large insects emerged from the Great Caves and tormented Carovela each night.

Chrysos had kept the match in a small box made from the same crystals that made up their arms and legs, for they were their most precious resource.

The animals of their land heard that the humans planned to cut away the trees and grew terrified of the future.

Chrysos decided that participating in the war would be against the better judgement of their forest, but their animals thought otherwise. They had been too excitable with their blade, and they found that their subjects no longer trusted them. A fox found them as they foraged and spoke.

"Why do you ignore us?"

"I have not ignored you, I have answered you."

"You answer our need to fight with silence."

"You needn't."

"We need to fight for our trees."

"They will learn soon enough that we don't need to."

"Sweet Chrysos, listen to our plea." The fox never dared to show Chrysos their neck.

The next day a moth found them while they watched the match in the lantern and asked again, "Why do you ignore us?"

"I am biding my time, we needn't feed their flames."

"But if the flames burn for you alone, what use is it to let them light for mankind?"

The moth flew around her head as it began to panic. It didn't dare get too close.

"Do not question me, lest you wish to be my opponent instead." They told the moth, and it flew back to a tree.

"Mighty Chrysos, listen to our plea."

The day after, a buck found them as they fished in the Great Caves. Its antlers were curved and covered in moss. It had only one set of antlers. It was also much smaller, more closely resembling a fawn than a full-grown deer.

"I suspect you wish to ask why I have not acted, stag." They said, keeping their eyes on the water. But to Chrysos's surprise, the buck did not ask about the war.

"I am not a stag, I am a doe." It said simply.

Chrysos looked away from the underwater lake.

"I am sorry, doe."

The doe leaned her neck to the water, allowing it to be open to Chrysos's attack if they wished, but they did not. They watched as the doe drank from the lake.

"It matters not what we do, I will follow you," the doe said once it was done.

"What do you think I should do?"

"It matters not what I think."

"I would like to hear it."

The doe stared into the crystalline pool.

"It would be kind to speak with them first before acting."

Chrysos did not respond, but stood with the knowledge of what to do. They motioned for the doe to follow her, and she did. They walked in silence to Carovela and watched the people congregate in the centre, huddling in fear before the night descended. They felt a pang in their heart at the sticks strewn about, but they did not wish to disappoint the doe. They held the match's lantern box and wondered if this was what Vera wanted all along.

When they emerged from the wood, the townsfolk screamed in terror, but the doe assured them that Chrysos was a messenger for Vera.

"Spare my trees, and be free from the forest's torment."

The humans looked at each other in their town square, nodding as slow as the setting sun. Chrysos opened the box they had held for many years and gave it one last parting kiss before bequeathing it to a human child.

Chrysos said, "It is a small piece of Vera's flame, it will protect you from the cold and darkness."

The human children began to jump for joy, and Chrysos made sure not to kick any that came close to them. It seemed difficult until they remembered how easy it was to handle bird's eggs or fawns. They were all the same.

Chrysos was kind to humans from that point on, keeping their word no matter what.

Sir Crowden the Capricious

Sir Crowden the Capricious
Made the home facetious,
His plan did work, he married gold.
And with his wretched tongue,
No song went unsung,
'Bout his awful whispers of old.

Lit among the flowers,
Lay wizards and lay cowards,
Tangled in the vines of 'Drangea House.
He killed and he spat,
All for his Crown de Alley Cat,
And for a life not made for a brat, like he.

For while Sir Crowden was strong,
It did not take long
For people to notice beneath his crown.
As there lay the bones,
The Antlers of Stones,
Above his deer-brown eyes.

And while his rhymes crumble,
Sir Crowden did stumble
And away fell his Crown de Alley Cat.
So the people saw the bones,
His Antlers of Stones,
And soon the deer became the rat.

They chased the liar through the forests,
Through his house and through the floor; it's
Key he kept by the door.
So through the cellar, they went,
And for days the town spent,
Beneath his manor, and beneath his gaze.

Sir Crowden the Capricious,
Took his time with walls siliceous
And trapped the townsfolk in his maze.

And Sir Crowden the Capricious,
Took all of the suspicious,
All of the ambitious,
And all of the malicious,
Into his maze,
To be trapped forevermore.

And again the deer would graze,
And again his candles blaze,
Below his Antlers of Stones,
And his Crown de Alley Cat.

Chapter XIV: Escapade

Clematis

Clover did not sleep much that night; they could not bear to. They were far too confused with everyone's varying riddles and speech, and at about two in the morning, Clover decided that they were going to pretend as if Aster's strange outburst had never happened. They attempted to sleep off the discontent, but couldn't stop their nerves' sabotage. They debated taking a walk throughout the ship, but they changed their mind after listening to the rain clash against the deck above.

Aster had fallen asleep hours ago with his stuffed bear snug in his arms. Clover began to think of how foolish they were to have been jealous of Chariot, this family was not theirs, and the Williams (plus Dorothy) were free to accept whomever they'd like into their lives.

They worried about what would happen if– in reality– they were only being humoured by everyone around them, and they were being sent to their death.

On second thought, perhaps a walk couldn't hurt.

Clover crept down the ladder and towards the door. But, before doing so, looked one last time at the cramped room.

Rose told them that it was called a berth, but they didn't really believe her. They felt the golden-coloured plating of the doorknob. Was it real? Was any of it real?

They grabbed Dorothy's coat on the way out.

The hallway was cold and damp, and waves crashed against the hull like loud strikes of lightning. After climbing the steps, they opened the trapdoor, and in an instant, they were bombarded with violent rain pouring out.

They shut it with a muffled *thunk*. The silence hurt.

They sat there on the stairs for a long time, thinking. It was the sort of empty silence that made it easy to wiggle loose from time.

They were not aware they were asleep when they began to dream, and what a wonderful dream they had. Waking in a field, with dew-laden grass below them, was almost enough to make them cry. They were not tired, or hungry, or in need of anything. They were a singular feeling, warm and solid; they found themself within the weight they held between their ribs and their spine. An ancient, golden feeling they began to inhabit.

In an instant, they were back on the boat. They opened the trapdoor once more and walked out onto the deck. They were soaked, but it wasn't as cold as they expected.

The wind howled salty air into Clover's eyes, and their long coat rustled in what was soon to be the storm's domicile.

They thought of Crowden, despite not knowing where they learned of him. They felt the wind on their face, drying their eyes and burning their skin.

"Hello?" A gruff voice shouted from upward, near the captain's quarters. Clover jumped. They did not know how to respond.

"Hello?" Clover yelled back.

"Get out of the rain, you're going to get sick!"

Clover didn't want to get out of the rain. They didn't want to do much of anything.

"No?" They faltered, remembering to stay polite, "No, thank you?"

"What's wrong with you?" The person shouted once more. Clover debated replying with "Quite a few things, as of now!" But they decided that maybe that was not the best impression to give a stranger. They stumbled to the wall below the captain's quarters where there was an overhang. It only magnified thunderous rainfall.

Heavy footsteps descended the stairs nearby, rain ricocheting off of their boots.

"Are you insane? You will die out here!"

Towering in front of Clover stood a strong man of about middle age. He had dark red hair, just red enough that it wouldn't have been classified as brown to the naked eye, and his beard and moustache were not any darker. His right arm, from his wrist to his elbow, was replaced with a wooden prosthetic held to the upper arm by leather straps. He stood untouched by the rain, so his hair was blemished only by the ink of time. He was wearing what looked to be a sailor's uniform, and although Clover could not recognize it, they assumed from Aster's descriptions that he worked for the king.

Clover recalled the presence of King Valentijn in their mind, *that* they had not lost.

The man scoffed when Clover did not reply. He waved his hand, signalling Clover to follow him, and they did. In fairness, it was not the most intelligent thing for Clover to do, but they were soaked, and did not have the energy or mental cogs to think much about anything.

The man led them to a room labelled *Wheelhouse* and opened the door to unveil the control centre of the ship.

At the wheel stood an older woman with long, unstyled, black hair. She wore the same uniform as the man but with enough badges on her sash to decorate half of the king's police in Dolston. Other parts of her uniform differed as well. Her hat wore an embroidered lily on the ribbon around the base, and she had a sheathe tied to her belt. Pockets were also tied around her waist, the kind that would've been hidden beneath layers of skirt.

There were two other people in the room, a person in the same uniform eating an apple with a knife and– confusedly enough– Chariot Cross. He stared at them, and they were suddenly hyper-aware of the fact that they were drenched from the storm outside. The cold burned.

They couldn't remember what led them to walk into the rain in the first place. Chariot gave them a swift, polite nod, which Clover mimicked in turn, pausing to shiver.

"Found them outside in the rain, do you believe them to be an intruder, Lorelai?" The red-haired man asked her, Clover realised that he must've thought them insane, which would've been a fair assumption. They found madness– or the illusion of madness– was a strangely comfortable feeling.

The captain, Lorelai, turned around, hands leaning on the wheel. She stared at them for some time before shaking her head with a laugh.

"Look at their coat, you think someone with a coat that nice needs to break in?" Her voice was raspy, and she spoke with a strict formula, carefree words that were spoken with purpose.

She turned around again, facing the storm on the other side of the window.

"My name is Sinclair Bronte, captain, I was just trying to clear my mind."

"With a walk?"

"Yes."

"A walk in the rain?"

"Yes." Clover grimaced, it sounded much worse out loud. Lorelai snorted.

"Get them a towel, Heath."

"Right away, captain," the red-haired man quickly ran through a door opposite the one Clover entered.

The person eating the apple stared at Clover with silence as they quietly sat on a barrel in the back of the room, promptly regretting ever getting out of bed. Unblinking, the person continued to place pieces of apple into their mouth, making the silence agonising.

"My name's Reaper," they took another bite of the apple, "Reaper Malady."

Clover would've been afraid if that wasn't the coolest name they had ever heard. Reaper picked at the badges on their sash. Clover had begun to think that, perhaps, the crew was not hired by the king at all. They looked more like common criminals than royally appointed commercial sailors. Or privateers? Clover was unaware of the correct term.

"Sinclair." Clover offered their hand to the privateer proclaimed Malady. Reaper shook it with a toothy, apple-filled grin.

"This is my last trip, then I'm taking off back home." Reaper looked up, and Clover understood that as a sign. *They want you to ask about it.*

"Do you live in Avindre?"

Reaper set down the apple, but they kept the knife in their hand.

"No, I live in Doveport!" Like a proud lion, shoulders back. "When I return I shall see my fiance again. You've probably heard of her. Ever heard of Carolina Wright?"

"What were you doing out there?" Chariot interrupted with a whisper, as if scared Lorelai would catch him speaking. Reaper scoffed.

"I was telling the truth, I needed to clear my head," Clover whispered back, offended that he would assume they were up to something. Beside them, Reaper attempted to join the conversation once more, but was interrupted again.

"Well, if you *were* doing anything, and you needed help," Chariot looked around cautiously, "You know where I'll be."

Clover was taken aback but nodded anyway, "Out of sheer curiosity, why do you suggest such a thing?"

"These people are *nice*, Bronte, they aren't like the folks downstairs."

They nodded, again, far more pleased.

"Thank you, Mr Cross, I will keep that in mind."

Ignoring Reaper and Chariot's continued looks in their direction, Clover inspected the wall. Their clothes felt heavy with rainwater, as if they were pulling them down to return to the ocean below.

The wheelhouse was quite different from the other rooms in The Marianne, it was unlike the ones the passengers lived in. There were no lavish embellishments, or even proper insulation, but perhaps Clover's perception of temperature was warped in their state.

Heath ran back into the room carrying a grey towel, which

he handed to Clover from afar, as if holding meat to a leopard.

"Where do you know our friend Chariot?" Lorelai called out, assumedly to Clover.

"He was first put in the same quarters as my family, I believe it was a dorming error."

"Dorming error?"

"Yes, captain," Chariot clarified.

"How polite of you!" Lorelai mused. "Call me Lorelai."

Chariot did not speak. Clover still shivered despite the towel.

"It's strange, I can't recall any Brontes," Lorelai said honestly, Heath shrugged as well. Clover panicked.

"My sister-in-law brought the status," they stuttered. Captain Lorelai hummed, they didn't know if that was a good sign. "She doesn't have the same last name anymore."

It made Clover uncomfortable to speak as if they were married, especially since they were so young. Even knowing it was pretend did not help. It was even harder to come up with a lie so quickly, they had almost forgotten their alibi again. They did not like lying.

"You should go back to your family now, Sinclair, the rain's simmered down," Lorelai said. Clover looked out the window, she was right. They were suddenly filled with panic, unsure what to do with the towel. "Drop it in the basket, dear."

Following her order, Clover could not help but feel as if they were being talked down to, but if they had to hurt their pride in order not to get sick, then so be it. Rain did relate to sickness, did it not?

197

Chapter XV: The Glass Woman

Belladonna

The library of the manor on Palmond Cliff smelled of smoked leather and dust. It was the only part of the house that had sufficient airflow, which was one of the reasons why Aster favoured it over the other rooms. At least, that was what he told Clover the first time they walked in all those days ago in search of Rose's journals. Tall bookshelves lined the walls, and long windows peeked through the spaces with carved pillars and marble trim. When the sun set or rose, the light reflected off the smooth rock, and highlighted the clouds of dust wafting through the room, as if they were small planets orbiting the library. It was like the Marianne's ballroom, in that way.

On one of the desks built near the windows was a book, *Rogue's Voyage*, dusty and forgotten beneath empty journals. That was where Clover put it before leaving for Dolston. They weren't sure why they felt their mind wandering to it at the time. As they ran through the rain on the deck once more, they felt a strange clarity that was unlike all felt before.

Rogue's Voyage was a book about a young thief on a quest to kill the terrible queen of the land and claim her throne. They found alliances with a band of pirates, a gang of orphans, and a group of foul-playing ballet dancers. It was an odd book, but a good one.

As they walked through the ship's hallway, they wondered if they were dreaming. Perhaps all of their experiences thus far had been a collection of nightmares, all merging together to create one strange cacophony of noise and velvet.

They knew the wise decision would be to go back to their room immediately, but as they walked through the long hallways they were drawn to stay longer. It was as if the walls of the boat were alive and begging Clover to keep them company. It wasn't the same when with other people; perhaps the boat was shy.

They stood in the centre of a hallway and closed their eyes, breathing in the smell of ocean and mildew. It was a diatribe against humanity; mankind was never supposed to cross the ocean. Their covered feet sunk into the rug laid across the hardwood floor, and Clover thought about who was paid to decorate the boat. Were they paid well? Clover hoped that was the case.

A scream rang out through the halls, and Clover was shaken out of their nothingness. It was a terrible scream, one that broke glass and held up the thoughts of even the most jaded person.

Clover ran towards the sound, despite knowing how foolish it was. Strangely, it comforted them to know that they had made such awful decisions and were still alive. They allowed themself to believe someone was looking out for them.

The hallways were confusing at first, but as they continued to run, the walls seemed to straighten in front of their eyes.

Their still-cold clothes weighed them down, but they were thankful their boots were dry enough to keep them from slipping. Once they neared the edge of the ship (as told by the windows on one side of the hall) they heard a loud crash: the shattering of glass. It was much closer, and came from the room to Clover's right. Entering the room, they had to allow their eyes to adjust to the darkness.

Someone was lying on the floor, or– more accurately– someone was dead on the floor.

The person's hair was done up and had begun to grey at the roots. She was laying face down on the dark floorboards, which creaked with every step they took. They could hear their own heartbeat. The closeness of the body to their hand shortened with the same haste as one would attribute a doctor doing an amputation. They felt the urge to turn her over, to make sure that she was actually dead.

Their hand trembled as they neared the dead woman, but the closer they got the easier it became to continue forward. With a gasp, they turned her over. Her eyes were open, and terrified.

She lay like a fallen log, unheard by the rest of the world, the rest of the ship. She, like many others, had been failed by the unsinkable Marianne, for she had sunk. The Countess had been failed by Clover's inhibitions. The dear Countess, no matter how trivial and crass she had been in life, did not deserve that fate.

A shattered visage was hidden in the broken mirror underneath her. One shard lay bloody inside her stomach. Clover felt the rising heat of sickness enter their throat. It was as if they could feel the glass in their own stomach, digging deeper and deeper with every breath. The room felt as hot as the sun.

A sudden voice echoed through the room, but Clover was unable to hear over the sound of their own breathing.

"Hello?" The voice said again, and Clover realised that it was not the monster they expected. But they still did not respond. Footsteps roamed closer, until each step was so visceral and clear that Clover felt their heart beat with every sound.

The steps emerged as a familiar figure, the strange one in Lorelai's group. Clover couldn't remember their name, but they knew it was something absurd. It was the one with black hair, whatever their name was.

"Sweet Xana..." They whispered, not nearly as terrified as Clover suspected them to be. Shock covered their face, making their eyes wider as they watched Clover hover over the corpse. Clover realised how the sight must've looked, and began to stutter an explanation when they were interrupted. "Did you *kill* her?"

Panic settled in their chest as they shook their head. They were so close to making it to Avindre, they made it to the boat without struggle, and now they were sure that they would be arrested for murder. Even worse, Aster, Rose, and Dorothy would have to go through questioning, which would almost certainly get them caught as well. Clover felt like they were at the bridge of spewing sick all over the floor.

"I found her here while trying to go back to my room," their voice was choked and quiet, but they were unable to control it. They were just too frightened.

"All right, all right," they said, "I believe you. Are you very sure she's dead?"

Clover thought that the sharp piece of glass sticking out of her stomach and her wide, unblinking eyes were enough to prove her departure, but they shook their head nonetheless. The person placed their hand on her wrist, listening to her nonexistent heartbeat. Clover saw their eyelids flutter with panic. They turned to Clover and spoke slow and quiet.

"My real name is not Reaper Malady," Clover was surprised they had forgotten the name, "It is Ellis Syme, and as long as you listen to me neither of us will be arrested. Now answer me: Did you attack her?"

Clover's lungs took in an involuntary breath; their words scraped their throat, "I thought you believed me?"

"I do, but I also know that she may have been," Reaper paused for a moment, "Judgemental of certain sorts of people."

"Are you magic?" Clover said before their brain could catch up, and they would've slapped their hand over their mouth if Reaper didn't do it for them.

"Are you mad?" Reaper shouted as loud as they could without the possibility of being heard outside the room. "You'll get us both killed!"

"People have been asking that quite a bit lately, if I'm mad," Clover replied, pulling Reaper's hand from their mouth. It smelled like mould. They understood that they were in shock, but there was nothing they could do to stop their mouth running without its usual filter.

"Well they'd stop if you'd quit acting like it!" They stared at Clover like they were insane. "You have a family, don't you?"

"Yes," it was a miracle Clover could remember that, "I do."

"And you wish to protect them?"

"Yes."

"All right," Reaper cleared their throat, "You are going to go through the door in the wardrobe, it leads to a storage in the west wing, after that you must go to your room immediately without making any noise. If anyone speaks to you, you must tell them you went out to get water from the kitchen. There are kitchens in each corner of the wings so whichever way you go it will be on your way. You go to your room, sleep, and never speak of this to anyone. Do you understand?"

Clover tried to keep up as well as they could, but with the state of their head and the confusion of the entire situation, it was difficult to recall any of what Reaper said. They nodded and turned to the wardrobe before remembering their excursion outside.

"But surely they'd see my wet clothes?"

"They look dry to me." Reaper gave them a puzzled, exasperated look.

Clover looked down and felt their coat, it was dry. They were most *definitely* mad. Once more they turned to the wardrobe.

They didn't want to ask why there was a secret passage to a storage room, not from a lack of curiosity, but because they didn't want Reaper to think they were procrastinating.

Clover's hand curled over the handle of the wardrobe, and they were shocked to feel a terrible coldness attack their fingers. They attempted to push through, but it was so cold it burned. They took a handful of fabric from their coat and fashioned a glove, finally wrenching open the door of the wardrobe.

A strange mass fell onto Clover's shoe. A heavy mass.

Whether the scream came from their own mouth or someone else's they did not know. But when their elbows scraped against the cold floor of the room, they understood that the lightness in their heart was an experience solely theirs. Reaper simply stared at the body of the Countess's husband.

203

"I'm going to prison," were words spoken by Reaper, Clover understood, "Undoubtedly."

The moment the feeling of speech left Clover's ears, they felt a separation of their mind and body. Their head didn't hurt, but it burned with a rage so intense that for a moment they thought they had fallen into an open fire. The fire was not a physicality, but instead the manifestation of a dream-like state.

In a sudden, consequential moment, they were both asleep and in the mind of another person.

Chapter XVI: A Mouse of Soot

Asphodel

Countess Alexandra Rivera was a fan of gatherings. She enjoyed listening to the people around her, how they engaged in their mental battles. She felt almost drunk with it.

When she left the party in search of her husband, past conversations were all she could think about. He looked sick, Peter. She hated the boat, with its winding hallways and foul-smelling carpets. It was all so overwhelming.

She assumed herself to be somewhere between a kitchen and a games room when she decided to give up and allow Peter to come to her on his own. Up to that point, the only noise she could hear was her footsteps. But as she attempted to find the door out to the main hallway, the walls of the room grew darker. The Countess assumed this was due to her multiple levels of nausea, but as she neared it the walls did not clear, and instead elongated, a long everlasting mist. She felt her hands shake as she fixed her shawl to better cover her cold shoulders. A whirring sound began and she questioned if she was still upon the Marianne, it smelt only of sick where she stood. She wished for a drink of water, or perhaps a lay near the fire to get the blood back to her head.

In her disarray, she almost didn't see the shadow-like figure at the edge of the mist. It was taller than her, even taller than the ceiling. Its hands– or in the place where hands should have been– were as large as the wardrobe visible before the darkness.

All the same, she was reminded of a story her sister told her before she married Peter.

It was the night before her wedding, and they had just lifted the bed warmer from the fireplace. She wasn't so young as to be completely infatuated with the idea of marriage, but she wasn't old enough to be desperate either. She knew she would grow to love Peter, especially since he was only one year younger, much different from her other suitors who– on average– were a ghastly ten years her senior. Their home in Arnott, West Plicitar was not lavish, but it was home nonetheless.

While the church of Vera showed no bias, the rich, nonreligious traditions of East Plicitar bled to the West. There was a curse placed on the eldest, cursing them to a life of misery and dissatisfaction. Alexandra didn't believe in it at first, but her parents placed great pressure on her for it. Marriage was a good enough accomplishment.

"Did you know," her sister, Alice, began, "That a woman in Kivet gave birth to a mouse of coal?"

"A mouse of coal!" She snorted, "You watch your tongue, Alice, or you shall make no friends, much less be married."

"I needn't get married, you shall be married enough for the both of us," her younger sister gave her one of her smiles, the kind with too many teeth, and Alexandra wondered if she made a mistake, leaving her so soon.

Alice wasn't like the other kids in her room of the school-house (it was unnatural even for rich schools to have multiple rooms, their parents were greatly surprised.) They always spoke to her as if she were more animal than child, and while Alexandra could admit Alice was brash, she was not vulgar. She always had a story to tell, and no matter what it was, it was assured to go against all expectations.

She pulled the blanket up to her chin and turned back to her sister.

"How did she have a mouse of coal?"

Alice's eyes lit up like the candle beside her before it was blown out. Her face was still visible by the fireplace on the other side of the room.

"She was cursed by the mother mouse living in her stove for lighting it and burning her nest. She could choose either to have mouse ears bigger than her head twice over, or to have a mouse child."

"You are so strange."

"It's true! And she chose the mouse child, so in six weeks she had a mouse of soot. It was the size of a baby with the nose of a bat and the ears of a mouse."

"Don't mice and bats have the same ears?"

"No, no. Mice have round ears. Bats have points."

"Oh, all right, then."

Alice held her hand up, making a shadow from the fire-place's light. She touched her thumbs to make a winged creature out of their shadow. She continued the story as the shadow puppet flew across the room.

"She named the baby Esmerelda, and while she didn't speak Kivitian she was a very talented artist. She would get many

207

awards for her art."

"Well, how did she hold the paintbrush?"

"Her mouth, of course, don't be silly," Alice giggled, "And stop interrupting me!"

"My sincerest apologies, please continue."

"When she came of age on the day of her twentieth birthday, she told her mother that the curse would finally be lifted due to her diligent love for the mouse. But the mother had forgotten that it was a curse in the first place, and told her that it was a gift that did not need to be lifted. But Esmerelda shook her head, gave her mother a hug and told her she did not have to pretend anymore, and like that she disappeared into a cloud of soot, never to be seen again."

When Alice finished the story Alexandra did not speak. The story had become so melancholic, she did not know how to respond.

"She didn't know how much her mother loved her," she said finally, "She thought she was only tolerating her."

Alice nodded. "It's easy to ignore what you believe is impossible."

Alexandra closed her eyes and thought about something that would bore her to sleep, like getting married, but she was unable to get Esmerelda out of her head.

"You'll visit me everyday, Alice?"

"When Father will let me."

"Good, don't let him hide you away while I'm gone."

She heard Alice giggle. She always laughed in the same way, without shame. Alexandra smiled into her pillow, and soon after, they both fell asleep.

The wedding was normal– they were married under Vera's

candle– and her dress was prettier than she ever imagined. Her imagination once again proved to be less than Alice's, as she gave a plethora of new ideas on improving the sleeves.

Her mother put her hair up in a ringlet-clouded bun, and when she looked in the mirror, Alexandra saw her mother's face in her own. Her black hair was just as neat as hers, and her eyes fluttered around in the same way.

When the veil was lifted over her head, it granted her passage away from her last island of childhood. But even as an adult, she was afraid that she had made the wrong choice. Was it her choice? She didn't love Peter, but she didn't have any skills. Nothing she knew could be pursued for a career. She supposed she could've become a professional mourner. She was quite good at being pessimistic.

Alexandra didn't remember much of the wedding itself. At the end of the veranth's speech they picked dandelions from the ground. Linking arms, they blew the petals over the other's shoulder, just as they were taught. Her mother told her to wish for something, but her mind was empty as the petals flew.

A week later. It was a hot autumn, and Alice had somehow caught a cold. Alexandra first realised it when Alice was visiting her at her new home, not long after she told Alexandra all the new schoolhouse spectacles.

"Back when you taught nothing ever happened, but the moment you left everyone has gone entirely mad!"

Alexandra laughed, despite her knowing that she better not. To be a good adult, she must be gentle and proper at all times. She had already embarrassed herself enough at many of the tea parties she had been forced to attend with the other couples of the town. Perhaps she had spoken too strangely, or behaved too crass, but she understood the faces the other attendees made to each other when they thought she was preoccupied with putting sugar in her tea. She wondered if that was how Alice felt all those days in the schoolhouse.

"They aren't giving you any trouble, are they?"

"No, no, don't you worry about me," she took a bite of pastry, "If anything they have been better to me, they all ignore me now. Besides, I can always fight them."

Alice held her fists up in a vulgar way, she always knew exactly what to do to make Alexandra exasperated.

"Well, that's good, I suppose." She fanned herself with her hand in hopes of calming her nerves, and prayed to Vera that Alice was only joking.

Alice shrugged.

"Never mind about me, where's Peter?"

"Hunting with his father."

"Not with guns, I hope."

"Goodness no!" Peter would never. Or, at least, he *could* never. His hand had a horrible tremor. "At least, I know *he* isn't."

"He worries me sometimes."

"Whyever so, Alice?"

"He's just very…" Alice grumbled a bit about finding the correct word, "Simple– and dense."

"Dense!" Alexandra scoffed. "And you didn't think to tell me this *before* I married him?"

"No." Alice gave her a mischievous smile. "Of course not, you're perfect for each other."

They both erupted into improper laughter, filling the empty estate with their joy until Alice fell into a fit of coughs. It started small with light hacks, but quickly turned into a bombardment of wet, raspy wheezes.

"Alice? Alice!" Alexandra stood with such a suddenness that the teacup she balanced upon her knee crashed to the floor. She ran to her and supported Alice's back as she settled her against the sofa.

The coughing stopped as quickly as it had started, and Alice assured her that it was just the autumn's fane getting to her. Alexandra believed her, sending her home with a basket of scones for their parents and an apology for breaking one of their gifted teacups.

That was until Alice grew sicker with the mysterious illness, or, at least, it started mysterious. She was in bed all day, and even when the doctor prescribed her medicine for her "moonly troubles," nothing helped. One day, during Alexandra's visits, she noticed her sister had grown paler, and her cheeks were slim where before they were soft and full. She was being consumed.

It happened back when doctors thought the consumption was hereditary, so there was nothing Alexandra could do in hopes of her sister's betterment. But even still, if it were modern day she doubted doctors' abilities. 1894 was not so different from 1867 in terms of empathy for the ailed.

She could do nothing but watch as her sister became frail and desolate. She no longer joked or danced, nor did she laugh at Alexandra's feeble attempts at cheer. Alice just stayed there, flat on her bed, staring at the ceiling. The same ceiling Alexandra stared at for the first twenty-two years of her life. She could almost feel her sister's disease suffocating *her* as well, but even when she left the room she was not freed from its miasma. In mere days, her happy life had transformed into one of nightmares.

One day after a visit with Alice, she found herself sitting on the steps of her old home, bonnet in hand, her hair down with all the grace of an old soldier. With languid motions, she phased through moments in time.

She wondered at that moment if what her mom said about Vera was real. If, as long as the sun was out, there was someone watching them, Beyond. Alexandra supposed that she must've believed in her when she was younger, but with Alice as she was...

She had seen her cough up blood and vomit into foul-smelling pots despite her empty stomach. When she thought about those things, it was difficult to imagine that such a sweet someone looked at her fondly.

Perhaps it was payback for leaving Alice so soon. She wasn't yet of age, so perhaps Alexandra should've waited until Alice was older to get married. It wasn't her choice, but perhaps it should've been.

It was difficult to imagine that anyone could be so cruel as to abandon someone so amazing; Alexandra preferred to think that coincidence was the only thing working against Alice. But even if she had begun to lose her faith, she did not stop speaking to Vera, even if it was just to say that she did.

She remembered how Alice would record the sermons told in the town church in her journal, each word the veranth said would be copied down in an excitable script. She would say, "Vera means true in Old Florien, that *must* mean something."

She also remembered Alice's fifteenth birthday, when she was made a true member of the church. In churches under Vera, there were four categories of people. Lilium: feminine. Dianthus: masculine. Asteraceae: pertaining to neither or both masculine and feminine identities. And Syringea: for children under fifteen. On the fifteenth birthday, children would choose which group to sit with, and once they chose their family would hold a celebration where they gave gifts pertaining to the group. Blue for lilium, pink for dianthus, purple for asteraceae, and white for syringea. The gifts usually consisted of clothing with floral embroidery of the group they chose or food for the family.

Alice was dressed in blue for her post-ceremony party, and Alexandra helped do her hair like an adult. She wore a light blue dress with daffodils, dandelions, and other yellow flowers. She looked like a princess, and Alexandra knew that Alice was excited from the way she spoke with such frivolity at the party. It was like she was playing the character of a grown woman, making sure to dust off her gloves and check her curls in the reflection of her glass. It was cathartic to see her sister grow up so swiftly when she herself still clung to her childhood. The day was filled with such happiness, such hope for Alice's future. If someone had invented a way to relive a day forever, Alexandra would've been the first in line.

She stared at the sun until dots floated in her vision and tears burned in her eyes. And once her eyes realised they were able to cry, she did not stop until she went to bed.

Peter wasn't absent during Alice's sickness, but he might as well have been, for Alexandra did not remember much of anything apart from her sister's face. It was like her little sister had aged quicker than her, with wrinkles leaking onto her poor face. She was once such a large voice. No matter where she was, Alexandra knew she was alive and well, despite the distance. It was the sort of ability older siblings possessed when put in the position of both mother and sister. She felt a warmness in her heart and a possession of her blood, but as

Alice fell more into sickness, Alexandra could feel the warmth leave.

Alice would die at night, Alexandra knew.

How she knew wasn't important to her, but she knew it was true. One day whilst watching her sister writhe in agony, the thought materialised in her head. "She'll die at night." It was a terrible thought, but she believed it to be a true one.

Alexandra had lots of time to think about what she'd do once Alice died, but anytime she tried to imagine it she pulled blanks. She had hit a wall in her mind that could never be broken.

After their mother had her second daughter, she gave up on having anymore due to the sickness that followed each birth. Her moods were almost as unbalanced as her humours, rivalling the most arduous of mental ailments.

Thinking of it more, it made Alexandra's head hurt trying to wrap her head around it, but her mother still spoke of her two daughters with an air of disappointment. She wondered how she felt once Alice became too sick for saving. She would go from two disappointing daughters to only one.

Alexandra couldn't leave her home during the few hours she was not at her parents' house, but the one time she did she felt like she had fallen deep into the ocean. She walked through town like an apparition, and when she looked at the faces of her neighbours, she saw no defining features. It was as though she had died and was unable to be seen, which made her think about Alice even more. If she died– no, *when* she died– would she feel the same way? Walking absently through endless halls of empty faces?

It was impossible to imagine that the people walking past her were real and not figments of her imagination, that they might've had their own problems. Maybe some of those people were having a good day. The only time Alexandra had thought of the possibility she became sick, so much so that for three days Peter had a doctor watch over her, not allowing her to visit Alice. She felt like a prisoner on those days. Being near Alice was awful, but being forced away was even worse when every minute could bring news of her death.

She couldn't bear to think, and yet she could never stop. The days began to meld into one mass of failing memory; no matter how many times she tried to read or do any of her usual activities, it was shut down by the constant reminder of her sister's closer nearance to Crowden's maze; too far from Vera to be saved, but too far from the ocean to be truly lost.

When she was admitted back (by the doctor, not by Peter,) Alice had gone even further in her transformation. Blue tinged her lips, and the red on her cheeks contrasted the white paleness of her skin. She no longer moved or groaned in agony, she was silent. The only indication that she was alive were the whispers of breath that expelled from the blue of her mouth. No matter how many times her parents called for the physician, there were no new answers. No new cures were found. When Alexandra spoke to her it was with the same voice she used to use when she spoke to Vera. As she lost her faith in Vera, she gained one in Alice.

"She is to be your saviour when you return to the ground," the doctor had said, but Alexandra didn't want to be saved when she returned to the ground, she wanted her sister. How selfish would it be for her to shape Alice's death as a good thing for *herself*? Alexandra would rather fall to the ocean than view her sister's death as anything but the most tragic event.

She sat with Alice one night, and there was something in the stillness of the air that made her know it would be the last time. But Alexandra told no one, for fear that if she spoke it then it would be true. Alice sat silent, no thrashing, no screaming, just silent. It was there that Alexandra realised she no longer expected her to get up and be fine, to start joking as if nothing had happened. She couldn't dream of it any more, and she realised that it was because she could no longer recognize the body on her old bed to be her sister.

It wasn't supposed to be her. Alexandra was supposed to be married off, moved away, while Alice was to pursue her passions, that was the life of the older, untalented sibling. What was the point of marriage if not to get out of Alice's way? She was supposed to be a painter, or a dancer, or anything at all. She was supposed to live.

Staring at Alice was like watching her own heart stop beating outside her body, and when she tried to breathe there was no oxygen in her blood. But with a suddenness, Alexandra's old daydreams began to blend with reality.

"Alexandra?" Alice wept, her eyes still shut. Alexandra ran to her from her spot on the floor and held her cold hand.

"Yes? Alice?" She asked, and she hoped Alice couldn't feel her shaking. She had forgotten that it was night. "How do you feel?"

Alice shushed her and whispered, "Listen."

A bird's song soared through the air and into the crack of the window, filling the room with music. The haunting melody made Alexandra's heart beat out of her chest.

"I hear it."

"Don't worry," Alice returned her weak smile. "You don't have to pretend anymore."

"Pretend? Whatever do you mean? Look at me, please Alice."

"You were always so fond of him. Your Peter."

"Peter?" Alexandra answered, if only to keep her sister talking. "We don't need to speak of Peter, don't force yourself, Alice."

"I thought him daft but…" Her voice trailed with a rasp from her cords. "He is never without ink on his sleeves– letter writing I'm sure– but he has the callous on his centre finger nonetheless. You have the same one." She let out a deep sigh. "My pain, it has affected you to the same degree as it has I."

"I'm fetching the doctor, I'll be back sooner than you'll know," Alexandra choked on the words as she wrapped her scarf around her sister's neck.

"No."

"No?" She faltered.

"No." Alice opened her eyes fully. "I will be gone by then."

"Don't speak like that!" Alexandra shouted, and suddenly she was ten years younger and telling Alice off on her misbehaviour. But gone were the days where they lived in childhood peace, and gone were the days of Alice yelling back. "Please."

"Stay with him if you wish, leave him if you wish. It doesn't change who you are," Alice's throat struggled with each noise. "Keep going, do not end with me. You can't end with me."

Alexandra couldn't reply, so she answered only with tears.

"I have been thinking this entire time. That's all I can do. I have been saving my strength to–" she was cut off by a hacking cough, "–tell you this."

Alexandra once more stayed silent.

"Don't stop in this room just because I have. Look at me in whatever you see. I will be there. Find me in the flowers and birdsong, or even grime and jokes, whatever you need me to be I will be there. Just don't stop."

Large, swelling tears grew in Alexandra's eyes, until her vision was so blurred she couldn't tell the difference between the bed and the wall.

"What will I do without you?" She said between sobs. She held onto her sister's hand as if it were a rope pulling her back to land.

"Life is memory. Do enough for both of us." She wiped a tear from below Alexandra's eye. "And, Alexandra?"

"Yes?" Alexandra felt close to vomiting.

"Cry for me."

That was all she said before being taken out, through the window, and with the birdsong by the hands of a goddess Alexandra no longer believed in.

Alice died on the first cold night of autumn, 1867. Alexandra refused to leave her grave for almost a month straight in case of body snatchers. Peter brought his friends to stay with them, but no one tried to speak to her. The only thing she could think of was how funny Alice would've found it if she had known her prim and proper sister had become the founder of a cemetery club. More often than not she was overtaken by shattering sobs, but no matter how hard she screamed and begged, she knew nothing would change. She would not wake up.

She had come across a poem about the consumption long before the thought of sickness was even considered. It was short, and like all poems it was dreadful, but after seeing the sickness for herself she couldn't stand to think of it. For such a disgusting disease to be spewed up as a beautiful, romantic tragedy made her hands shake with an anger unknown to the rest of humankind.

Alice was not flushed, her cheeks were filled with diseased blood. Her skin was not clear, it was blue. She had not turned beautiful, she had lost everything. Not a single piece of her was saved, none of her humour, none of her laughter, none of her smile. Her body was trapped under cold dirt, never to be shown again. As her skin left her body Alexandra could do nothing but imagine it, imagine her poor unaccompanied baby sister under the ground, without a hand to hold.

There was no time to mourn, as only six weeks later the fighting began between East and West Plicitar, and once more Alexandra was unable to remember it. Tension had been brewing for years between where she lived in the west and the blossoming soon-independent nation Eleuthero. Both she and Peter were spared from the draft due to a life-long tremor in his left hand and her being in mourning, and while Alexandra wanted to feel happy for it she was no longer able to see his face, no longer able to see anyone's face. She was in a constant state of solitude.

Her parents wanted her to leave, as their neighbours in the north had begun to allow fleeing Plicitarians in to escape the conflict. Terra Florens, under the reign of Augustus I, had just cured themselves of civil confrontation not many years prior. But the thought of leaving her lifelong home– of leaving Alice– was too much. Her parents couldn't afford to leave, and Peter had only his estate in resources, which would not be much in Florien currency.

Plicitar had not outlawed guns as Terra Florens had, so

when fear of her family being destroyed along with her home became too strong, she began to see the faces around her once more. If she could not save Alice, nor Alice's home, she could at least save her parents.

She did all she could to stop her parents from selling their belongings, starting with the selling of her own. Her clothes, ribbons, even half of her hair. She spoke to the Florien soldiers stationed at train stations that her parents were too afraid to speak to. She filled out documents and received loans in her name. When the train set out with Alexandra, Peter, his father, and her parents, she felt the ice in her heart begin to melt.

She didn't think about the possibility of never visiting Alice's grave again, and, in reality, it was the least of her worries. She knew Alice wasn't there.

Peter was not visible for the first year of their marriage, and by the time they had moved their family into a small room above a family of eight, Alexandra still did not see him as such. He was not family to her, for she was afraid that if she allowed anymore family there would be a greater risk of their demise. She still held a grudge towards her parents for their blatant ignorance towards Alice's condition, and a part of her blamed them for not being there during her last moments. While they slept upstairs, Alexandra was hearing Alice's last words.

It changed once they both acquired jobs in Terra Florens. Alexandra as a hat-maker and Peter as an assistant at the bank. Due to his high education in Plicitar he was quite good at counting, so he was able to pay for better lodgings, while she struggled to pull a thread through a needle. She couldn't bring herself to be upset by it.

They were less partners and more roommates with a

toleration for one another. Alexandra could see Peter's regret and pity each time she looked at him, but she was too preoccupied by the excitement of seeing another person's face.

Peter proved himself to be a hard worker, and in their new house she began to hear the words he had been saying every day. He said the same quote each day before leaving, but she could never bring together the effort to process it.

"I must be off, I'll see you all tonight. Wait for spring."

"Wait for spring," she repeated, which stopped him with one foot out the door. Alexandra was afraid she had startled him, or– the more terrifying thought– offended him, so she attempted to alleviate the darkness in her voice with a smile. "I like that saying."

He shut the door and went to her at the stairs. Peter looked terrified, which was strange, as she was sure she had spoken to him since the move. Well, she must've, at least once or twice. Or had she? She began to worry more.

"Yes," he stuttered, "I do too. How do you feel?"

"I feel…" She was unsure how to respond, "Tired, I suppose."

She could see tears form in his eyes as he smiled, which then became laughter. Large, pure laughter that was so rare, she could not remember the last time she had heard such a thing. It was as if a veil had been lifted from her eyes.

"Tired, yes." He wiped a tear from his cheek, and it was her turn to stare. "Yes, I'm tired too."

"I never thanked you for what you did for us– do– what you do for us."

Peter looked at her like she was a new person, and she understood why.

"Surely you know why I've done it."

"Why?"

"Why?" He echoed. "Alexandra, I would take Vera's flame from the wick if you asked."

"Don't let my mother hear you." She joked for the first time in a year, but he did not laugh. She joked as Alice would joke.

His expression was so unadulterated, so real, Alexandra grew overwhelmed, and tears left her eyes in large drops. Peter dropped his old briefcase on the floor and wiped her face.

"Peter," she said, "I have been so blind."

When he hugged her she could feel the warmth that she had wished to have back for what felt like an eternity. It would never be the same, but it was there. Love was still there.

"You had good reason to be."

Alexandra didn't see her life flash before her eyes, but instead a scrapbook of her worst memories shown to her in perfect detail. Fear drained from her mind just as blood would.

The monster was encircling her where she had fallen, but she could no longer feel sad. She knew that what happened was meant to be, she had finally come to peace with it. She thought of Peter, with his eyes forever red with tears, and she began to cry. She thought of their wedding, then of their second wedding, after the war was over. She thought of her lack of children, and Peter's reclaim of the Count title. She thought of all there was and all that could've been. And then, she thought of the pain. All of the pain she was experiencing in that very moment. A pain so searing, so violent, her head spun. She understood pain, but what she could not understand, as the shadows morphed into something greater, was what stood beyond her.

It was a peculiar sight, not only because of the size of the creature but also because of the large yellow circles that were its eyes. *Inebri*. A manifestation of darkness, a representation of magic's horror. She knew Alice was waiting for her, even if she would die at sea. She knew Vera would make an exception.

"Look at us both." She said to Alice. "Wouldn't mother be proud?"

Chapter XVII: Crucibulum

Foxglove

Clover was unable to understand what they had seen, but beyond that, they didn't want to. Whatever Esme had done to them, whatever spell she had put in their tea or whatever charm she had bound to their heart, they were done with it. They wanted nothing more than to retire with no prior knowledge of the world apart from the softness they liked in a towel. Adventure was too much for them. If terrifying premonitions containing the last thoughts of a dead woman were what knowledge was, then they would be content in having none of it. No thoughts, no feelings, no friends, and no family.

The Countess had lost her family, hadn't she? Clover would never have to experience such a thing if they had no family to begin with. But... if they did have one, that family would lose them. Wouldn't they? That thought would haunt them, just as Alice haunted the Countess.

Life was far too tough, they couldn't take it.

Above all, they weren't sure how to process what the Countess had seen. It wasn't human, but what else was there? Fairy? God? Clover let their body lay flat on the wooden floor, but felt nothing meet their skin. The numbness of their mind had spread, and they feared a cure.

"I am an officer, stand back."

They didn't know how long it had been until they were no longer alone, but when their brain caught up to their body they found themself in a room full of onlookers, staring not at them, but at the body.

The voice they had heard came from a woman Clover had never seen before. She was wearing a similar uniform to the sailors, but in a different colour, and atop it lay a thick wool cloak. Her hair was the colour of stale bread, moulding at her roots. Her nose was sharp and her mouth was in a grimace, but what Clover noticed first was what hid beneath her left glove. Her ring finger was almost rectangular.

"*You're* an officer?" Someone said as she weaved through the crowd.

"I'm sure you've taken notice of my hand," she replied as she kneeled near the corpse to inspect it. Without a glance away from the corpse, she removed the glove, revealing a wooden prosthetic. On the back of her hand, where the prosthetic met flesh, was a healed gash. "Former magic, I lost it with the rest of the soldiers. I assure you we are no different."

Former magic? They could do that? Clover thought about Aster, and what would've befell them if he was not there to rescue them from the carriage. They wished he hadn't.

"Well, what is your name, *officer*?" Another asked.

"Officer Harrison. Now, once again I must ask you to stand back."

"What was your power?"

"I will answer every question as soon as I have room to

inspect the body. Or have you all forgotten one of your own has died?"

The whispers ceased, although the crowd's faces did not seem pleased with her outburst.

"Two," Clover whispered.

"What was that?" Officer Harrison whipped around to face them.

"The..." Clover swallowed back their fear. "The wardrobe, officer."

"The wardrobe you say? Where?" She accepted the lit candle that was offered to her by one of the children standing nearby. Clover pointed behind her with a shaking hand, a hand they did not feel were theirs.

When light hit the body of the Count– like sunrise over a terrible sea– he was not bloodied, but instead drenched in what smelled like ocean water.

The officer placed her gloved fingers upon the fabric at his wrist and felt for a pulse. A sour face morphed her features before she set the candle on the floor and began to lay the Count beside his wife. Clover didn't dare think of anything, they should've run, but after seeing the Countess's– no, Alexandra's– life flash before their eyes it would've been equivalent to abandoning a dear friend. The officer did not seem surprised at the bodies. A veteran of war and another failed by Terra Florens. Clover didn't know if she fought in the same war that further split Alexandra's family, but the moment they were done with their personal matters they felt an obligation to learn more of it, if only to put the Countess to rest.

"You must be the witness, I assume?" She asked. Clover looked up, they didn't know how to respond, for only one wrong word could tear the plan apart.

"I heard a scream," they replied, their voice so soft they weren't sure she heard them. "I was on a walk. I went to get water."

They didn't know if she believed them, but as she turned to the crowd Clover could see canary hair peek through the darkness.

"Excuse me, you can't come any closer, this is now a crime scene." Officer Harrison told Dorothy, and she looked at Clover with such fear they worried about what they must've looked like behind the crowd. But the mob quickly parted when a shout erupted from behind Dorothy.

"That is my husband! You will let me in!" Aster– Jonathan Bronte– yelled from the door where a soldier stood. When Clover saw him, they were thankful they could see his face, it meant they were not so far gone as Alexandra had been thirty years ago. He met their eye and ceased any attempt to charm the soldier. He grabbed Dorothy as well, who must've snuck in without attention, and hurried to Clover's side without any further interruption.

Aster examined Clover's face for wounds, his hands hovering over their face before his worry overcame his modesty and he was forced to feel where they hit their chin whilst falling. It stung, but he could do nothing with so many people around; Clover could almost feel the guilt swell inside of him.

"What happened?" He asked without a glance towards the corpses, so Clover didn't either. Dorothy lingered by their side, unsure of what to do or how to comfort an already deeply discomforted individual.

"Boats," they murmured, feeling tears rush to the surface. Curses. "Terrible, terrible boats."

Aster let out something akin to a dying breath. He felt their head for fever. It was strange to be so worried about; Clover wondered if Alexandra felt similar.

"Sir, if you'd let me question the witness, I will make sure all of your questions will be answered."

"I don't need you to answer my questions, Sinclair can answer them perfectly fine."

They were so tired, they could feel their muscles relax as Aster placed a reassuring hand on their shoulder. It was terribly inappropriate for friends, and even more so for people who met less than a month ago, but it was perfectly acceptable for a partner to act in such a way to comfort the person they were married to. What strange rules these people had, and that Clover had, for they had understood them so quickly it was an instinct.

"I'm sorry, but I cannot let anyone leave until this is settled." She turned to the crowd, "Is there a veranth on board?"

The crowd looked around, and some looked ashamed, whether out of guilt of not being useful, or guilt of not going further with their faith, Clover couldn't distinguish much.

"I am." replied a soft voice. A short brunette clothed in blue foliage stepped forward. She wore a long, beautiful light-blue doublet with flowers outlined in silver embroidery. Over her stomach was sewn a great eudel, with antlers sprawling across the sleeves, where more flowers grew. A scarf was wrapped around the top of her head which connected with an owl-shaped mask. Her tight-wound bun was visible behind it. "I am the Veranthium Lonicera; I was educated in Old Carovela."

She spoke in a whisper, like a light breeze. It was as if Clover was witnessing nature herself.

"Veranth, please save them from the ocean." Officer Harrison asks with the highest air of respect.

The veranth kneeled in front of the two bodies, put her head to her knees, and began to mutter something so quiet Clover only knew she was speaking by the sight of her moving mouth beneath the mask.

"If no one minds– I am a mage from Highland, may I say a gift from there?" A man said from beside the officer. His voice enunciated just as Chariot's did, with shortened vowels. He was dressed similarly to the veranth. Clover assumed the two occupations were about the same, veranth and mage, whatever it was they did.

"Do what you can." She replied with an equally respectful smile. The intimidated respect spread to the rest of the stuffy room.

A voice that sounded like the young Alexandra spoke in the echoing cave of Clover's mind. She whispered, "Highland worships the ocean, we fear it."

As the quiet blessings were told, a distant shouting was heard. It must have been across the ship. Not long after, the crowd parted to reveal Reaper Malady in the hands of two guards. Clover felt the bile in their stomach churn, and they could not bring themself to look at them. They grabbed for the sleeve of Aster's coat and pulled him in front of where they sat once more.

"What is it?"

Clover's head hurt from how wide their eyes became, and their vision began to blur from tears.

"Please," they muttered, "Don't make me lie."

They wished to leave, to go anywhere but the place they were at the moment. They felt like a child. They had messed things up for everyone; they would be arrested on the ocean without any clue who they were. Clover couldn't understand how they kept messing things up. Terrible. Terrible. Terrible.

Aster couldn't hide the fear on his face. He looked past Clover, to Dorothy, presumably for an answer. When he turned back to Clover they had begun to lose what little hope they had in him.

"Whisper to me what has happened."

Clover took a deep breath, but when they went to speak the air was knocked from their lungs by Aster's crude attempt at a hug. It took a few moments of recollection for them to realise this was so that no one would see their mouth when they spoke, so when they did answer Aster they did so from the crook of his neck, hot tears spilling into the collar of his shirt. When he pulled away he did not acknowledge what was said, but he kept close.

Reaper Malady did not squirm as the officer inspected them— assumedly giving in— until Officer Harrison pulled out a small syringe filled with a golden liquid. She gave it to a doctor. Clover knew it was a doctor by the mask they wore, a white mask which covered their face, but resembled the same bird as all other government officials: a crow.

"She's testing them," Dorothy said. Her voice was steady, but the melancholy was prominent. In the corner of their eye, Clover saw her hand clench on the arm of their chair.

They could not tear their eyes away from the terror which covered all of Reaper's shaking body. They repeated nonsensical denouncings at the doctor, who forced the needle into their arm without further questions. The orderlies around them scattered like roaches, their faces bare. Clover could see Reaper almost fold in agony as their wound turned a deep blue.

"Close your eyes," Aster whispered, but Clover ignored him.

"Higher pain levels than normal," the doctor told Officer Harrison.

"No, no it's not," Reaper said through gritted teeth. "I'm fine. Can't you see I'm fine?"

Harrison turned away. Clover couldn't believe it. She walked to them, keeping a respectable distance. Veranthium Lonicera, too, stared at the ground with shaking hands.

"Have you seen this person?"

Fane could hurt in the bloodstream as well, Clover realised. Without question, they restrained a civilian and forcibly injected a substance that would hurt someone even without usable magic. There was nothing else they could do. They would have to lie.

"No," they said. Harrison nodded, but the doctor still restraining Reaper scoffed. "I haven't."

"Then could you please tell me what you saw?" Harrison asked, looking tired. Reaper looked limp behind her, so much so that it was possible they had fainted. Clover felt close to fainting.

"I was on a walk, I had a headache, and I heard a scream. When I found her I must've passed out."

"Lying," said the doctor. The officer waved them off before returning to Clover.

"It checks," Harrison said shortly.

"I saw them," someone else said. A young person who couldn't have been more than seventeen. He wasn't with a family, but he was dressed so dapper that Clover had grouped him up with the people next to him.

"What did you say, boy?" Harrison snapped. The boy

pointed at Reaper.

"I saw them kill those two people. I was so tired from the dance that I fell asleep next to the bookshelf." The corner where he pointed was just out of sight. It was believable that Clover wouldn't have noticed him, but Reaper's jaw dropped with a horror Clover could only understand as that of deep betrayal.

"Do you have any proof of this?"

"They're magic."

Officer Harrison did not speak. She knew she was outspoken in a room full of people who did not take her seriously. People turned to each other and covered their children's eyes, as if the heinous crime of being born magic was worse than the bodies only a glance away.

"It isn't true! Please!" Reaper shouted before the doctor shoved a handkerchief in their mouth. Clover's heart pounded in their chest.

"Even if it isn't, we will try you the moment we step back in Terra Florens. The crime of breaking onto this ship would be reason enough to send you to the Cynosure," cried the doctor.

When the name of the place was said, Reaper's eyes widened, and their brow quivered with the doctor's hoarse laughter. Without eyes to look into, it was as if the voice of the very gods they respected moments before were cackling at the idea of peace, and although minutes ago Clover had witnessed the collision of two separate beliefs come together to ensure safe passage to the recently deceased, they were snapped back into reality. They were not in a beautiful land of peace and humanity; they were trapped in a web of death.

They couldn't hear anything after Harrison turned away and the crowd twisted their attention to Reaper. Reaper stared at Clover– pleading– but they knew they would be compromising Dorothy, Rose, and Aster's life. With each passing second they felt time slow down, but they could do nothing but watch as their power left their hands like sand. Aster did not watch, and Dorothy closed her eyes, but Clover couldn't blink.

Reaper spat out the handkerchief and shouted one last thing before succumbing to the fane, but Clover couldn't hear it over the beating of their heart.

Chapter XVIII: King of the Gilded Throne

Hydrangea

Humanity lived between the borders of the mystical and the realistic, between the severance of life and death, of magic and blood. Some believed there to be ways of harnessing magic into a third-party element, usually in the form of sticks or sceptres, but the relationship between such things and the magic inside a person was purely decorational.

Magic relating to the blood, such as distasteful spells or rituals of the like, had been taboo even in the nations friendly towards magic folk, and in some kingdoms– take the everlasting Avindre– it was considered a terrible crime the moment blood spilt upon stone. Grass, however, was entirely allowed.

In a land such as Terra Florens, blood was to be spilt wherever the king desired.

Dr Folly Hallworth– for that was what he called himself at the time– stood tall above the passing guards, but he did not look to be anywhere near as strong. His hair was yellow, and his skin was tawny, but despite those attributes, his true body was invisible to the people of Palperroth. He could hear hidden servants whisper hushed observations to each other just beyond his eyes. A jester on break exclaimed to someone Folly could not see.

"The king demands I work without end! But–dear– how I long to sit and read until I rot. It is an awful life to laugh all day, when your mind is filled with great ideas. If only I could be both! To have the mind of an intellectual, but the joy of a fool!"

Before he arrived at the castle, he spent days walking from Tambury to Palperroth; crossing even the Montgomery River without assistance. It was a terrible feat, but not a new one. Hundreds of people living in the make-shift community outside Tambury had been making the trip for the past year in hopes of bargaining with the king.

But Folly was not there to bargain, he made the trip for a very different reason. He was there to give the king his final warning.

Just outside the bridge to Bellerose Castle stood a very disgruntled-looking man. He looked much older than Folly– and he might have been if not for Folly being much older than he seemed– and was speaking aggressively to a guard dressed in mail. He was a large man, and his thinning hair was red. The closer Folly got to him, the more he began to resemble the young general from many years past. And then Folly realised that it was, in fact, the very same "young" general.

General Wesley Aberdail was an army legend and an old friend of Folly's, as they were both put into Augustus Senior's army many years past. Aberdail as a soldier, and Hallworth as a physician. Wesley rose through the ranks quickly, helping the king create a compromise for the three parishes. He became the general of a small army after the last war. Wesley was still just as scary as before Folly's departure, but he wore a look of such complex melancholy that Folly could not help but frown. Which was a mistake, as that was the exact moment General Aberdail took notice.

"Hallworth?" He shouted, startling the foot traffic of civilians and servants, and making the knights around him jump. "What are you doing here?"

Wesley Aberdail was not a normal person by any means. When Folly caught up to him and his group on the side of the gate his old friend's eyes widened. Behind him, Folly could see the knights-in-training take in the breeze, yet strangely they did not take off their helmets.

"I am here on request of all of Tambury," he told his old friend, careful to speak in the way the people of Palperroth found proper. However, he wasn't sure his words were even heard.

"Sweet William! Hallworth, do you age?"

Folly ignored the exclamation, instead turning to stare at the great bridge to the castle. Palperroth was a beautiful city, but he doubted even the greatest magic could save him from the cumbersome situation he had placed himself in.

"The forest's air has been kind to me," Folly looked around at the sweating knights, "Unlike the city."

Wesley made a strange whistling noise before saying, "You've been there all this time."

"I cannot part from it."

Folly looked at the water around the training area. Insects rippled the water's surface and created varying reflections of his face. Across the water lounged a group of Vera's devoted followers. They wore long white dresses with embroidered blouses and green and red stained hems, decorated by wet grass and wine. Ribbons tied their shoes to their legs like the stems of flowers. They devoted their lives to taking care of Vera's flowers, and when they weren't doing that, they sang. They hung dried lavender in their braids and carolled about Palperroth. No one paid them any attention, even when they sat loudly on a pile of hay. One of the children of Vera joked with a bottle of something or other waving in their hand. Apparently what they said was very funny, as the rest of them quickly joined in on the laughter.

"I suppose the gate hasn't been opened yet, then?" Wesley's eyes were small; Folly understood that to be a sign that he was concerned.

"Not yet, no." Folly said, and changed the subject before he could speak again, "I see you're doing well for yourself, friend."

Wesley looked around as if he had to remind himself of his occupation.

"Augustus Senior created a place for me, he needed someone for his new army of knights."

That explained why knights were running around again after four hundred years.

"You are a royal general now." He meant for it to sound like a question, but he feared Wesley would take it as jealousy. It was difficult for Folly to understand conversation, and he could not risk having his old friend think him envious of his position. Thankfully, Wesley only sighed.

"My knights are special, I could not have taught them anything if they did not have it in them already."

"I see."

"No, Folly, I don't think you do."

Folly felt the lines of his mouth fall into a frown. It had been a long time since he spoke to someone.

"I don't think I do, Aberdail."

Wesley held his chin with his hand, and said to the stream, "We live in a desolate time, Hallworth."

Folly pretended not to understand, but he did. And he knew Wesley knew.

"I heard about the missing investigator."

"Yes," he pinched the bridge of his nose, "The detective. I met them once."

"It's been in the papers longer than Tambury."

"Despite the king's wishes."

Folly scoffed, it was a rare noise. He didn't want to mention that he too met the detective many years ago, he didn't think it was of import.

He said his goodbyes to Wesley and watched as the group of knights collectively winced at their general's sudden energy when he announced to them that they would be doing a new training routine. At least he had seen a friendly face before being thrust into the fire of the castle. When he finally turned his back on Wesley, he wondered if he also remembered the last words he said to Folly after the war.

"Don't come back."

Folly went through the paperwork of a royal audience, then the weapon search, then the junolian concentration test. It made him sick to see what the city had become since the throne was defiled. Up close to the guards, he was still taller than them, and he wondered if his cover could be broken by such a thing. He didn't want to kill the guards, it wasn't their fault.

A sharp pain stabbed his lungs, causing the air to get caught in an invisible wall of dust in his throat. The gates opened as soon as he turned to cough, and he sputtered as his eyes met with a version of the king painted at the end of the room. His hair was light with age and his eyes were nothing but black dots from where Folly stood. Fitting.

Folly hadn't met the second Augustus, but he had seen a portrait once or twice in Tambury, and he could hardly believe the two were related. Augustus Jr had a friendly look to him, and dark curls without even the slightest grey tinge. He hadn't had the chance to grow old. Folly remembered him smiling in the portrait with a quizzical brow. It was the sort of smile you could learn a lot from. He looked eager.

Valentijn did not smile in his portrait, and he was paler than those who had fallen ill with the Grating Death that Folly treated during the war. It was like his blood was permanently drained.

The castle's interior was dark and omnipotent. Red patterned wallpaper peeked through the black-glazed pillars. Beautiful stained glass windows let coloured light ooze throughout the room, creating a dreamy film over the hallway. Royal guards spoke to knights and footmen with harsh, quiet words that reminded Folly of the school built in Tambury long ago.

"He comes from Tambury in want of an audience with the king." A guard whispered to another, one of the ones posted on the other side of the unscrupulous gate.

"He comes from Tambury?" The other repeated with anticipation.

"Outside Lignis's Gate, fratrem," Folly corrected, using old

Florien, "Outside Limbus."

"Haven't you family in Tambury, sister?" The first guard asked as they escorted Folly through the hall together. Neither of them seemed to understand old Florien; Folly surrendered to silence, not wanting to embarrass himself further.

"My father and two siblings."

"May Vera guide them."

Folly did not understand why the guard blessed his fellow soldier but not the messenger from the very same town. He did not understand how they spoke of Vera– the same Vera Folly loved with the entirety of his heart– like someone ashamed of him. They arrived at the door to the throne room and pushed Folly in without a second word. He went through a smaller door built inside the large decorative one, the one built for servants.

King Valentijn– the real one– sat in a room larger than all of Limbus. The throne upon which he sat was made out of fine redwood, the bumps and accents gilded with golden plating, the flowering wooden legs spindling about the room like the joints of a fairy. He wore a deep red gown, which filled and flooded the elevated stage like a pool of rich human blood.

He was looking at a large painted landscape of Everil, at least that was what Folly assumed, for he wasn't allowed to go any further than Palperroth. A loud noise from a trumpet-player sent the king back from the field and once again inside his castle. Folly looked around at the empty walls and wondered if Valentijn had redecorated since Augustus's reign. The room looked dusty.

"Who is this?" The king asked a guard. His voice was intimidating but soft. It was alike one of a family member Folly had not seen in years. Stern and paternal.

"Your majesty, he has come from outside Lignis's Gate for an audience with the king."

"And what is his name?"

"Folly Hallworth."

The servants surrounding the throne began to murmur with anticipation. The older ones were dressed in the bright colours of Terra Florens, with pale white sleeves with yellow trim reminiscent of daffodils, green dresses with the national flower (lily of the valley) embroidered on the waist, and dried flowers peeking through their hair, but the younger ones resembled the castle more than the land it sat upon. They dressed only in red and black. A woman stood at the king's side in perfect silence. Clothed in an owl mask and a simple day dress, she was most likely the Head Veranth of Terra Florens, the only human worthy of Vera's true light. How could she stand to be in his presence? Folly could not think of a reason other than power.

One of the younger people stood by a group of Wesley's knights, the ones dressed like historical reenactors. His expression was colder than the room. He wore red and black like any other servant, but he had a lily pendant on his long coat. It was red and covered in gemstones that shone in the sickly light of the stained glass windows. Folly had a sudden, racing thought, one where he wondered why the kingdom had ever stopped assassinating kings in the first place. It worked well enough with Queen Victoria during the wars.

Surrounded by both exciting colour and dark intimidation, Valentijn looked deified in his all-white coat, so much so that it made Folly uncomfortable.

"Why have you come here, Folly?" Hubris seeped out of each word.

Folly was dumbfounded that the king had spoken to him directly. He had even used his first name.

"One year ago today, you told Courtlan Edwards that you would have the gate opened by June," Folly began, stepping closer to the throne, careful not to alert the royal guards. The king nodded. "You haven't."

The king did not speak to him immediately, but instead turned to a woman standing next to the throne and asked, "Has my Marianne left, yet?"

"Yes, Your Majesty, last night."

"Magnificent!" He tapped a long nail against the arm of the throne. Folly stared mouth agape, at the ignorance in front of him.

"Your majesty."

"I do apologise, Folly Hallworth, but you have not asked me a question yet."

Folly took a deep, slow breath, and thought about his next words very carefully.

"Have you any update on the kidnapping of Tambury?"

"No, I apologise," he said nothing more.

"The forest has taken them for a year, your majesty."

"Yes."

"They could be dead!" Folly felt his anger overwhelm him immediately. A guard pushed him away from the king, knocking him to the ground. His chances of leaving the castle an innocent man had lowered exponentially.

"They have farms, do they not?"

"Humans can't eat fane."

"I distinctly remember leaving quite a few beet farms around, that and florissantia."

"That is hardly food, your majesty."

"Tell me, son," the king questioned, "how did your hair become that colour?"

Folly's hand felt strands of his hair without thinking.

"I was born with this hair, your majesty."

The king laughed, and Folly wondered if he should as well. "Your hair is yellow, son."

His Majesty began to stand before the smallest sign of pain slashed through his masque of neglect. A footman ran to his aid as his white cloak cascaded down the back of the chair. It was made with the fur of a white bear and the dyed feathers of peacocks. The golden clasp glinted in the same macabre way that the King's eyes did. It seemed that the king was sick, but Folly was not surprised. History had a tendency to repeat itself.

"Magic finds magic." He turned to the footman who held a small velvet pillow and took the blue dagger which was laid upon it. The wrinkles on his face became deeper in the reflection of the marble floor, and towards his eye, a dark tear smudged the makeup brushed under his eyes. Despite his light hair, his eyebrows were full and pulled to an intimidating point. He would've been handsome years ago, but it had been long gone when he took the crown.

Folly knew it was an attempt to scare him, but he did not move. His face stayed blank.

The cool crystal of Crysos's Blade was placed on the back of his hand, and up close he could see the magic pooling into the bottom of the rock, the blue swirled in Folly's eyes. The crystals of the western forest were said to attract magic. And if it was placed on the skin the magic in blood would rush to it. It was also said that the blue of magic can be seen through even the darkest of tones, but despite it, he was not afraid.

The king did not touch Folly, only the blade. It was a trained movement, and a dehumanising one. He wondered how Valentijn had managed to stay on the throne for so long, Perhaps everyone was too tired and sick to find their pitchforks.

When Valentijn peeled the crystal off of Folly's skin, there wasn't the slightest dusting of blue on his hand, and while he feared Valentijn's reaction, he also couldn't wait to see it.

"How?"

"My bloodline is very special sir."

"Not a single drop of magic in your blood? It's…"

"Unnatural." A new voice said.

"Oh, Simone! I didn't see you there!" The king giggled in a terrifying, inebriated way.

"I didn't mean to cause alarm, Your Majesty."

The man with the lily pendant stared at the king, unblinking as he bowed, which was something Folly had not seen before in the castle. The man looked to be in his thirties and wore his black hair in a small ponytail. He had spectacles that sat uncomfortably on the end of his nose, threatening to fall at any moment. Folly realised that the man must've been the new royal physician. From his research, he knew that Dr Simone Wright became famous for his studies on some random, unheard-of disease that affected next to no one. His flowery medical notes were so impressive it had even delighted the king. But Folly had begun to wonder if that was a difficult thing to do. Perhaps he could impress the king as well, with his notes on various poisons.

On second thought, perhaps not.

Once again the servants began to murmur, and the jingle of an old-fashioned jester's shoe rang somewhere in the throne room. If Folly hadn't known better, he would've allowed time to meld in his mind, unknowing of the historical aspects of the castle. Knights died out, but there they were. Jesters evolved, but there they were. It was like he was young again.

"Come here, please, Mr Wright." The king said.

"Doctor." he corrected, Folly could hear the arrogance seeping through his words. He was almost taken aback.

"Is there a difference?" Valentijn said, and Folly wondered if he had unknowingly begun a psychological battle. Dr Wright sighed like a teenager before leaving his place. The coat he wore had accents of velvety fur, which Folly envied with a shiver. The castle was colder than Folly imagined possible in late spring.

Along with the lily pendant, he also wore a silver one on a ring. The lily seemed preserved in metal, and Folly assumed the flower was a part of his family's crest. He could not recall any trends or new meanings which regarded lilies. Folly noticed that many of the young people in Palperroth were fashionable. He envied their affordance of luxuries like jewellery, or plumbing.

Dr Wright held the dagger given by the king in his small, undeserving hands. The rules of the castle must've changed much since Folly had last visited, as he couldn't imagine the king handing a weapon to a measly physician in such a context. Folly noticed Wesley creep in from a small hallway, and took Simone's place by the knights. Wesley could offer his friend nothing but a nod.

Wright inspected the crystal dagger with an intense look. One of his eyebrows lifted. He looked at Folly once, and his expression changed entirely.

"While it is unnatural, it is possible."

"Are you sure, son?"

"You've already done the test, don't embarrass yourself any further."

The king's eyes narrowed, and Folly prepared himself for bloodshed. It was like watching a rabbit insult a wolf. But, somehow, Wright made it back to the knights in one piece. When he stood next to Wesley, it became much clearer how. They had the same nose.

"Folly," the king said quietly, "If I may be frank with you, we have recently suffered a great loss, son."

Folly said nothing in repliance. He looked behind the king and caught the Head Veranth's gaze. With her face hidden, only her eyes could show any hint of expression, and yet there was no warmth for Folly to latch on to. Despite loving Vera, despite loving magic, she was as cold as the king himself.

"I have been putting much of the kingdom's resources towards handling the disappearance of a... great mind." Folly was very sure that the king killed that person, whoever it was. "No matter how many times we attack the gate, the trees grow back all the same. There is no escape from them, son."

Folly did not fall for the sad voice. He stayed polite and silent, allowing Valentijn to sit in his own failure. When he felt he had waited long enough, quietly he said, "It is disrespectful to refer to someone older than you as son."

"What?"

"May I leave, Your Majesty? If there is nothing else to be done?"

The king blinked, once, twice, and then no more.

"Yes, don't be foolish." He waved him away with a shaking hand, and his face became pale. Everyone stood still. Servants stopped moving, musicians stopped greasing their valves, and jesters stopped jesting. "Leave!"

Folly was hurried out before he could say another word. His leather shoes scraped against the hard floor of the outside hall until he was once again thrown through the doors. A second later his bag followed through a crack in the gate. The blinding light of spring's sun attacked Folly's eyes, and he dusted off his pants in humiliation.

He had half a mind to wait for the general, but he couldn't bear shattering his already wounded pride. Folly stood, stretched his legs, and took a deep breath. He wished it hadn't come to it, but he had been given no other choice. He walked across the bridge and sat under a tree near his children of Vera, who were still laughing at each other.

When he knew he was out of the castle's sight, he took out a small flask from his bag. It was made with the thorns which grew on florissantia vines. When crushed and fermented, the juice could help regain the magic Folly lost since he left the Pharaen Forest. Without help from his siblings, the castle was the farthest he could go without the risk of his forest wilting. Downing the contents of the flask, Folly felt the horns beneath his skin and the marks on his arms threaten to show, but he did not allow them to. He had one last thing to do.

Folly was the heart of the northeastern forest. The trees breathed as long as he did, and he could no longer watch as his home was desecrated by the human king. He lived there for thousands of years, and not once had he seen anything as ignorant and arrogant as this so-called king.

He apologised to the forest under his breath when he stood. Folly approached one of the fane trees which grew at every corner, and recognized it as one of the children of his forest. With one touch upon the bark, the yellow, flowering vines on the tree wilted with the breeze and fell to the ground.

When he created fane, he did not wish for it to be the downfall of magic, it was meant to be the opposite. He created it during his first studies of poison, but as the years went by, the humans took his creation and turned it into something of nightmares.

Of course, fane could not affect him, as Folly was its father, but without the help of his forest, he found himself wheezing by the last tree around the castle's perimeter. The small yellow blooms fell quickly and released spores as they hit the ground.

Finally, he had destroyed the cloud of fane which suffocated the castle, leaving it open to magic attack. Without fane to subdue magical ability, it would be much easier for King Valentijn to be stopped by one of the many people he had wronged.

Perhaps he would be bested by that one boy in the paper all those years ago. Or perhaps, more realistically, he would be defeated by Wesley and his army of magical knights. There was a reason their helmets had a filter.

Chapter XIX: Consequences

Yarrow

Clover awoke the next day with pneumonia. It felt like their body was aflame, but they couldn't stop shivering. They didn't know how they came to be in the ship's built-in hospital, but that was where they happened to be when they woke up to cough. It was strange how quickly the sickness took them, and if they weren't so ailed they might have even suspected magical influence.

The first day was the worst of all. They spent it in fruitless attempts to catch sleep's lips. Clover felt as if they floated between life and death, unable to stay in either place. When it was the worst, and they could seldom breathe, they would feel a cold hand against their forehead– which helped– but it never lingered. Clover remembered doctors entering the room wearing strange masks that resembled flowers and birds. It was all absurd, but Clover had grown used to it long ago. As Clover was finally falling asleep, they heard someone listing off many long, medical words.

"Inflamed... phlegmatic... choleric..."

Clover imagined someone with a long black cloak listing off their symptoms, ready to toss them overboard the moment they stopped breathing. The figure got closer and closer, and Clover's eyelids fought to remain open, or perhaps they had been closed the whole time. Their body ached and burned with fever, and every time they acclimated to one kind of pain, a new one peeked its head through the door of their mind.

The figure spun around and Clover saw themself at a wonderful dance, with people spinning in a waltz. There was a flute melody in the clouds above, flying in the fresh air of the sky. Away from the foul-smelling hospital; away from the horrific Marianne.

The door closed, presumably by the doctor, and they pretended to be asleep. It was not a struggle to keep their body limp in the bed, as weakness came as easy as breathing.

Once more they felt a cool palm against their cheek. A breeze went through Clover's entire body as if they were drinking water from a well, or swimming. Their head cleared, and they opened their eyes.

The first thing they saw were bright lights shining throughout the room, piercing their eyes. The Marianne could afford extravagant things like lightbulbs, unfortunately. The second thing they saw was Aster, his hand pouring green light onto Clover's face. He leaned forward, blocking the lightbulb's vicious glare.

"I'm sorry it took me so long, they wouldn't let me be alone with you," He whispered. His hand was heavy on Clover's cheek, and they felt their headache alleviate. "Were you all right without me?"

"Am I dead?" Clover muttered, it was the only thing they could have asked without throwing up. Aster smiled, his eyes scrunching. He began to laugh.

"Even in death, you are charming."

Clover remembered what happened, and pushed past their pain in order to grab at Aster's retracting sleeve. Their hands missed with rusty coordination, and it took all of the restraint they had not to let out an aching sob.

"Aster," his eyes went wide with fear when Clover said his real name, "Jonathan, whoever."

"Don't push yourself."

"The Countess, she's, she had a…" Clover spoke with a voice so frantic they did not realise they had begun to shout. Aster clasped Clover's hand with both of his own and nodded with a knowing glance to the door.

"You told me already, you needn't repeat it."

"But they– that person– they were innocent," Clover pleaded, their voice choked and dry. It still felt as if the water in their body had been replaced with that of the sea.

"It couldn't have been helped, there was nothing you could've done."

"I should've told them, I should've helped them–" their words were cut off by a cough rising out of their throat, attacking it on the way. Aster kneeled beside the bed and helped them sit upright.

"Clover, look at me please," he said when they were able to take a deep breath of dry, smokey air. They complied as best as they could. "You have done no wrong, there was no way we could've helped them without getting caught ourselves."

Clover attempted to swipe away the sweat accumulating on their brow. Anger filled their sickened stomach, making their fever feel as hot as it had been before Aster's interference. He took the rag from a basin next to him and began to dab at their forehead where they struggled to reach. It hurt to see

251

how easy it was for him to care.

"It isn't fair."

He sighed, setting the rag back into the basin, "Most things aren't, as you soon will remember."

"How am I to survive the rest of the trip?"

"Don't speak of it– don't think of it– at least for now," Aster's words were quiet but sharp, and his hand moved frantically to cover Clover's. "Do whatever you must in order to forget it, you'll have time to grieve later. You will heal, in time."

Clover nodded the quickest they could, which was really not quick at all. Their head began to droop, and their sore throat started rearing its head once more, but this time it was only a tickle.

Aster released their hand and walked to the small window to their right. He opened the curtains, and Clover saw a room on the other side where Dorothy and Rose sat. They entered the room along with a doctor when he waved them over.

"I think they're doing much better, doctor, I thank you," Aster observed. "Don't you feel better, dear?"

Clover was unable to reply, in shock and so out of it, they could not remember their cover name. They had the sudden urge to throw something at him, if only to make him feel as shocked as they were.

"That doesn't make any sense," The doctor remarked, feeling their forehead with a clammy hand, "They're no longer warm."

"How wonderful," Aster said, smiling at Clover as the doctor ran to update the charts.

"We were waiting all day," Rose complained, Clover realised it must've been night, "Teddy had to throw a fit for them to let him in alone."

"It was terrifying," Dorothy said, deadpan. Clover still felt far too ill for their antics. They answered with a series of agitated grumbles, their throat feeling less inflamed than before.

"Life will not give you a break, Clover," Rose sadly enunciated, her voice meek but playful, "You're like the main character of a horror story."

When she spoke and joked in such a light-hearted manner Clover was taken back to Alice. A person they had never met and yet felt so close to. When the Countess cried, so did they in their memory. And while they did not really know Rose, the part of their mind still housing the deceased Countess was drawing them to the unmistakable similarities.

"I feel like I'm living in one already," they replied. Dorothy walked closer to where they sat.

"Are you sad, Clover?"

"What?"

She looked serious, as usual, and as she spoke Clover felt as if they were being spoken to by someone far older than they were. Aster's back stayed facing the two of them.

"Look forward to the summer."

"Dorothy, are you all right?"

She puffed out her cheeks.

"You need to look forward to something, it'll help."

"I see," Clover did not. "Thank you."

"I look forward to summers. And to the solstices." Wait for spring, Clover realised.

Aster turned to Clover once more, taking a break from looking through the window.

"I've asked them to let you out two days before the boat lands, you'll be sleeping through most of it, I'm afraid," Aster said to them, and Dorothy took his declaration as the sign to back away. Clover attempted to ignore the questions that were born with Dorothy's suggestion. They were very excited at the prospect of sleeping for a week. "Just don't let them leech you."

Clover suddenly felt very awake.

Chapter XX: The House of Opulence

Orchid

"Have you heard, Sir? The Twelfth is back from Highland."

"Is she now? You would've thought she'd have made the trip by now, how long has it been?"

"One hundred and forty-two years."

"I suppose she has had much to do in those one hundred forty-two years."

"Yes, sir."

"Aminoff, we are beyond such titles."

"Of course, Mr Ollirye. But in a professional setting, it makes sense, no?"

Dionysus groaned. He was tired of being treated as if he were the king of this magical– somewhat illegal– Chamber of Hubris, or perhaps even Castle of Hedonism; that title was also fitting.

Perhaps changing the name of the gambling house was a good idea. He recognized the tackiness.

"Mister?"

Alas, he had zoned out again.

"Yes, Aminoff?"

"Please do not call me by my last name."

"Of course, Amir, what is the matter?"

"I said your brother has sent a letter."

Dionysus jumped up from his seat in the drawing room and grabbed the letter out of Amir's hand. The blood drained from his brain.

"Why would– how could he– How did he find me?"

"Have you not been in contact with him since you last spoke?"

Dionysus scoffed.

"In contact? He's in prison! The only way you could be less in contact than that would be if he was in the royal morgue."

"Sir, I don't mean to be rude, but how many Olliryes do you believe to own a gambling house in Cherin?" Amir watched as Dionysus read the letter. His hands folded in on it until it almost ripped. "Would you like me to administer the lock up protocol?"

Dionysus ignored the question and instead shouted into the hallway.

"If this place isn't spotless by Wednesday you're all fired!"

Amir decided that for the sake of his partner, it would be best to keep his mouth shut for the time being. No matter how long he had known Dionysus, it was not long enough to know the extent of his fear.

It was Friday, and Dionysus had informed his employees that they were free to leave after lunch. Throughout the day he sat restlessly upon his red armchair and awaited the return (or escape) of his brother. It was night when he realised that Olliver might not be coming. The weight of it hung on him strangely, as if he were disappointed. But he wasn't disappointed. Dionysus decided long ago that he would no longer allow people to hurt him, he knew better than anyone not to believe a thing Olliver said. He stood from his chair and took a turn about the room.

It was not difficult to imagine it being a trick all along. Certainly, with Dionysus and his tendencies to overreact, it was not a stretch to believe he was making something out of nothing.

Suddenly, with a deafening roar of its hinges, the door opened, and there he stood.

It was not a mirror that he looked into, but the sight of a man he could hardly recognize. His twin brother still had their childhood face, one that was taken from Dionysus long ago. But, looking past the rotted nostalgia, Olliver's face was sunken and bruised. Prison did not serve him well, even if his treatment was better than most.

"Hello, Dion!" His skin stretched as he smiled, too much pink, not enough teeth. Dionysus never showed his teeth when he smiled.

"You're late," Dionysus took a breath to steady himself. He forgot how nightmarish it was to reconnect with family. He hadn't had the chance, as the rest of his family had been dead for quite some time.

"How could I be late if I never specified the time?"

"What do you want, Olliver?" He pressed his thumb and pointer finger to the bridge of his nose to calm himself down, "I don't remember you being so friendly."

It was best to only ask Olliver the most important questions one at a time. As children, when given questions to choose from, he would always pick the one Dionysus needed the answer to the least.

"Can't I have missed you?" Olliver said, hands outstretched, palms facing the mural on the ceiling. Then his face fell. "I want to make a deal."

"Why would I ever make a deal with you?" Dionysus scoffed. He was too much of an adult to plead. If he were to have been honest with himself, he was angry Olliver never asked how he was doing. For a mere moment, he wondered if he could've forgiven him. He didn't know what family felt like, but the sincere familiarity of his brother was more than he had experienced since he was a child. It was too much to bear.

"I promise it will be worth your while."

"And what will you do if I say no? Or if I lie?"

Olliver laughed dramatically and tilted his head forward, eyes burning with a terrifying hollowness. Dionysus understood then; Olliver was the very same as he was before. Not even magic could bring the emotions he lacked. It wasn't his fault, but it was more draining than Dionysus remembered. They were both men now, but Olliver still acted like a boy.

"If you play me like a fool?" Dionysus forgot how much tears hurt when he held them back.

"Is that so hard to imagine?" Dionysus tried to ignore Olliver's scoff/

"Well then, I was always the smarter one. I'll tell you. I suppose I would have to rip out your throat, just as I did with your mother."

Anger rose up Dionysus's throat and it took all the power within him to stop himself from acting on it. Dionysus wanted nothing more than for Olliver to feel the pain he had felt, to challenge him there, but then he noticed an inconsistency in Olliver's threat.

"Did you?" Dionysus asked. Olliver's eyebrow quirked.

"Did I what?"

"Is that really what you did? Rip out her throat? That isn't how I remembered it at all." Dionysus said coolly. He saw Olliver's mask slip for a moment, it was a sudden jerk of his muscles. Dionysus wondered if he did that as well, he hoped not. "Because the way I remembered it, you had a tantrum and electrocuted her, or are you no longer proud of it? Your great power?"

Olliver scowled, eyeing the leather gloves on his hands that covered up the long scars, created by years of abusing his magic. Dionysus looked at his brother's face, *his* face, or at least what he would've looked like if Olliver never existed. What would his mother think if she knew they hated each other? No. His mother was dead, only they survived now.

"What do you need, Ollie? Do you need a place to stay? I won't throw you out on the street." Dionysus said exasperated, turning around to pour a dark liquid into one of his many golden cups. He understood the risk of leaving his back turned to Olliver, but it did not override his urge to trust. Again and again. He trusted.

Turning back, he was left with no one in front of him. Only the consequential slamming of a door and a few missing chalices. Once again, Dionysus was alone in his mind.

So much for his trust.

He had a game that day, one of the not-so-noble, not-so-legal ones, one with someone named Jasper Pendragon. There was another in a few days, his secretary had told him, their well-manicured nails clicking against the typewriter keys.

Dionysus was used to loneliness, but that did not mean he was fond of it. No amount of gold cups or fine coats could make up for the fact that he had no one to turn to. Except for Amir, of course, but it was different. Curling his fingers around the gold chalice, he stared down into its beautiful ripples. Swishing the liquid with a rhythmic waltz by his hand. He never went games without it, it was too easy.

Would Olliver kill again? That answer was obvious, but there wasn't anything he could do. Telling the authorities was out of the picture. It would open another investigation, forcing him to recite the night again. He couldn't do it.

He drank the chalice's contents with one gulp and let it crash roughly onto the table below. He prayed that Juno would guide Olliver, but more than anything he wished he wouldn't. His deep hatred towards Olliver had trouble staying still at the bottom of his stomach, it filled every crevice of his being. Dionysus didn't see him as a person, much less his brother. He was somewhat thankful for his scars, for now he didn't look like Olliver at all. Hate. That was all he could feel. He repeated it again and again.

Unlike the Florien fane which required a calmer climate, and made the magic in blood attempt to escape, faeberries temporarily nullified magic painlessly. That was what he poured into his cup. An ambrosia.

He didn't understand to a full extent *why* he did it, only that it was the only thing he could. There was an unaccounted sorrow forever anchoring him to his family's gambling house, and no matter how many changes he made to the exterior or how many people he paid to be near him, there was nothing to be done for his inability to cry.

Dionysus had been a tearless child even after he moved in with his adoptive family. He had been poisoned for too long at that point, but he respected that family too much to think about it any longer. They had let him keep the gambling house once he came of age. There was nothing he could do to pay back the lifelong debt.

He thought of his magic, how he created illusions to trick the other players, and for a moment he could not bring himself to breathe. It was all too much.

He drank another cup of ambrosia, it didn't matter. It was not his power that was keeping his victims' memories stolen, but his card dealer-slash-mindkeeper, Uriel.

Uriel Braithwaite moved to Avindre from Plicitar after receiving a telegraph via fire courtesy of Dionysus's secretary. Mindkeeper was a polite title for one who coveted stolen memories; the one who kept the game going. With more sisters than Dionysus could remember, Uriel knew a great deal about stealing. Dionysus did as well.

Chapter XXI: The Landing

Chamomile

Avindre was a land of dismal contemplation and drizzling wisdom. It was a hive of information, buzzing with opportunity in its arctic peaks. The mountains of Highland to the northeast and the hot forests of the Dahlia Empire to the northwest gave Avindre a unique perspective of the continent which held the majority of the world's gold. King Juno XII ruled with a fist stronger than iron.

The way of choosing the next king was unknown to the population, but that did not mean it was out of the people's choice. It was a lifelong job. Unless the chosen king was deemed incapable, in which case the people were under a moral and societal duty to forcibly end it. It also did not matter the name or gender of the person chosen, as they would always be referred to as King Juno.

The Twelfth (as she was called by her subjects) came to power on July 15, 1752. She was the longest reigning king of Avindre since the first King Juno. 142 years ago she was picked as the next ruler of Avindre, and when the Twelfth descended upon the two-century-old veranda, she gave the first speech of her reign. Mellowing in the applause of her people, her voice boomed throughout the kingdom without greeting.

"What do you believe in, Avindre? Is it a long-lost deity, simultaneously above and below you? Is it the promise of something better? Is it– perhaps– the very space we exist in, today and all days?" The crowd grew quieter by the second. "Or do you believe in something tangible?"

The crowd murmured amongst themselves until she held a strong hand above her people.

"This is what I believe in. Tangibility. What do you do with your two hands each day, I wonder?" She stayed silent for a moment, letting her words ring in the ears of the people around her, and staring at the hand she rotated absentmindedly in front of her. "It doesn't matter what you believe in, as long as it is something you would die for."

The crowd cheered for that, they knew very well that dying for a cause was something that warranted mindless support. At least, that was what the Juno before taught. The new Juno seemed upset with their support, but continued with a slight grimace.

"Who are we but peasant to the hand? What is our body but a minion to our mind? Working towards a goal that not even we are aware of. The quicker we come to terms with the peculiar peculiarity of our existence, the sooner we can thrive without self-punishment. It matters not what's in your blood, nor does it matter who you throw your coin to," she paused to breathe, "what matters is the feeling of life. The feeling of art!"

The crowd was silent, turning to one another and grumbling their confusion. Yet she did not react, and continued on.

"How lucky we are to live amongst change, to see the roots of the life and society your children will live in for years to come. Rejoice in your indecisiveness, revel in your terrific mortality." When the crowd believed she was done speaking, they began clapping and yelling their support, however, she was not done.

"Do not forget," she interrupted, "Do not forget your life. Do not forget the tragedy we endured in the war all those years ago. You are the only ones keeping us from ruin."

The first days of her reign were seen by many as the greatest of the kingdom. The Twelfth created reforms to improve trading, and solved the long-disputed troubles between Avindre and Kivet, a republic close by. She created friendships with the king of Terra Florens at the time, King Valentijn's great-grandfather. After he died she was friends with his daughter, then her son, and continued to keep a close positive relationship with all rulers until King Valentijn.

For the sake of continuity, King Juno the Twelfth (or the Twelfth, or the Twelfth King of Avindre, or any other name of that sort) would be referred to as Juno to any outside the nation.

It was a kingdom so beautiful, so rich in life, Cherin was the capital of art for hundreds of years. But as the years went by, the world watched as Avindre fell into disrepair. Poverty was the true king, with famine at his right hand. Beautiful architecture collapsed, and history began to move on from Avindre. King Valentijn cited it as the reason why he was closing the Florien border, for fear of attack. Somehow, this did not stop him from annually sending a ship there and back. Valentijn was called the King of Brotherhood in Avindre, because the only thing everyone could agree on was that they despised him.

Even those who were neutral (such as the resident empress of the Dahlia Empire, Esther) didn't enjoy Valentijn's presence. Esther was one of the most aloof leaders in history, and even she knew to politely decline every one of Valentijn's invitations.

Esther was also known for her deep history with Juno. The two had followed in the footsteps of the original Juno and Dahlia in the sense that they were the only rulers in the history of their lands who interacted with any semblance of friendliness. Some would say they were best friends. Sadly, things took a turn for the worse when Juno's obvious distaste did not meet Esther's morals of constant peace and neutrality. What resulted was a long, dramatic fight between the two. Juno stayed apathetic, saying only positive things about Esther, while Esther wrote twelve songs about how sad she was and performed them yearly to her subjects.

In the case of Juno's royal painters, they were happy Esther would no longer be attending the events, as her red hair was too frustrating to paint. They once requested Juno gift her a headscarf in hopes that she would be so grateful she would wear it every day of her visits. In their defence, it worked for three weeks.

In the modern day, the streets ran with shades of white, grey, and black. To those rich enough to pay for the expensive and restrictive imports from Terra Florens, it was almost as if nothing had happened, but to the poor, starving artists on the streets of Cherin, it was impossible. The days seemed to get colder, the coats grew thinner. Disease ran through the lower classes, and operating theatres had no shortage of cadavers.

That was the explanation Rose gave for why the docks had such a large population of suspicious cloaked people waiting for the boat to arrive. *They await the dead, Clover. Will we be next?*

Clover recovered slowly in a quiet stupor, being woken a few times a day for food and to rapidly shake their head at the ceramic tub of leeches the doctor kept pushing closer and closer towards their bed. The room had a lingering smell of death that they tried to ignore, but with each breath it came back stronger. They longed for the ability to breathe clean air again.

Finally, they were released, and not long after did the ship land in Cherin, Avindre. It was a large city that smelled of illness and strangely enough– poetry. The civilians had a greyness to their complexion that matched the bone-chilling snowfall. Clover wished for their coat to consume them. With their bright clothing and sun-rich skin, it was clear they were from Terra Florens.

They were bombarded with a bittersweet sight as they left the ship. On the docks, a group of children played. They did not play tag, cards, or the typical games children in Terra Florens would play. In the hands of a young girl was a ball of light, and she giggled as she threw it into the air for her two friends to toss to one another. The young Floriens gasped, their eyes wide and eager.

The population of people with high junolian concentrations in Avindre was almost tenfold that of Terra Florens, but the non-magical people didn't seem to mind. In fact, Clover couldn't tell who was magic and who wasn't, or if anyone was non-magic.

They could see a woman clothed in a thick furred coat dance in the sparkles of fire raining from her fingertips, the toddler wrapped around her chest grasping, pleading.

"Will we head to the gambling house first, Aster?" Dorothy asked as they trudged through the rotting roads away from the crowded port.

"No, we need a place for Rose's bags," he whispered back, patting Rose's hand as they walked arm-in-arm. Aster turned to Clover as they manoeuvred past the snow sweepers and lantern lighters. Their legs felt wobbly, like their bones were still riding the ocean waves. "Don't get lost now!"

Aster tended to expect nothing but the greatest effort in inconspicuity from all others, but when it came to his actions, Clover couldn't help but believe he begged for the attention of others. He was wearing a coat so brightly coloured it was screaming out to the whole city that he was a foreigner. It would've made Clover angry if he wasn't so kind.

In their distracted haze, Clover could not pay attention to their surroundings, and before they knew it they had knocked into someone. Clover was unable to see their face as they steadied themself, but the person's hair was as black as ink.

"Sorry," they muttered, but the person was already gone. Clover removed their hand from the shoulder the stranger bumped into, only to find grey ash on their sleeve. Clover looked behind once again and watched the person's retreating back, their clothes covered in ash. The air smelled of smoke, but there were no factories to be seen. Must've been a chimney sweep.

Avindre was nothing like Terra Florens. The cold was bone-chilling. Clover already missed the warmth of Vera's candle, despite not knowing if they believed in her.

Sorry, Alice.

The wind was stronger than they ever imagined, even Dorothy's coat couldn't protect them. The dirt on their boots mixed with the snow underneath, creating a discomforting sludge as they walked down the small road. Shops stood terrified in the howling wind as Aster hauled an old (and more importantly warm) carriage.

They hopped into the carriage, and thanked everything out there that they did not throw up. Clover was able to survive the two-week boat ride, but getting used to land again would be an entirely different story. They tried to calm their nerves as Rose was helped into the seat beside them.

"You smell like smoke, Clover, have you been smoking?" She asked.

"A chimney sweep bumped into me."

"Let me see," Aster said from the other side of the carriage. Clover showed him the mark that the stranger left on their sleeve.

"It doesn't smell like a fireplace, are you sure it was a chimney sweep?" He inquired. Clover shrugged, they didn't think it smelled any different from regular fires. Was it them? Did they smell strange? Their stomach churned further with the thought.

"It doesn't smell like a chimney sweep," Rose drawled in dramatic impersonation.

At the inn, Clover was faced with four beds, each holding a blade-thin mattress. Not the most comfortable of arrangements, but it was better than being in a hospital bed. Clover sat on one and pushed their hands against the fabric. It was as hard as a rock.

"Is that all right with everyone?" Clover heard Aster say from across the room, "Clover?"

"What?"

"I asked if tomorrow we should head to the House of Opulence?"

"Yes, of course, I apologise," they leaned against the wall behind the bed "I am very tired."

"Me too," Rose agreed with a yawn. Aster stared at Clover.

"Will you need something to wear tomorrow?" He said.

"Is what they have already not good enough?" Dorothy asked while going through Rose's many scarves.

Aster pondered. Clover could tell he was looking through the eyes of an artist.

"Would you be open to a skirt?" he asked. Clover was taken aback. Could they wear a skirt? They had never thought about it before. It didn't sound too horrible.

"A skirt?"

"I've always wanted to style a detective," he looked sheepish, and Clover began to believe that they were the only one taking the situation seriously.

"Do you have something like that?" Clover asked with a quirk of their brow. Aster nodded and began to look through his bags. "Nothing velvet!"

"Of course, of course. You needn't worry." They could hear the smile in his voice, his face hidden behind a pile of coats.

As everyone got to straightening out their arrangements (except for Rose, who fell asleep the moment her head hit a pillow,) Clover decided they would take a walk. One last bit of peace before the final hour.

They left the inn and breathed in Cherin, it felt as though ice water entered their lungs. They watched flakes of snow catch on their hair and melt away, and it made them think of death. People scurried about on foot or horseback, and Clover thought about how those people each had lives of their own, families, magic, and problems. They wondered if anyone was going through the same thing they were. Fluffy, comforting thoughts were spun like silk. Clover lifted their hands to the sky and closed their eyes.

It would be over soon. Their jumbled thoughts– which paced to and fro in their mind– would soon be straightened out. No longer would they feel passive in their life. They did not wish to die, but they could not continue to live like this, forever missing.

The street was beautiful, in a way. It looked older than Dolston, but the buildings were still charming. They were made of brick and had an archaic quality to them. If only they were more taken care of, perhaps their beauty would be even greater. Clover wanted an older house, they decided. Once this was all over, they would be able to do whatever they wanted.

A loud metallic crash made Clover return to Lethe.

A man with shoulder-length black hair stood on the ground nearby trying to pick up the fallen contents of his box, it was the same person from before.

"Are you going to help me, or are you just going to stand there?" The man said. Clover could hardly hear in the snow, could hardly see. They kneeled and began to help the stranger. The contents were mostly loose pieces of paper, but Clover also saw teacups, goblets, and golden plates.

"Are you a chimney sweep, sir?" They asked. Clover understood it was impolite, but they couldn't stop their curiosity.

"Sure, right." He lifted the box once more, and a piece of paper flew out of it, causing him to swear. Thankfully, Clover caught it. It was a napkin with a small crest, red words encircled it. *The House of Opulence*, it read.

"Here you go!" Clover said. The man snatched it out of their hands, his nails were strangely clean. The rude man walked away without another word.

This man, Clover realised, was *not* a chimney sweep. He was a thief! Not only that, he was also related to the House of Opulence. This was exactly what Clover was looking for. Before they knew it, they were following the man down a side alley.

They felt the act of stalking to be as easy as breathing, and they wondered if they were a good detective. They hoped so. It would be embarrassing to go through all of this to find out they were boring. They wondered if their father was awaiting their letter. They wondered if any friends wondered where they were.

The man turned into another dark alley, with Clover only a few paces behind. They followed him down a maze of roads and alleys until he finally entered a strange building. It was tall, skinny, and made of the same rotting brick as the rest of the town. It was a strangely elegant building, with gold plating on the door glinting in the dark. He shut the door swiftly behind him.

Clover crept up to the door after waiting for a moment, and turned the doorknob ever so slightly until it clicked. Locked.

They could not help but be disappointed.

On the side of the building, facing another alley was a window, which they crouched in front of. They hoped no one went on walks in this part of town.

271

Looking through the grimy window, Clover saw a small store. Someone wearing a grey hood sat at a desk in the front, but they were unable to see the face of the person wearing it.

The person in the hood broke from their stupor when they noticed the man had walked in. Clover could barely hear as the man said to them,

"I have it, just as you asked." The hooded figure did not respond. The man placed the box on the desk loudly and Clover realised that this was a pawn shop.

It was illegal, but not necessarily Clover's problem. That was until the man revealed a mangled hand. Thick scars wrapped around his fingers and palm as he gave coins to the pawn shop owner.

They gave them a bad feeling, those scars. Like runes pressed into the flesh. And, wait one moment. Why was *he* paying the shop owner?

Suddenly the hooded figure began to change. The shadows of the room grew darker, and they saw the man gasp. Large, yellow eyes opened in the darkness.

A bird began to caw, then another, then many more. The windows rattled and the man...

The man *disappeared*. He exploded into darkness, without another trace. The figure turned to the window, and Clover ducked below the window, their heartbeat loud in their ears. Suddenly a crow flew into the window, and Clover felt their heart fall to their stomach. They feared the window would shatter upon connection, but it stood strong as the bird threw its body into it. It fell beside Clover, but it did not move.

As the crow bled there, lifeless, Clover began to panic. They heard the door creep open and ran behind the shop and through the alley.

As they ran, Clover could feel the cold air scrape against their lungs with a harsh vigour, and with each step they could feel their body sink further and further into Lethe. Tears grew in their eyes, the same ones which threatened to spill when they thought of the people lost to the ocean.

When they finally returned to the inn, it was past nightfall. After apologising to the innkeeper for returning so late, they opened the door to their room and sighed as they allowed the warmth of the fire to consume them. Everyone was fast asleep, exactly as they thought. Everyone but Aster, who perched on the windowsill.

"You don't sleep much, do you?" He asked apathetically, as if he had been practising. Given the amount of time they were gone, he probably did. The light of the fire did not reach where he sat, but they could still see him in the moonlight.

"Do you always sit in dark rooms waiting for me to walk in?" Clover teased. They did not lack evidence for that claim.

"Only when I want you to find me."

Clover quirked their brow. It was not difficult to find him when he put such little effort in hiding.

"You speak as if you've known me for long," They said, half joking and half only now realising it was a possibility. "Have you?"

"Clover." He stayed silent for a long time. Clover could hear birds outside. *Crows.* When he did speak, his voice trembled. "How I wish I could say."

He undid his necktie in one motion as he left his spot at the window. There was something bigger going on, Clover feared. Still, they could not help but be frustrated with him. Why couldn't he just speak?

"I hope we did know each other," Clover spouted, "You're a very interesting person, Aster. I've enjoyed being your friend."

Aster only stared. They began to wonder if they had said too much, he looked as if he were about to cry.

"You are too kind for your own good."

"I don't know anything right now, but when I do," Clover tried to find the right words, "When I do, I will find you."

Aster's eyes widened, and he smiled with an intimate understanding that made Clover feel sick, as if the cold from the outside rushed into their stomach all at once, making it drop.

"You already have."

When they went to bed, their heart beat faster than it ever had before.

Chapter XXII: Dreams

Moonflower

Among the body, past their rotting bones, the ineffable expanse of all they knew was born. It was more than the world, a greater blue would never again be found. Full and empty, they flew through cerulean skies, the line between it and the sea unknown. Their senses were left behind. They plunged into it.

The feeling of it was unavailable, but the water pushed forward their lungs and pressed their stomach deeper into the horror of their mortal body. Bubbles of past thought rushed past them, swallowed by what they could only assume was the sky.

Bound only by the past, they felt the world pass by with a school of nightmares, their childhood nestled in a cavern at their feet. Moving pictures of their scars' stories took hold of the space behind their eyes, but the shapes were indescribable. Below and above, there was no difference. Water was air, and air was all around. Their sleeves were fins.

A castle of gold replaced their ocean. The light of the candle reflected off of its surface, blinding. Their lungs collapsed in. They wished to shout, but the words mixed in awful, unnatural ways.

In a single moment, the light burned more than the first time their fresh skin touched flame, during the birth. They understood, now, what the sight was. The City of Gods had come to accept their newest citizen, but they could not get past their humanity.

"It is human to long for this," the city said, "you are going against your nature, refusing."

They knew it was a trick. They did not speak. Words and languages came and went in the time they waited. The Sun fell behind the spires of the gold city's walls, and they were no longer harmed by its beauty.

"We will wait for you," the doors said.

"We will wait *with* you," the walls said.

They were in the ocean once more, it did not matter. The scenes bled with each other like smeared ink. They were the very time they longed for.

There was a strange creature in front of them, one with strings extending from their hands. Canary locks and a painted face. The strings forced her to dance in the dark, the curtain daring to open behind her.

There was no need, for Clover could see behind the curtain all along. The man pulling the strings had a face which changed like water, in one moment speaking the truth, and in the other spouting lies with his sweetened tongue. It was no longer in their nature to hold a grudge, they had lost the passion long ago. What was the point of violence if it all led to the same thing? There was no time to clean the blood from their hands, so they preferred not to be in situations which dirtied them. Clover was a detective before they were a child, but they were not a child for long. Children did not see the things that they had seen, children did not speak in the way they had spoken, children could not pull the trigger the way they had all those years ago. No, they were never a child, just a changeling pretending to be one. It was a shock it took them so long to know who they were truly fighting.

They needn't worry about that now. They watched the doll dance in front of them, grey eyes watching in the distance, beyond the lying man, and they looked at their body. It was still their own, despite their waking mind not recognizing it. Did they have a good time, so far? Did they enjoy noticing the clues placed for them? It did not matter to them, they knew a greater game was still to be found. There was always a new game to be played.

For once, they wondered what it would be like to live simply, to notice nothing. They could never exist that way, it was not in their nature. They were the detective's kid prodigy, the star quickly burnt out, like a cigarette. They could almost hear his voice.

"One more case and I'll retire." He paced to and fro. "One more, Clover."

They knew it wouldn't be the last, they knew he could never stop. It was in his nature as much as it was in their own. It was their life. A soldier of the mind, and a tool to whoever held the most gold. They could not think, and yet they thought. They could not move, and yet they ran. They always ran.

"Did you have a good time?" The doll continued to dance. The eyes continued to watch. The man continued to puppet. The king continued to kill. The shadows continued to lurk. It was as natural as the moon, or the ocean. It was the very heart of Lethe. They were Lethe, they had always been Lethe, ever since they were born.

"Was it a good run?" The voice kept speaking. *Can't you see I'm busy?*

"I think you are quite done, now." *No!* "I think it is time to stay asleep."

Clover could not give up, not when they were so close to winning. They only had a few more steps until they reached the end.

"Did you get what you wanted?" They realised that it was Esme's voice.

No, not yet.

They awoke, living once again.

Chapter XXIII: The Eleventh Hour

Edelweiss

To Floriens, Avindre was a terrifying land; to the people of Seraphine, it was the capital of art. To Clover Page-Bettencourt, Avindre was to be their deathbed. Whether it would be their body or their amnesia placed in the coffin, they did not know. What they did know was that they finally had a chance to feel whole, and they were not going to waste it.

On that important morning, Clover found themself staring into the cracked mirror above the wash basin in hollow disbelief. They began to think Aster had gone crazy. Instead of giving them advice, or planning, or doing anything of import, he fussed with Clover's outfit. They wore a brown tweed coat with a matching cycling skirt. Upon their head was a strange hat with a feather, one of Rose's. It felt strange to dress up so nicely for what may be their last day alive. They felt once more like one of his dolls, but they did not mind.

When he left, Clover tucked their silver pocket watch in their vest and smoothed it out, making sure it would stay put. It was their only true possession, not including their clothes. In the reflection of the basin's mirror, they stared at a distorted version of themself. In their hollow gaze, they saw an expression similar to the young Alexandra that they could hardly recollect after their fever.

Their face was different, cadaverous. It was like they were at their own open casket. The candles nearby flickered, creating shadows on their face like a reflection in moving water.

In Terra Florens, the sun would've been up by that point, but Vera did not care for Avindre the way she did across the ocean. It was all so confusing.

They were back on their bed and barely conscious when Aster handed them a box of matches and a small dagger to put in their pocket.

"Just in case," he told them. The matches were for (in Rose's half-asleep words) if they were trapped in a cave and needed to build a fire, and the dagger was for (in Aster's more conscious words) the obvious. Clover nodded and returned to the dark expanse of their mind.

Clover's hands shook and wept with perspiration as they again traced the metal of the watch, and it was then they realised they had never opened it before. There was no specific reason as to why they never thought of it before, perhaps it was simply the quickness of it all. The silver gleamed in the candlelight as it opened. On the inside of the watch's lid was an engraving that read, "*Paradicaelum.*"

They traced the words with their fingers. Was it their own handwriting? Clover stared at the room as Dorothy fussed with the fire, Aster buttoned his coat, and Rose snored.

Aster wore a red ulster coat with golden thread weaving the image of wheat on the fabric. Clover wondered where he found the time to make such things. As Aster focused on braiding his hair, Clover contemplated asking.

They decided they would rather wait until the end of this madness. They had many questions they still wished to ask, but something made them feel as though they should wait. It was good to have something to look forward to, even if it was small. Wait for spring. Wait for summer.

His cool, angular face looked soft in the candlelight. His translucent cheeks glowed with the morning chill, and his light eyelashes batted against his spectacles as he struggled to keep them on his nose.

It was strange, Clover was sure Aster could not see them stare, but despite it, they still felt as if they had been caught. Aster leaned closer to the oil lamp lit on the windowsill. It was at that moment that Clover truly saw him as another human.

Clover appreciated Dorothy and Rose– their help could not be ignored– but they felt a deeper attachment to their friendship with Aster. Perhaps it was due to their closeness in age, or his magic. Aster's magic was something embarrassingly fascinating to Clover. It was so embarrassing to them that when they realised where their train of thought had gone, they felt a sudden longing to be back on the ship, if only to make it easier to jump into the ocean.

"Will all of you be going with me?" Clover asked as the sun rose.

"Of course, we've made it this far," Dorothy replied, "Can't be worse than what we've handled before."

"Do you really think we'd leave you to fend for yourself?" Rose said, her hair sticking all about from how she slept. They all turned to her, amused, and Clover was sure they heard Dorothy giggle. They caught her eye, and Dorothy smiled.

Clover realised they were surrounded by friends, people who wanted to help them, people who risked their lives to help them. They felt their face burn with emotion.

Clover didn't want to die.

They did not want to die.

I don't want to die, Clover thought.

The House of Opulence was located on a large road off from the port; it was one of the older, nicer buildings. Walking inside, Clover felt every breath grow cold in their lungs.

"Welcome to the House of Opulence and Opportunity, how may I be of assistance?" The secretary said, her eyes hidden behind her uncomfortably large smile. Her teeth swallowed the rest of her face in plastic joy. She was shrewd, and as short as Rose, but far skinnier. She was like a strange bird, an omen of death. With pale skin and eyes, Clover shuddered beneath her stare.

"We're here to see…" Clover realised they did not remember his name. "Your boss?"

The secretary's eyelids drooped, mask falling onto the tiles as if it had physically manifested. She smiled once more, and signalled for them to follow as she entered a side hallway.

Gold and bronze statues watched them in every direction through the long hallways. Tiles cracked and echoed as the secretary's heels marched along. Rose clung to Clover's lapel with a shaking hand. There were too many thoughts around her, they suspected.

Dorothy walked beside the secretary, as she was the only one able to keep up, Aster trailed behind, and Clover was comforted by the feeling of his eyes. His boots clicked in a rhythm opposite to the secretary's; it made Clover's ears ring, and his cane only magnified the noise. Clover looked at their surroundings constantly, but no matter how many times they attempted to memorise which rooms and hallways they entered it was impossible, the memories falling out of their grasp.

A large golden door stood valiantly at the end of the large hallway. The secretary knocked quietly on it, so quiet that the largeness of the door would've surely muffled it unless someone stood directly on the other side, ear to the door.

The door opened, and the head of a dark-haired man peeked out from the other side. The secretary whispered into his ear and he nodded, inspecting them all with one swift motion. His glasses were small, circular, and balanced on his nose, which was as straight and imposing as a statue. He wore the same smile as the secretary, but his was genuine. Clover understood, by just a single sighting, that they were in front of a man who loved his life.

He slipped out with a large chain of keys around his wrist, the keys jingling like sentimental charms on a bracelet. He was wearing a suit the colour of crushed dandelions; it was the brightest colour around.

The secretary turned to leave, but the man shouted at her with strange joviality.

"Thank you, Niamh!" He called to her, mispronouncing her name seemingly on purpose, saying it more like "Nymph" than "Neeve." At least, that was what Clover presumed, perhaps she actually was named Nymph. She must not have minded, as her laugh rang through the hall just as Clover's footsteps once did. The man looked at Clover with wide eyes. "Nice to see you, Detective."

It is a trick! Clover realised. They had to be very careful with how they acted.

"Nice to see you too," Clover noticed the name tag pinned

to the man's coat, "Mr Amir Aminoff."

Apparently, that was not the reaction that Amir expected, and his fingers stopped locking the door suddenly, he then– for the first time– looked into the eyes of Aster, Rose, and Dorothy.

"Ada?" He called out to the hallways, and an older woman popped out of a small hallway.

"Yes?"

"Bring these lovely people to the drawing room," and to Clover, he continued, "Come with me."

"Wait, I haven't–" Clover began to say, but was interrupted.

"Only one can play at a time."

They walked in silence, and Clover began to wonder if they had made a mistake in coming there together. The feeling of incoming danger crept through Clover's heels all the way to the tips of their ears and the ends of their curls. After the feeling became tangible, it was given more ammunition when they thought of where their friends could be because of them. What if they were being led to a death trap?

Amir led them to a different door, a smaller one made with dark-stained wood. He looked at Clover before opening the door.

"Is this visit a personal thrill, or a message from Valentijn?"

"Valentijn, what?" Clover's brain stopped working. "Of course not!"

Amir squinted with confusion.

"Is that not why you're here?"

The two looked at one another in the doorway, each inspecting the other's features for evidence of falsities, but both gave up fast.

"Something of mine has been stolen," Clover said.

"Really?" He asked before shrugging, "All right. Luckily for you, he's accepting all visitors today, said he's about to go on holiday. *Absurd.*" The last part was said almost silently, and Clover knew they were not supposed to have heard it.

"That's good, I think."

Amir's smile grew, the rest of his face overwhelmed by his glee.

"I am incredibly impressed by your handling of our language, most Florien tourists never bother."

Clover's head hurt. Amir opened the door to reveal a small office. He did not look in.

Inside was a man sitting in a red plush armchair with his back turned from the door, he faced a golden fireplace. Statues held up podiums on either side of it with a brazed plate on the side which read *Ollirye*. Underneath was a small engraving.

"Mindreading, mindkeeping, mindholding."

"Mr Ollirye?" Clover said slowly, hesitating with the hope that it was his last name.

"Are you here for a game?" His voice rumbled. Mr Ollirye turned to face Clover with the speed of a lethargic snail.

His study was kept very clean, with each surface reflective. Mr Ollirye had jet-black, pin-straight hair, which fell undone at his shoulders. He was wearing a beaded mask which portrayed a phoenix, but underneath they could see sepia-toned skin. His skin looked smooth, smooth to the point where Clover began to debate his humanity. Either that, or he was inebriated. They did not know how to respond. Clover felt a strange connection to him, and something told them that they had been in the same situation many times before.

"You stole my memories."

Mr Ollirye held his head in his gloved hands, swaying ever so slightly.

"That means a game, you win the game, you get your memories."

"What's the game?" Clover asked. It was met with a groan.

"Chess, you make a move, you give a memory, I make a move, I give a memory," he sighed. "The employment of the mind, that whole thing. I never understood it."

He began to mutter something incomprehensible.

"What?"

"Do you want your memories or not?"

Clover stood in silence. They assumed this would've been a great deal more dramatic, even a bit dangerous. It was underwhelming, they felt like something more should've happened.

"Better yet," Mr Ollirye said suddenly, "how about I just give it to you?"

It wasn't supposed to be this easy! Clover had been preparing for this moment, they did nothing but prepare. They couldn't let it end in such a way. They needed to *earn* it.

"What?" They tried not to shout. "No! I want to play."

Mr Ollirye's head rolled on his shoulders.

"M'kay."

He attempted to stand but was met with great struggle, and Clover stood in silence as he writhed.

"Do you want me to get someone?"

"No."

Luckily, the game was to be held in the drawing room across the hallway. Inside the room, Rose, Dorothy, and Aster were sitting on a large pink sofa. Clover was beginning to rethink their decision. Was their pride worth the humiliation of dragging an intoxicated adult man across his own hallway?

"Dionysus?" Amir said as he leapt from his chair. Clover assumed he was attempting to make small talk with their friends. They doubted it went well. Dorothy looked uncomfortable, Aster had a polite smile (but was no doubt uneasy,) and Rose was stroking the fabric of her skirt.

"Who is Dionysus?" Mr Ollirye grumbled. *Dionysus*, that was his name! How could they have forgotten?

Amir took Dionysus to a chair at the chess table. Clover could hear him whisper things. It became clear that this behaviour was not normal for the richest man in Cherin.

"Are you sure you want to?" Was the only full sentence Clover could hear. They looked at the couch in hopes of some guidance as Amir and Dionysus whispered to each other angrily, but Aster seemed much too busy looking at the floor to make eye contact. Dorothy gave them a weak grin. They always had Dorothy.

"I am truly sorry for my friend's behaviour," Amir exasperated, "You can play if you wish, but we will compensate if you would like to another day."

"Today," Clover said immediately, "I want to today."

Dionysus adjusted his mask clumsily.

"Well?" He said, his words slurred, "Go on, don't have that much to lose."

Clover thought otherwise, but sat nonetheless.

"I was talking about myself," Dionysus explained, "Explain it please, Whatever-Your-Name-Is."

"Mr Ollirye!" Amir cried, but continued nonetheless. "This form of chess acts differently from the normal version, and was taught only for games of grandeur. In this case, each piece represents a different memory you give up."

"Wait," Clover gasped. "You give them up? Forever?"

They only had so many.

"Don't worry, detective. You'll only feel a little confused if you lose. You consent to the game the moment the first turn is played," he smiled at them, and despite Clover knowing they shouldn't trust him, they couldn't help but feel comforted. "Make a good move, give a good memory, make a bad move, give a bad memory."

One of Dionysus's employees placed shining pieces on the square board; it was easily the most refined chess board Clover had ever seen, especially since the only other one they had seen was sitting dusty in Aster's room. The pieces had a strange pulsating light beating in the golden veins of the marble pieces.

The air went from warm to cold as another employee opened the large floor-length windows. Thin white curtains began to dance in the wind, and Clover watched them waltz for a moment before looking at the sad man in front of them.

"You may go first," he said.

Clover licked their lips and took a deep breath, they at least understood the basics of chess, but even still there was a part inside them screaming that something was wrong. They decided to play it safe and moved the middle pawn a space up.

The game had begun.

Clover awoke in a strange room, they saw beautiful walls embossed with grey flowers blooming as if it were a warm spring day. They had a moment of peace before their brain kicked in.

Dionysus played in the snow with his brother when they were very young. He hid a rock in a ball of snow.

Clover went on a walk in a strange forest.

Dionysus got perfect marks on his research project on Dahlian agriculture. His family was very proud of him. His brother did not do as well, but the tutor only took ten points off.

Clover learned what a raccoon was, they still didn't quite understand the concept.

Dionysus's cat died, and his family couldn't talk about animals for two months without him bursting into tears.

Clover went to a magnificent ball.

Dionysus woke during a storm, he was becoming more and more like his brother every day.

Clover had a nightmare about a large red eye.

Dionysus kept hearing the storms even during the day, he didn't understand how someone could be so angry.

Clover saw a woman's life flash before her eyes.

Dionysus woke up early the morning of the ceremony, a storm was coming. He was the only one who could hear it. Each step brought him closer to something fatal, and there was nothing he could do to change it. Blood seeped through the wallpaper of his room, he was the only one who could see it. The ceremony came, and he stood upon the small platform in the garden. He was made the chosen heir of the Ollirye's fortune.

"Clover!" They heard someone shout.

Dionysus watched as the lightning came, he stood still as it struck his family, and then him. He was the only survivor, apart from Olliver. Olliver was sentenced to spend the rest of his life in prison. The years passed, and Olliver began to forget his life before.

That was until he escaped. Finally, he was free, but there was no one to greet him. He watched his brother in his new life, and realised just how much time he had missed out on. He couldn't handle it. He began to hatch a plan. He could finally have the fortune he deserved.

But he couldn't kill him, no matter how many times he tried. Out of sight, he waited for his chance for weeks, but he could not do it, so he thought of something else. He would find an illusion-master and become the true heir of the Ollirye fortune.

But it hadn't worked, he was consumed by something greater, the shadows which hid in disease-ridden streets and dangerous alleys.

"Clover, move!" Clover was snapped out of the game's trance as Dorothy dragged them out of the chair and onto the floor. As they hid beneath a table, lightning erupted and roared throughout the room. Dionysus was still at the table, his hands gloveless and gripping the tablecloth. Electricity hummed in the air.

"It's not him!" Clover yelled. "It's his brother, an identical twin!"

"Olliver?" Amir shouted back. *Olliver*.

"Don't do it. Don't do it. Don't do it," he kept repeating. His eyes were hollow, "Please don't do it."

Amir, Aster, and Rose were behind the couch, and Clover could see Amir whispering to Aster, who nodded before beginning to take off his gloves. Clover's stomach dropped, they didn't understand how Aster could hurt the man with his powers, but something in Aster's expression made Clover certain of the action he was going to try to perform.

"Aster, don't!" Clover shouted. Aster turned to them, his hand trembling as he tried to decide what to do.

"It isn't him, Clover," Aster yelled over the strikes of lightning, "he tricked us, don't you see?"

"That doesn't mean we have to kill him!"

As Clover said that, a burst of electricity sent the table they were hiding under, and pain shot through their entire body as they were knocked into the open room. Amir and Aster pulled them from behind the couch quickly, but not before they were struck by a small ball of light. It felt as if their body had been lit on fire. All at once they felt their skin grow cold and yet also searingly hot.

Sleep was something they had grown fond of in their short time on Lethe, but this was different from sickness or slumber, this was death. They had not thought in detail how they would die, or what it would feel like, but it wasn't so much different from their other dreams. They felt so weak, so nauseous, like they were slipping into a large body of water.

"I don't want to die!" Clover shouted despite the pain. "I don't want to die! I don't want to die! Please, someone, anyone! Vera, don't let me die!"

Someone—Vera— grabbed them with a small hand, and pulled them back to the surface.

They woke up sore, seconds later. Clover looked at their arm to see new skin growing over the recent wound. They weren't hit anywhere vital. Perhaps they were not so close to death as they had thought. Aster looked over the couch as lightning continued to strike with his hand resting on their shoulder, he looked at them swiftly and nodded when he saw Clover was conscious. Next to Clover, Rose rocked back and forth trying to keep calm, They covered her ears, ignoring the pain.

"Aster?" They called out to him, but he was distracted. Amir was at the other end of the couch and Clover could hear him muttering something, but they couldn't hear the words over the screams of electricity.

"The plate," Rose said quietly, "Tell Dorothy to grab the plate."

Clover looked over the couch and saw Dorothy under another table, on it was a glass plate holding a bowl of ice.

"Dorothy!" Clover shouted, ducking from the electricity. "The plate!"

She snatched the plate from underneath the bowl, letting it fall and shatter on the floor. Clover could see lightning strike near her arm but she didn't flinch. Clover saw Aster shift to follow her until lightning struck again, hitting Amir beside Rose. Clover could see his breath quicken, Aster was panicking.

This can't be happening, this cannot be happening. They began to spiral into fear and confusion before slapping the fresh wound on their arm. Folding with the pain, their mind finally cleared. Clover took a deep breath and spoke to Aster.

"Help him, I'll go."

Clover moved to the end of the couch closest to Olliver and ran behind the table. They felt electricity in the fabric of their clothes and where their hair brushed against itself. Dorothy's hair began to rise with static electricity. They watched as she held out the plate to the incoming lightning strike. When it finally hit, she was unharmed. She had found a shield.

"What?" Olliver sputtered, and the electricity faltered for a moment. The dagger was heavy where they kept it in their coat, but a single thought of using it caused a resurgence of nausea. At that moment, Clover caught sight of a book that fell off of a shelf in the mayhem. They picked it up and stood. Before they could think twice they felt the book in their hands collide with Olliver harshly, and he fell to the ground like a stuffed animal. Clover heard nothing but their own heavy breathing.

Amir awoke as well, sputtering thanks to Aster for saving his life.

"How did you know you wouldn't get hurt?" They asked Dorothy, their voice trailing with an empty breath. Dorothy put one of Aster's gloves over the hand she used.

"Glass is an insulator."

The door swung open, and there stood Dionysus– the real one– and Niamh. His outfit was fitted better than the one Olliver wore. He ran to his unconscious brother, taking off his mask. Olliver's face was smooth and scarless, unlike Dionysus's. Olliver's hair was also shorter and less well-kept, for it had grown out in prison.

"Why did you do it?" Dionysus sat next to Olliver, his voice pained. "What did you want from me?"

Olliver's eyes opened momentarily, but he did not respond. Dionysus began to cry, and he held his brother's head, gasping for air. Removing one of his hands, he revealed blood on his fingers. Clover met Aster's gaze.

"He's hurt," they said, which was obvious to everyone who had seen Clover hit him with a book, "heal him."

"You are a healer?" Dionysus demanded. Aster nodded. He looked awestruck at the situation. Dorothy must've been incorrect in her assumption that they had dealt with worse things, or at least more confusing things. Leaning over Olliver, Aster held out his hand, and the beautiful green light surrounded him. He swallowed and looked at Clover wordlessly. Dionysus paid no attention to them.

"Sir?" Amir asked quietly, "What are you going to do?"

Dionysus sniffed and held his brother's hand in his own, he shook his head.

"Why did he do it?"

"He paid someone with illusion magic to make himself look like you," Amir answered, "I believe there was a mishap, it must've connected your feelings somehow."

Dionysus laughed, but it was weak, like the closing of one final door.

"I must have a higher tolerance," He looked up at Clover, "I found out days ago that he escaped, but..."

"It wasn't his fault, sir." Clover interrupted him.

"What?" They tried to remember what they had seen, and how to say it without admitting they were following him the night before.

"I was in his mind, he was consumed by something– this

shadow– it was terrifying. He meant to rob you, I'm sure, but I don't think he meant to be violent, Mr Ollirye." It was difficult to think of the shadow for too long. It must've been the same thing that killed the Countess. "He was possessed. He might've been even before he escaped."

"A shadow?" Aster gasped. "What did it look like?"

"It had..." Clover's mind was jumbled. "Yellow eyes, I think."

"Inebri." Dionysus exhaled.

Everyone stewed on the feeling the word brought, as though the shadow were in the room. Perhaps it was.

"Dionysus?" Olliver said quietly, waking up from his stupor. "Where am I?"

"You did something bad," Dionysus choked, "I don't know what I can do to help you this time."

Olliver hummed and looked at the people surrounding him, his eyes half-lidded with pleasant sleep. Clover could not imagine the disorientation he felt, him being drunk, missing memories, and likely concussed.

Clover only related to two of those feelings.

"This place is a mess, I see why you drink," Olliver said, his voice was small, and with those final words he fell asleep once more.

The room was silent.

"You could have his magic taken away," Amir finally suggested to Dionysus, and Clover saw a vein in his forehead twitch. Aster tensed in the corner of their eye. *Like taking away a cat's claws*, their brain supplied. *A cat who killed before.*

"It wasn't his fault."

"He's killed people, sir. He killed your parents," Niamh said quietly, "You know what they'd do to him if you don't."

"I know," his voice was barely audible, "but I can't."

"I agree with Clover, he didn't want to hurt us, I heard it." Dorothy said, and Dionysus smiled at her. "He kept repeating over and over again, trying to make himself stop."

"Thank you."

Clover understood, as Dionysus sat beside his unlucky brother, with Niamh's hand on his shoulder and Amir by his side, that they were witnessing a family. Clover looked around, at Dorothy's tired face, at Rose– who was once again distracted by the fabric of the sofa– and at Aster. They were a family, as well. Clover tried not to cry as they realised they had missed their chance at saving their memories. Their clothes felt heavy against their skin.

The game was over.

Clover had lost.

Chapter XXIV: The Truth

Forget-Me-Not

There was nothing more for Clover to do than sit outside on one of the gambling house's many balconies. The door shut behind them with a soft click, cutting them off from the rest of the world. The door separated the silence of the outside from the mayhem of the inside, creating a quiet paradise.

As they waited outside, hopelessly, Clover counted the stars. Whenever they saw a new one, they tapped the cold balcony floor; it helped Clover distract themself from the fog of unknowing. They did not think of the future. For now, there were only stars. Nights in Avindre came earlier. They were grateful for that.

When looking at the stars, Clover found it easy to believe in the Goddess that had both saved and cursed their quick life.

The wind was audible, and with it brought chills. The stars created small shapes speckled in the blanket of night that covered them all, and with every glint and sparkle from the inconsequential diamonds sewn in, Clover could see their future. They could see their fate. If magic was a mistake, all of existence had to be as well. And if fate was a fallacy, then there was nothing Clover could do to control it. They could only change how they reacted to it. Aster, Rose, Dorothy, Countess Alexandra, Alice, Reaper, every wronging they had witnessed did not matter. They were nothing but a glint of crystal in the night.

The door creaked open, and Clover knew who it was by the light clicking against the limestone floor. Aster's boots stopped, but he stood out of Clover's sight. They noticed that they were only able to hear Aster's approach when they were on Avindre soil.

"May I join?" Aster asked with his familiar politeness. Clover nodded, although they didn't know if Aster was able to see in the darkness. Regardless, Clover saw him lay beside them in their peripheral. The two sat in silence.

The time they had spent searching for answers seemed too quick; there had to be something missed. But above them was a picture made in the stars, two people in the sky. Twin boys. The moon was not far, either, and shed light over the quiet night spread above Cherin. Their problems seemed so silly when the stars were so bright. They were content with lying on the floor for the rest of their life. Their short, fleeting, incredible, impossible life.

Clover turned their head to face Aster, and they were not surprised when their eyes were met immediately, he– of course– had been staring the whole time. The red of Aster's heavy coat swam in the light like wine in a glass, or perhaps a field of wheat soaked in the light of a blood moon.

"Did you know that staring at the night sky can fix your eyes?" Clover spat out, they had no idea where they had heard that. Aster blinked.

"Really?" He asked earnestly, "Is that true?"

His eyes twinkled like a geode reflecting light, but perhaps those were just tears. "Yes– well– I think so, at least."

Aster removed his spectacles with haste.

"Like this?" His eyes looked strange, perhaps they were reflecting the stars. Could he see anything? Clover had half a mind to wave their hand in front of his face.

"Yes," Clover looked at him in the corner of their eye, he looked ecstatic. "And just stare at a star."

"Any star?"

"I would believe so, just focus on one."

Aster looked at the sky with his eyes wide and sparkling with anticipation. He looked so enchanted, Clover began to second-guess their suspicions on life's meaning. Maybe it wasn't how they thought at all, for how could fate be a fallacy when it had led them to this moment? A moment so picturesque they doubted their state of mind. He then met Clover's gaze. Had he, too, felt the very same wave of emotion that almost brought them to tears?

"I'm not so sure it's real, Aster," Clover admitted with a laugh they hadn't expected. Aster did nothing but stare, a smile on his face.

"I need you to promise me something again," he said quietly.

"What?"

Aster's face began to shift and Clover could see him take a deep breath before speaking once more. His words came out slowly and his voice stuttered slightly with every other word.

"When you remember everything–"

"*If* I remember everything," Clover interrupted.

"When," Aster corrected forcefully, "When you do, you will realise some things weren't as you thought, some people."

Clover didn't interrupt anymore, confusion eating at them like a parasite. This was a conversation that had happened before, and yet this time it felt final. "You should be prepared to see who I really am."

"Aster, if you're embarrassed about something, it's all right," Clover began to joke.

"I've done bad things, Clover, things most wouldn't forgive."

Clover didn't say anything. Aster's eyes searched frantically for any sign of understanding, but Clover could not give it. They knew there was a reason for Aster being in a wanted photo, and even though they were not aware of that exact reason, the reminder of that photo conflicted with everything they knew of him. The memory of it was hazy, but Clover could remember the face of a young boy with large, faded eyes and lips turned downwards in an overzealous frown. He wore a white uniform. It must've been the first– and only– photograph of Aster Williams.

"What if I did something bad too? What if I find out I had done something terrible, or unforgivable?" Clover finally said.

"Oh, Clover," he said with a shaky voice, "Nothing you do could deter me from seeing you in the..." He shuddered a breath, "The highest respect."

Clover was ready to go home, wherever it was. "I hope to one day remember why you would think that."

The door opened with a bang, and both Aster and Clover recoiled.

"Detective?"

Clover turned around to see someone they did not recognize.

"I'm sorry, do I know you?" Clover asked, they hoped no

one could see how on edge they were. The person had short, doe-coloured hair, and if they weren't wearing the clothes of a distinguished party-goer, Clover would've rudely assumed them to be a farmer. Their freckles were visible even in the darkness.

"What are you doing here?" The person whispered, and then their eyes darted to Aster, "You found him?"

Aster's hand moved to the front of his breast pocket, ready for conflict. The person swiftly threw their hands up in the air.

"I didn't, that isn't–" They stuttered. "You really don't remember me?"

"Who are you?" Aster demanded. The person lifted their hands higher as if Aster didn't see the first time.

"I am Uriel Braithwaite!" they said quickly, "We met in Terra Florens a few months ago while I was on holiday. We met in a pub!"

Amir walked onto the balcony through the still-open door.

"I see you've already met our mindkeeper?" He said, his voice audibly fatigued.

"*Mindkeeper?*" Clover spouted, and the puzzle pieces came together in their mind. "You have my memories?"

Uriel nodded frantically.

"It was off of the books, I was told not to come in today, but I lingered just in case something was wrong," they flinched when they made eye contact with Amir, "I see I was correct."

"I am embarrassed I didn't notice, Dionysus told everyone to let him be this morning, he's always been self-conscious about his face. I just grew used to not looking at him. If I had just…" Amir began before shaking his head, "I was so blind."

"Wait," Clover said to Uriel, their mind spinning. "You have my missing memories? Right now?

"Yes? You asked me to," Uriel now also looked perplexed, "Wait, why did you think you were here?"

"I woke up from a carriage accident and was told by," they didn't know how to describe Esme, "*someone*, that the House of Opulence stole my memories."

"Have, not stole." Uriel corrected.

"My, this is peculiar. Do you understand any of this?" Amir asked Aster without much care, who replied with nothing but a confused squint. Amir sighed and finally returned Uriel's arms to their sides. People had begun to gather on the street to watch the confrontation. "You all may continue your collective crisis elsewhere, preferably inside."

Seeing the crowd below, Clover began to wish they were back fighting Olliver.

To those watching, it would seem like any other meeting in one of the gambling house's parlour rooms. However, the observant (or those willing to take a second glance through the window) would find a complicated cast of strangers. A frantic detective, a hysterical farmer, and a doll with the hair of an old man. Amir was not included in the list, as he was not considered a stranger in any regard, everyone in town knew him, as he was the only one in the room who was raised in Cherin. Dionysus and Olliver were raised far away, in a town called Radium. The family business had always been in Cherin, but the Olliryes took to raising their children in a house in the countryside.

After the deaths of the Olliryes and the incarceration of Olliver, Dionysus was sent to his late father's right hand, Sasha Aminoff– one of Amir's mothers– to be raised as one of her own. Dionysus always saw himself as a burden to them, and he was constantly trying to make it up in absurd ways.

When he turned twenty he was given ownership of the abandoned family business and the desecrated estate. Dionysus refused to even visit his childhood home before deciding to sell it. Using the money, he rebuilt the gambling house which had been under his family's name since the founding of Cherin. As the docks were built and roads were set, his family stood at the top, watching it all. In the time of his rule, he wished for no part of the building to resemble what had been before. There were no more Olliryes, there was only him.

Before the renovations were complete, Dionysus decided to cease his burdening of the Aminoffs for good. He purchased a house a few blocks away without telling anyone, and he planned to slip out of their lives forever. But on the night he planned to leave he received a knock on his door.

No one ever knocked on his door, no one acknowledged him; it was what he liked about living there. He finally had something to busy him away from a home that he never felt belonged to him. That wasn't to say the Aminoffs weren't kind, they just weren't his.

But that night Amir knocked on his door in a shaking panic, muttering nonsense which Dionysus did not understand.

"It's Niamh," he sputtered, "they've got Niamh."

Niamh was the name of his fiance, but Dionysus had never met her. It wasn't that he never got the chance, he just didn't wish to.

"Who? Calm down, now." He said, but Aminoff did not.

"The doctors! There isn't any time. They got her, and they're going to amputate..."

"Slow down! What's wrong with her?"

"There was a stabbing, I think. Just come on, we need to leave!"

He chased Aminoff to a dusty, decrepit hospital in the centre of the city, and in a small room among many other patients was Niamh. She looked just as Aminoff described, apart from the wound on her arm. The beds around her were disgusting, most likely hadn't been cleaned for weeks, and the doctors around did not take a second glance even when she screamed. Dionysus thought about illusioning the other patients invisible, but thought better of it. There was an easier fix.

"Is it infected? Is it infected?" Aminoff urged the doctor with a cry, but they did not respond. Dionysus was not familiar with medicine, nor was he of infection. But two things that he *was* aware of were money and bribes. He had to know it, given the reputation his family had.

He knew that if Niamh stayed in a house of death any longer there was a large chance that she would only get sicker, so Dionysus felt for the pockets in his coat and took out some coins. His inheritance was plenty for the new casino expansions, so he was positive there was enough to get Niamh a personal doctor.

"Aminoff."

"What?" He shouted back in hysterics, and while it was a reaction Dionysus could understand he was still surprised by it. Aminoff was usually the calm one out of the two of them. The terror of the situation mixed with the constant bustle of the hospital made it an overpowering sensation.

"How are her comforts at home?"

"Well, she has a bed, but she lives alone in a boarding

house…"

"Any stairs?"

"To get to the room, yes."

"Have them stay with us, I'll pay for a doctor," he called over a nurse. "Have their wounds dressed and I'll pay you twice your wages."

The nurse nodded quickly at the mention of payment, and hurried off to prepare the dressing.

"Stitches?

"Whatever's necessary, I'll pay extra for disinfection."

Niamh peeled open her eyes as Aminoff spouted grateful praise at Dionysus. She did not speak, but nodded at him as much as she could, and for a moment he experienced the feeling of having his debt cleared. Only for a moment.

"How did this happen?" Aminoff thought out loud.

"You may ask her later, for now, make sure she stays conscious." He began to pull his coat back on. "Have her discharged in an hour, I should be done by then."

"Where are you going?" Aminoff asked with a frantic squeeze of Niamh's hand.

"I am going to inform her board-lord that I will be paying for her room for the time being, and then having a room prepared, of course."

"Dionysus!"

"Yes?"

"Thank you."

But his thanks expanded rapidly, and Aminoff was soon convinced that he was indebted to Dionysus. Amir Aminoff vowed to repay him in any way possible, including joining his efforts to rebuild the Ollirye family business. It was a story widely told in Cherin, and one discarded by Dionysus himself.

Amir thought of this as he listened to the new story being told in the parlour. It was almost relaxing compared to the Olliryes.

As Amir pondered the far past, Uriel explained to Clover the scene that happened a few months before. It was the week before Uriel was set to go to Avindre for their new job, and Terra Florens allowed citizens of Plicitar to enter the kingdom due to the allyship, so Uriel decided that it was the perfect time to visit before they left the continent. Their family was in the inn, their mom, dad, and four sisters, and Uriel was wandering the town.

They came across a slimy pub named "The Jabbering Raven," it was about three in the afternoon, and there was only one person at the bar.

The reason that Uriel decided to go there out of all places was because of its location far from any fane.

The person inside was wearing a long tweed coat and cap, a right detective's outfit. Uriel sat a few seats down, but they were intrigued as to why an official was in such a place. So– much to their chagrin– they asked the stranger exactly that. The moment the words left their lips, the detective's eyes began to well up with tears. They told Uriel a long and painful story about misery and murder, and how they knew something they weren't supposed to. They were conflicted between their sense of justice and their love for their friend. Uriel felt bad for them, but they were more curious than anything. The detective said that if there was anyone with magic that could change memories– the words were said with a plastic venom– they would do anything.

Uriel knew that the person was drunk, heavily so, but they couldn't have ignored the request. Before explaining that they had that very ability, they asked for the detective's name, and Clover was not surprised by what came next.

The detective's name was Clover Page-Bettencourt.

"I could give them back, if you still want me to," Uriel asked them. Clover looked to Aster and watched as their eyes slowly met. Aster looked dead, as if the cogs in his brain were working so painfully that Clover swore they could hear it through his skull. His eyes shimmered with the promise of tears before being replaced the moment he blinked. Now Aster looked as clueless as Clover was. Clover was then certain they needed to learn of their past, they needed to find out what Aster was reacting to, what he was thinking about so furiously.

Clover felt sick, they didn't even know if the crash was real. They didn't know anything.

"I need them back," Clover pleaded, "Please, give them back."

Uriel nodded and stood from the couch, Clover did as well, their knees cracking. The tea Aster was drinking sat in his hands, cold. Amir hadn't said a word since Uriel's story began. Uriel led them to the space next to the couch and Clover watched as they touched their forehead.

It was happening, after all this time, it was finally happening.

In a sudden panic, they shouted, "Wait!"

"What?" Aster stood with haste.

"Where's Rose and Dorothy?"

"The girls? They're sitting in a parlour room nearby, do you need them?" Amir asked, agitated. Perhaps he was just as anxious to see what would happen as Clover was. Or– the more realistic reason– he was tired and wanted to go home after a long day of dodging man-made bolts of electricity.

"Yes, I think so." It felt wrong for them to not be there. Amir nodded and left the room. Clover stood there quietly, staring at the floor. The tiles were hard beneath the soles of their boots, and they felt as if they were sinking into the engravings of horses and griffons.

"Well," Uriel said awkwardly, "What do you both do for a living? Apart from being a detective, of course, I know what you do."

"I don't understand the question," Aster muttered.

"What do you spend your days doing?"

Aster sat in deep contemplation before a sheepish smile grew on his lips.

"Hiding."

"Oh."

"He also makes dolls," Clover reminded, unable to stop themself despite the sensitive situation.

"Lovely," Uriel looked at Aster with fear, their brow quivering upward. They almost laughed at how absurd it was. Something in the air stuck to the inside of Clover's lungs and made it hard to breathe.

Rose and Dorothy entered the room quietly, and while Clover saw their lips move, they could not understand what they were saying. Aster looked at Clover in anticipation as Uriel began to reach out again.

Now, truly, it was going to happen.

The moment Uriel's hand connected to Clover's forehead, their eyes closed, and all of the pressure that had been put on their mind for weeks had finally made it to the surface. A migraine floated to the top. Suddenly it felt as if there was a brick wall behind their eyes, and each time they moved they could feel the migraine move closer.

Then their head grew warmer, as if with fever, and in space, perhaps their consciousness, an image was curated of bright light. It was a white light, maybe, Clover couldn't discern the colour. No matter the colour, it overwhelmed all of Clover's senses, burning their eyes and filling their ears with a low ringing. They stepped closer to it, despite their mind telling them not to. It was a familiar light, a good light. A light that would help.

They took another step, then another, and then one last one. They were now before the light, in all of its blinding ineffability. They opened their eyes, but they were not in the room, they were still there with the light. The warm light encased their limbs and mind, embracing them, and making them stronger. Clover now understood why they did not remember anything. They felt at peace for the first time in what felt like an eternity; they felt free of it. There was no one else, there wasn't even Clover. There was nothing apart from the light, it helped them to think like that. It helped them wait for the light to come closer and closer. As close as it could go.

And for a second, there was nothing at all, no light, no darkness, no Clover. No metaphorical nothingness, no utter somethingness. Simply the complete lack of all things. Whether they stayed there for a second or for a lifetime they did not know, and perhaps they had done both, but it did not matter. Nothing mattered in the nothingness as there was nothing *to* matter. There was nothing to be, or not to be, and there was nothing to want.

Want. That was what came first. A strong trickle of wanting, a want for a bigger home, a want for better food, a want for something more. It was a faint feeling in the beginning but shortly grew into something greater than the nothingness that they had accepted themself to be. There was a room of nothing beneath their feet of nothing. There was a creature of nothing beside a fire of nothing, and when they tried to pet it they found they had no hands, it was not shocking, for it was nothing.

Beyond nothing was something, but beyond that was dangerous. It was a lackadaisical danger; it couldn't be bothered to hurt, but it did nonetheless.

As Clover felt the light pass through their body they began to remember. It started small, remembering their favourite park, their hometown. Then their adoptive father. Their job, their friend, Ellawyn, had she been waiting for them? Had their father? They felt the light go past their eyes and into their mind.

There was something important that was soon coming, Clover could feel it. The memories flooded back, settling into their comfortable positions in their psyche once again. They were once a respected private detective. They weren't a prodigy, but their father wanted them to be. They specialised in cases dealing with magic users, just like the people around them. Their favourite colour was still yellow.

They remembered a case they did, all those years ago, when they were soft. When they were weak. It hurt them more than they wanted to admit, they were only a child. They didn't know any better.

They did a case on a series of murders; they stayed with a family who made them long for one of their own. They remembered years of beautiful memories and years of horrible ones, of their greatest accomplishments and worst mistakes, and they were so happy to reunite with them. They had a song their father hummed to them when they were young. Their dad taught them all they knew. It was like meeting someone for the first time in years. But the wonder of reconnection was soon met with confusion as they were hit by a brick wall.

"Go through it," a voice said, it was their own, "it cannot hurt you anymore."

They were scared to go through; they felt that if they did something terrible would happen, but they answered the call, they would make it through no matter what, it was the only thing left for them to do.

They awoke feeling wind tickle their face, and warm sun on their skin. Although they were conscious, they waited to open their eyes. Not out of fear, nor to eavesdrop, but to spend just a few more seconds in their magical slumber. When they felt they were ready, they opened their eyes. They were in a sea of whispering white fields. It was soft under their fingers.

Clover– for they knew that was their name– felt a rumbling beneath them. Breathing. The fields of white morphed into a much smaller form, and they understood that it was an animal they were sleeping on.

How rude of them to do so without thanking the creature! They didn't know what they were doing before, but it couldn't have been so important as to fall asleep without properly thanking their bed. They couldn't remember thanking them, so a post-nap apology would have to do.

But they could do that later. They were so comfortable, it would be a shame to interrupt. The grass against their legs moved in the wind, and Clover's hair was picked up by the long rivers of breeze. Their hair was long again, like it was during their days in the academy. They remembered cutting it after graduation. It had become too much.

The slow breathing beneath them began to pick up, and the creature awoke, but it did not sound as content as Clover. A deep growl ripped through the air, gnashing teeth they could not see. They stood quickly as a sudden burst of fear forced their brain to panic more than they had ever known. Searching for an escape, Clover realised there was none. They were in a field surrounded by thick brush, not tall enough to hold back the sun, but just enough to hold back Clover.

The creature they were using as a pillow turned out to be a great white wolf, and when it stood it opened its large eyes. Large green eyes, like arsenic.

"You're beautiful," Clover said, and while they did hope to disarm the wolf with their words they were truly shocked, "I'm sorry for sleeping on you."

The wolf looked at them and stopped growling. It turned its large head to the side before huffing, as if too tired to bother. It sat once more and blinked.

"We have been fighting for so long, Clover," it said to them. "I can help you put an end to this."

They did not say it at the time, but what they truly thought was, "What is there on the other side of this?"

They thought he wouldn't have an answer for that.

"Do we need to know?"

"I want to," they said without thinking, "I want nothing more than to."

"That's how you know you are something, Clover. That's how you know you are alive."

"How?"

"You want. Plants want, animals want, and you want. Shadows could never do that, they could never dare."

"Please, Wolf," they pleaded, "Help me."

The wolf smiled, or at least Clover thought he did.

"You've already been helped. You have no need for me, now."

Clover stood silent. They supposed they felt happy, help was what they wanted. It was just embarrassing to know they had asked for nothing.

"Could you stay, nonetheless?"

"Once again, Clover, you have proven you are alive." The Wolf turned to Clover, showing its eyes in the brightness of the ever-rising sun. "I will stay, but when the greyhound comes to chase me away, it will be at your heels as well."

In an instant, they were back in the light.

They walked through it and found a woman. It was a strange woman, she stood there for a very long time, taking in the sights of Clover's mind, it made them upset. The woman was not a familiar one, it was a stranger. Thankfully, Clover was used to strangers. They tried to call out to her, but their voice was lost. Suddenly they remembered the most important things. They met a friend in an unfamiliar town, the most important town, how could they have forgotten?

"We have been fighting for so long, Clover." It told them. "I can help you put an end to this."

They felt hungry, they felt scared. But most of all, and more importantly than anything else, they felt like Clover. They hadn't felt that way in some time.

And there, holding his words closer to their heart than anything else, Clover remembered Aster. Their friend both then and now. Then they remembered the Vampire, and the reason they came to Dolston two years ago.

To find the Vampire of Palperroth.

And to kill Aster Williams.

Epilogue

Trifolium

Night fell on Palperroth like a heavy blanket on a sleeping child. As it did, a young woman, far from home, waited for the physician's file-clerk to unlock the filing cabinet, her palms perspiring.

"Here you go, Daisy," she stiffened at the name, but nodded in the hopes that he hadn't noticed.

"Thank you, Marlow," she replied, feigning a light optimistic tone, "I must apologise once again."

"Nonsense," Marlow waved it away, "I was a student once."

He smiled at her, unknowing of her true purpose, her real motivation. When he left she tugged on her hair to tighten the bun required for the uniform of a physician's apprentice.

Her name was not Daisy, it was Octavian, and she had become one step closer to reaching what she had been working towards for the past two decades. To find the identity of her missing sibling.

To say she was dedicated would've been an understatement. It was considered the utmost important thing since the night her father died and her uncle stole the crown, *her* crown. That night ruined Terra Florens for the foreseeable future. Not only was she sure that her sibling was alive, she knew they would've been the only one who could have understood what she had gone through. Octavian was told that they had died, but no one would tell her how. That was before Valentijn took what was rightfully hers. He destroyed not only her home, but everything her father had worked towards, and she had been too young to do anything about it.

Only she knew what her father told her that night before he died of that quick curse. It had been storming, a dark, brutal storm that had plagued Terra Florens for three whole days. On the last night of the storm, she snuck into her father's large bedroom, no one but doctors had been allowed in since they diagnosed him with the contagion.

Octavian sat on her father's bed, and he opened his eyes slowly. His face had shades of purple and blue mixed into his normal hue, but back then she didn't know why.

"Octavia," that was what her mother would call her, "would you like to hear a story before bed?"

She nodded, basking in the room's warmth.

"There was once a cat named Henry, who lived in a beautiful field in Everil. Do you remember Everil?"

"That's where I made my daisy crown." Octavian answered, she remembered it from their tours of the kingdom.

"Good." He began the story.

Henry ran through the fields every day and every night, he had many friends in the field. Mr Mouse, Harriet Hare, Captain Raccoon, and many, many more. Octavian's favourite was Mr Mouse, who was the field's doctor. He had a little office in a tree, and made sure all creatures there were healthy and well.

One day, when Henry went back home to his family, he could not find them. They lived in an abandoned barn which they had turned into an inn for animals visiting the field. Henry asked their chef, Gertrude the grasshopper, where his family had gone. She told him Mr Cat was very sick, and left for Mr Mouse's office while Henry was gone. With haste, Henry thanked Gertrude and ran through the field to the tree Mr Mouse's office resided in. There he saw his family surrounding the makeshift bed for the large Mr Cat. Mr Mouse told Henry that Mr Cat had bad berry disease, an illness contracted by eating poisonous berries.

"I don't like this story, Papa," Octavian cried, "I liked it better when Henry was playing."

"Would you rather he spent all day in the field and not know his father was sick?" Her father replied.

"No, of course not, I'm sorry Papa, you can finish the story," She once again snuggled next to her father.

Henry asked Mr Mouse if there was any way to make him better, and Mr Mouse said only one, to destroy all the berry bushes in the field, that way the air would be better for him. Henry immediately got to plucking out every bad berry in the field, leaving behind only the blackberry and strawberry bushes. It took him many days and many nights, but finally, after a very long time, he completed his task. Dashing back to the doctor's office he found his family still there.

"Did it work?" Henry asked Mr Mouse, and Mr Mouse told him that while Mr Cat was getting better, the air was still very bad.

"Come here," Mr Cat told Henry, "I will be better, but you have to find your sister, she will know how to stop the miasma."

Octavian didn't know what a miasma was, but she didn't want to interrupt the story.

"Octavia, when I die," Her father said, "I want you to be the next ruler of Terra Florens."

She felt her heart swell with conflicted feelings. On one hand, she would be like her papa, but on the other, he would be gone. She wasn't quite sure what death was, but he looked so sure of what he said that she only nodded, and he continued his story.

Henry searched for his sister in the field, but could not find her. Next, he searched in the lake in the centre of the field, but she was not there either. Finally, he realised that he must search for her in the sky. He practised for many days, jumping up and down over and over again. He tried as hard as he could to reach the clouds but to no avail. So, he tried another tactic. Henry asked his friend Mrs Raven to fly him up to the clouds.

"Fly you up to the clouds?" She asked, "Wouldn't you fall? You do not have wings."

"I will not, I am light enough to stay on the cloud."

Mrs Raven thought for a very long time before agreeing to fly him up to the clouds, but if he were to go through the cloud she would catch him and make him promise to never try again. Henry accepted those conditions. She held him up with her talons and began flying up and up into the clouds.

Before her father could finish the story, her uncle walked into the room, beckoning her to leave and let him rest. Octavian now knew why, it was then when she left the room that her father had been murdered. Every day since she regretted leaving that room. No one believed her when she told them her dad entrusted her with the crown, and as she sat in her room during the coronation she decided then and there that she would run away and find her sibling. She knew her father didn't tell her that story for nothing.

Her mother had died two weeks prior during childbirth. She overheard her father being told that the child didn't survive either, but the screams of a baby echoed throughout the castle for hours past.

For the many years since, she was left to the care of Palperroth's streets. She acquired the acquaintance of a local apothecary, where she introduced herself with the false name she had used since a small child and the promise of hard work. She did not think anything of it, until one night during a storm, when something thundered about her boarding house hall. A darkened shadow approached her door with echoing footsteps.

Octavian could not remember what she said to it, perhaps she called out in questioning, or even in warning, but no matter what she did it responded all the same.

"Open the door." An airy whisper told her. The voice crackled through the memories frozen years before. It was the voice of her late father.

She assumed herself to be dreaming, paralysed upon her borrowed four-post bed. She watched as the door opened itself in silence, quieting even the loudness of the door's usual squeaking. Had she been cursed? Had her father come to take her with him to Crowden's cellar, a place between worlds?

Her fear did not stop the door from opening further. A tall, hidden shape appeared behind it, but she could not see any defining features.

"Octavian," it said, the voice mixing with the thunder outside. "Princess of Terra Florens."

"Father?" She said to the opened door with the same voice she used the last time she addressed her father: weak and crying.

Lightning shot through the ground, shaking her room. As it slashed through Lethe it flashed a great light through her dreary window, and like Vera's candle it lit awake the secrets of her terrarium. And there– in her rented room– stood the ghost of her father. She was filled with both a sudden burst of exuberance and a shocking fear, and she sat frozen under her threadbare blanket. He looked just the same as he did the day he had died. He wore the same expression he did on his deathbed, when Octavian saw his blood leak through the quilt she had sat upon her whole childhood. His hair was long and black as the shadows around them– just like her own– but his curls were wet, as if he had just been outside.

"Octavia," it repeated coldly, "There is a shadow upon your birth, and a stain upon Terra Florens."

"Father, is that you?"

"There is no time. You must listen to what I say." Thunder cracked once more, but it was farther than the last, and only partially lit his face. Her blood was as cold as the room around her. "The lines through Lethe have already been set. The first blood has been split, and it will not stop until Valentijn is dead. Kill him as he killed me."

It was just how she thought. Somehow– without the doctor's notice, or perhaps *with*– her uncle had murdered her father, and now she had to murder Valentijn. Kill him just as he had killed her father years ago.

Sitting in the dark office, she held the file matching the exact day after her sibling went missing, two weeks before her father's death. Octavian had searched every clinic in Palperroth for adoptions, check-ups, and deaths of children under five. Every time she was met with rejection and failure, but she knew in her heart that they were alive somewhere. In her hands was the file of a newborn baby found in the rain on the street.

Her breath stilled as she opened it, and she could feel her heart rate quicken. Octavian took one more deep breath as she read what seemed to be the summary of a check-up– and an adoption. The blank where the child's name would go was empty. She scrambled to find the name of the person who brought them in hopes of more information and was stopped by the description of the child for the record. *Hair: Black; Eyes: Brown; Nationality: Florien.* Exactly like Octavian. She tried not to get her hopes up as she continued to flip through the pages.

Stapled to the back page was an old certificate confirming the adoption of this mystery child, and as she read, her face swollen with deprivation, she felt a change in the stars. That with those words a new mass of life had burst into creation; a new heart for a new body. Finally, she had a lead. A reason to live once again. She knew that right there, in the dark film of night, she had found a string to pull.

"I, hereby certify the birth of — born on 20th of May 1872;
District: Palperroth.
Signed, Markham Page"

Acknowledgements

I would like to start by thanking all of the friends, family, and teachers who have had to sit through my ramblings about detectives and flowers, and while I am sorry for that, I fear that it will only get worse.

Special thanks to my favourite (and only) writer friend, C.M. Field. Thank you for sitting with me every morning before class and listening to me talk about how I once again didn't do my homework so I could finish writing another chapter of Clover passing out. If you ever go to space, I hope you bring this book and use it to trick aliens into believing that magic is real. As– of course– aliens from Mars were always the targeted demographic.

Thank you to all of my friends! You all mean the world to me, even though I know the majority of you will never make it this far into my book to read it (I would say I understand, but that would be a lie. I will never forget this betrayal.)

Thank you to everyone who read this book before it was published, I am so sorry. I promise I (kind of) know the English language now.

Thank you to my amazing editor: myself. I don't know what I would do without you. (I had a joke in here before about sending twenty bucks to whoever finds the most grammatical errors, but my mom said it wasn't a good idea. Sorry if you wanted those twenty bucks. If it makes you feel better, I probably wouldn't have been able to pay you anyway.)

Thank you to my parents. If the money from these books buys us a house, please frame this section so I may forever brag about it. If the book money *doesn't* buy us a home, ignore this. Pretend like I never wrote it.

Thank you to the teachers who pretended like they couldn't see me writing in class.

On that note, thank you so much Mrs Baxter, Mr King, Mr Liner, and all of the other amazing people who came together to help me fund my dream, I never thought something like this could happen to me, but because of you, it is real.

Thank you to my siblings, I promise I'll visit while I'm at college. However, if I come back one weekend to find you both taller than me, I am running away.

Thank you, everyone. I hope you liked reading it as much as I liked writing it.

Here's to as many more books as I can stomach!

(For legal reasons, Ad Arnold does not, and has never, eaten a book.)

(Okay, maybe *one* book.)

(Fine! They have eaten a lot of books, are you happy?)

About the Author

"Ad Arnold is an inspiration, a magician, a young, tall, handsome man of few words." (Rad Rarnold, 2024)

Ad Arnold began writing *Detective Clover and the Mystery of the Manor* in the summer of 2021 when they were fourteen years old. They continued writing until they finished it the summer before twelfth grade. They currently live in the U.S. with their family and mischievous cats.

Arnold gets inspiration from everything they read. Currently, their favourite genres to read are historical fiction, horror, and Victorian-centred non-fiction. When they aren't writing, they enjoy drawing, playing video games, and staring at various walls in their room.

Although *Detective Clover and the Mystery of the Manor* is Arnold's first novel, it will not be their last. They plan on publishing many more works in the *Detective Clover* universe, as well as short stories in various genres.

Last but not least, they would like to note that if any critics are offended by their superfluous use of Ad-verbs, they are willing to negotiate as long as they are paid fifty dollars for every deleted adverb. They would also like to note that this work alone has over one thousand adverbs.

You can connect with me on:
🌐 https://www.adarnold.com